The Sa
Corruption There

The Same Corruption There

Joanna Trevor

**PIATKUS
CRIME**

To Liz

'Twas grief enough to think mankind
All hollow, servile, insincere;
But worse to trust to my own mind
And find the same corruption there.

Emily Brontë

Copyright © 1996 by Joanna Trevor

First published in Great Britain in 1996 by
Judy Piatkus (Publishers) Ltd of
5 Windmill Street, London W1

The moral right of the author has been asserted

A catalogue record for this book is available from the British Library

ISBN 0–7499–0355–4

Set in 11/12pt Times by
Action Typesetting Ltd, Gloucester
Printed and bound in Great Britain by
Biddles Ltd, Guildford & King's Lynn

Chapter One

The fog, creeping over the city from the river in the west, had grown thicker since he left headquarters an hour ago to collect his things from his flat. Streetlights hovered at an indeterminate height above and he was forced to drive very slowly on dipped headlights, carefully guiding himself by the white lines in the centre of the road. Traffic lights glowed in a lurid red haze and he came to a halt before turning west again towards the university buildings. It was not an auspicious start to his leave, this creeping, uneven pace, and after he had picked up Jessie, things might get even worse, because they were going on to her home further west, across the river and the low meadowlands notorious for impervious winter fogs and traffic pile-ups.

Not that there would be much traffic at this hour. He glanced at the car clock. Quarter to nine and he was already late and unsure how far he still had to go. Suddenly the sign to the university emerged from the fog, forcing him to make a rapid turn to the right before pulling into the car park of the psychology department. The low white lights around the edge of the parking area created an uncertain world at knee level. A black vacancy separated it from the glow of rooms lit somewhere above.

As he opened the car door, the interior lights of the vehicle next to his came on and a figure got out at the same time as he did. He heard a grunted acknowledgement of his presence and they both headed for the dimly lit entrance of the building. The man held the door open for him and gave an ironic grin as if to take away any offence in his words.

'The fuzz!'

The man was less tall than Detective Chief Inspector Simon, a fact that gave Simon some compensatory satisfaction in being able to look down on him with an impassively enquiring countenance and ask, 'Night porter?'

'Dr Peter Dawson of this department.' The man was no longer smiling as he turned and led the way up the stairs towards the sounds from above. 'Coming to collect the fair Jessica, are you?' he asked over his shoulder.

Simon had not had occasion to meet many of Jessie's colleagues and was surprised that Dawson knew who he was. Still, associations with policemen tended to be noted.

'Yes. You missed the party then?'

'It's just a start-of-term meeting with drinks thrown in. I had to go out for a short while.' Dawson threw open a door at the head of the stairs and a barrage of voices brought an end to casual conversation.

Simon immediately spotted Jessie at the far end of the common room, speaking with a woman with red hair. As if by instinct she looked across and waved to him waiting by the door, uncertain whether to struggle through the press to join her. He saw her speak again to her companion and watched them both begin to move towards him. Peter Dawson had disappeared into the throng as soon as they had entered the room and he saw him now reaching over someone's head and handing a book to another man. Simon had, in fact, known who Dawson was. Dawson was a man who liked to be known. He was the media man of the department – of the university, even – available to television, radio and the press for comment on the psychological afflictions of all and sundry, writer of popular psychology guides for the masses and lately presenter of his own television series. He had the right kind of image, sleek with a careful disarray of overlong hair and expensive casual clothes. Despite his boyish good looks, he must, Simon thought, now that he'd seen him up close, be well into his forties.

'Chris?' Jessie had arrived at his side. 'This is Hermione. Hermione Roe. She wanted to meet you.'

Slanted green eyes looked him over. 'She's kept you quiet. And now I see why.'

2

'It's a terrible burden to her, my being a policeman,' Simon agreed.

'Yes, I can see that. She's been looking positively hagged.' Hermione glanced smilingly at Jessie, who was looking, as usual, anything but.

'You're going to stay with her for a few days, she tells me. Not very well timed at the beginning of term.'

'No,' he agreed. 'But things were busy as usual over Christmas and the New Year so I'm taking some leave while I can. At least I can cook dinner for her when she comes home from work.'

Jessie pulled a face. Simon's culinary expertise gave no cause for pleasurable anticipation. 'He's coming for the country air, Hermione, and to make sure he doesn't feel obliged to mend a leaky tap or some other job that needs doing at his flat.'

Green eyes widened up at him. 'And where's that? Could we be neighbours? I have a flat in town myself.'

'And more *pieds en lit* elsewhere,' Jessie said drily. 'Stop vamping it, Hermione.'

Simon cleared his throat. 'The fog's getting thicker,' he said prosaically.

'We'd better go then,' Jessie said promptly.

An arm slid round her shoulders and Peter Dawson's head appeared close to hers, too close.

'You're not running off yet, are you, Jess? I haven't had a chance to talk to you.'

She moved to face him so that his arm was obliged to slide from its resting place. 'I've been here all evening, Peter,' she said.

He made no reply to that but stood staring into her eyes as if no one but they were present. A faint smile began to curl about Jessie's mouth. 'I'll see you tomorrow, Peter. Shall we go, Chris? I'll just get my bag and coat.' As she turned away, Dawson made a brief move to follow her, then seemed to think better of it.

Hermione moved in closer, her head at Simon's shoulder height. She had the most glorious red hair and it looked unassisted. 'Where did you say your flat was?'

Simon grinned down at her. 'I didn't. You lecture in

psychology too? Any particular specialism?'

'We all have those,' she said, deliberately throaty. 'What's yours?' Her expression changed abruptly and she said contritely, 'Sorry. I've probably had too much to drink. You know, I've never met a policeman before on what might be called pleasurable terms. It would be interesting to talk to you about your work some time. Forensic psychology, now ...'

Simon looked about the room for Jessie. She caught his eye from her position near the door and signalled to him. Dawson was once again at her side.

'Got to go,' Simon said hurriedly to Hermione, touching her shoulder in farewell and pushing through the crowd again.

'She's all yours,' Dawson said, as if handing over something of his own, when Simon reached them. Simon ignored him and opened the door for Jessie to go ahead of him.

The damp chill of night fog reached into the brick-lined stairwell.

'Wanker,' Simon said. He heard a stifled laugh from Jessie, preceding him into the swirling mist, and quickly lost sight of her.

'Jessie! Whose car are we going in?'

'I've been drinking. It'd better be yours. Where is it?' Her voice was distorted by the strange acoustics of the fog.

'Where are you? I'm over near the entrance.'

They found each other at his car. 'You'll have to drive me in tomorrow morning,' Jessie said, buckling her seat belt. 'Will that be all right?'

'We don't have much choice.'

'Look, I haven't had a lot to drink. Probably still well within the limit.' She moved as if to get out of the car.

'No.' He put out a hand to restrain her. 'What time?'

'About nine thirty?'

'Civilised enough.' He was forced to give his attention to driving the car, and he was glad of the excuse for silence. His ill-concealed irritation at Dawson might evaporate more quickly if they could just quietly resume their usual intimacy. It didn't occur to him that Jessie might have equal, and equally absurd, reasons for annoyance at Hermione's overt interest in himself.

He straightened his back and shifted his tense posture, the

slowness of speed matching the ponderousness of his thought processes. As he relaxed a little, he wondered whether part of his unease was the result of an unhappy awareness that Jessie related to her colleagues at work in a way that he did not. But he was on leave and not inclined to explore that particular train of thought.

Out of the silence, Jessie said, 'Dawson's probably going to get the chair when Lamb retires. That was the general rumour tonight.'

'So, Professor Dawson next? No stopping the man. And how do you feel about it?' Simon tried to keep his tone neutral.

'How else but a degree cynical personally? I'd prefer someone with a rather more original mind and a greater commitment to the students and their needs. On the other hand, he has a name and he'll attract students and funds. And financial survival is first on the agenda these days.'

Her equally neutral tone cheered him. 'Pushy, isn't he?' he said.

'In all directions.' She chuckled in the dark.

'Doesn't he get up your nose?' he asked cravenly.

'He obviously got up yours.'

Simon didn't respond, peering with overt concentration into the mist. They had left the uncertain haze of city lights behind, having crossed the river into the country, shrouded in dingy cotton wool. He hadn't a clue where they were. Had it not been for the reassuring drum of rubber on tarmac, they could quite possibly have been toiling across one of the wide flood meadows. They were down to a slow crawl.

'You'll have to open your window, Jess, see if you can guide us by the kerb.'

The cosy warmth inside the car was quickly annihilated by dank, chill air. They were both glad to focus their attention on something other than the nebulous discomfort of the mood between them.

'Move this way a bit. You must be at least six feet in.' Her head was out of the window, her voice muted. 'Slow down!' she said sharply. 'I think that was our turning.'

He manoeuvred cautiously. The road to Oxton, the village Jessie lived in, ran uphill for some distance before it descended again to the more level agricultural land beyond.

This was a narrow road, crowded by high hedges, but less alarming than being on the main highway under these conditions. He drove steadily, still in silence, her window wound up again, her attention again detached. Then they came up out of the fog, magically into a starry moonlit night, as they reached the top of the hill.

There was a parking place a little way on, with a viewpoint. On impulse, Simon pulled over and stopped the car. They opened their doors in unison and stepped out into the night. It was elating, liberating, to be able to see clearly again, and such a sight. A bench faced back over the direction they had come from and they sat huddled together gazing over the fog bank rolling away before them, lit weirdly from below by the neon lights of the distant city.

Jessie said, 'I've never seen this before. In daytime I've been above the fog, but never at night.'

They sat in companionable silence amid the greater silence, city sounds deadened by the fantastically illumined cloud forming a frozen sea below them. From up here among the bright stars and clear moon it seemed like a view of hell from heaven. Simon's dark thoughts detached themselves like leeches, fell away in the tranquillity of the night. When the chill sent them back to the car, his arm was still comfortably, gladly, resting on her shoulders.

Chapter Two

They were within half a mile of Oxton when the phone buzzed.

'Oh, no,' Jessie groaned.

It was Detective Sergeant Longman.

'Suspicious disappearance!' Simon said irritably. 'What do you mean, suspicious disappearance?'

There was a crackle on the line, but Simon caught the name Bradley. Something had happened that Superintendent Bradley thought serious enough to warrant dragging him back from a leave that hadn't even begun.

'Can you hear me, Geoff?' A buzz and a crackle responded. 'Ring me on Jessie's number. We're almost there.'

At the cottage, Jessie slung her coat over a chair and went upstairs, calling, 'I'll get Sid to take me in in the morning.' Sid was a neighbour a few doors down the lane, retired and now semi-official taxi driver for the village. Simon heard the bath being run and sighed, picking up the phone on the first ring.

A few minutes later he went upstairs, carrying fat Flossie, Jessie's cat.

'Shall I feed her?'

Submerged in soap bubbles, long curly hair piled high, eyes closed, she nodded.

'I'm sorry, Jess.'

'Can't be helped,' she said neutrally.

He looked on longingly, wanting to throw off his clothes along with all other commitments and climb into the large, old-fashioned bathtub with her. There were times when his duty to his job called up a resilience he didn't know he had.

'It's a student,' he said, as if in greater mitigation.

'What, dead?' She opened her eyes.

'Looks as if she may be. She's disappeared. There's blood but no body. That's about all I know.'

'From the university?'

'I think so.' There were a lot of students these days at a plethora of post-school institutions in the city.

'You'd better get on then,' she said. 'Come when you can.'

He bent over her in the bath and kissed soft, warm lips. Flossie mewed protestingly as her bulk got squeezed in the process. 'OK, Floss,' he said, carrying her downstairs. Murder could wait on the prosaic dietary needs of a feline. It was one of those things that helped give life a sense of proportion.

The fog had lifted slightly but it was near midnight when he arrived in Acacia Road, a pleasant, tree-lined thoroughfare on the north side of Westwich. There were several cars, including marked police cars, in the road concentrated about number 25, a large detached Victorian house with an elaborate porch. Longman was waiting in the spacious hallway, tidily groomed and unusually smart in a charcoal suit. It looked as if he, too, had been called away from more pleasant pursuits.

'You look different,' Simon said to him.

'It's the eyebrows,' Longman said self-consciously. 'The wife made me trim them.' The famous wild eyebrows had indeed been tamed.

'They'll grow back,' Simon said, comforting.

Longman gestured towards a room on the left of the hallway and led Simon to the open door, pointing silently to a zigzag trail of blood that traced its way down the large mirror and over a grey marble fireplace below it. Stains could also be seen on the enamel and chrome of the unlit gas fire. A hardback chair stood in an odd position, its back to the fire on a cleaner area of the light-brown carpet. At the nearest side of the pale patch was a dark stain with a straight edge in line with the edge of the cleaner oblong.

'The rug's been taken, the landlord says. A brown one, apparently,' Longman volunteered.

'Has anything been touched?' Simon asked, his eyes on the chair.

'The chair was in the way of the door when Edwards the landlord unlocked it. He had to move it to get into the room. It had fallen over. He put it upright and got blood all over his hands. So he didn't mess about. Called us straight away.'

'The door was locked, was it?' Simon looked at the door which opened into the room, the key still in the lock on the hall side of the door. 'Had her key been removed, then?'

Longman indicated an old-fashioned iron key that had been placed on the small table to the right of the door inside the room. 'No. He had a bit of a job unlocking it with his own key because her key was still in it.'

Simon looked across at the curtains covering the tall window opposite. A faint movement of air disturbed them. He had had only the briefest of information over the phone, the emphasis being on Superintendent Bradley's wishes that he, Simon, deal with it, rather than any details of the case. The chief constable was a friend or acquaintance of the vice chancellor. The police were supposed to cast an avuncular and caring eye over that vulnerable section of the population, the university's students.

'So why was the landlord so concerned about his tenant that he went to such a deal of trouble?'

'The girl's sister insisted on it.'

'And why was she so concerned?'

Longman shrugged. 'It seemes she phoned earlier in the evening, at nine o'clock, from London, to speak to Emily – Emily's the name of the girl that's missing. This was apparently by arrangement. Anyway, Emily wasn't in. One of the other tenants, a Mr Richard Lee, answered the phone and knocked on her door. When Charlotte Sanderson, the sister, rang again at half past nine, Mr Lee tried the door again and still couldn't get any answer. So the sister insisted that they should check that Emily was all right.'

'Protective big sister,' Simon commented.

'Sounds as if it's just as well. Anyway, Mr Lee fetched the landlord to the phone and she persuaded him to open up and check on Emily. Edwards told her he'd ring her back after he'd managed to break into the room. He phoned us first, then contacted her again.'

'He told the sister what he'd found?'

Longman nodded. 'The blood upset him, I think.'

'Understandable,' Simon said.

'Anyway, the sister's supposed to be on her way here.'

'And where the hell's SOC?'

'Also on their way.'

Simon took the opportunity to examine the room while it was still unoccupied. It was typical of most bedsitters in its cheap furnishings and general decoration. One window faced the street, a divan bed beneath it, its orange nylon counterpane disordered, as if someone had restlessly slept on it or, more likely, fallen on it in a struggle. The rest of the furniture was minimal; a flimsy wardrobe at the bottom of the bed partly hidden by the open door, a grey velour-covered armchair, which looked as if it had once been part of a suite, to the left of the fireplace, a rickety coffee table beside it. Yellow chip paper covered the walls. In the alcove to the left of the fireplace and to the right of the other window was a table with a laptop computer placed on it, incongruous and prominent. The alcove on the other side of the fireplace contained a small sink and draining board and a tabletop cooker with a cupboard underneath.

Longman waited with him by the door, watching where Simon's eyes went and following.

Despite the elements of disorder, the room didn't look lived in. The girl, Emily, had made none of the usual marks of student occupation.

'Had she just moved in?' Simon asked.

'Moved in on Monday, the landlord said.'

'So where was she last term? What year is, or was, she in?'

Longman shrugged. 'I don't know.'

Bradley had apparently spoken to the landlord, set up a search of the local area and hurried back whence he had come, leaving all further dispositions to Simon.

They heard voices in the hall: the scene-of-crime team had arrived. After speaking with them and disposing of available personnel to start questioning the residents, Simon went with Longman in search of the landlord.

The down-curved mouth and close-set, narrow eyes conveyed the impression of one generally at odds with the world. He was short, his body showing the soft, almost feminine lines that overtake some men in their late middle years. His hair, an artificial-looking black, was long on top, short at the sides and glossily flattened to his head by some greasy embrocation. The cheap, smart clothes had gone shiny from

10

overuse and too little washing. Simon uneasily sniffed the stale air, sickly with the smell of fried food, as they entered his basement flat.

Edwards looked ill at ease and said nothing as he gestured towards a tatty vinyl sofa and seated himself in another auction-room reject chair opposite them. Simon observed the large television set and video machine, the bookshelves filled with videos and the little piles of magazines, tabloid newspapers and other rubbish.

'When did you last see Miss Sanderson?' he began.

The man clasped his hands around one bony knee. 'I saw her going out this morning, or yesterday morning, whatever it is – around ten o'clock.'

'Tuesday morning, then. Did you speak to her?'

'No.' He gestured towards a window at the front of the room. 'I saw her from down here, going down the front steps.'

'And you didn't see her return?'

Edwards shook his head. 'No.'

'Do you have your own entrance?' Simon glanced around the room. There was a door to the left of the window.

'Yes, I have. But I use the main door sometimes, just to keep an eye on things, like.'

'How many tenants do you have, Mr Edwards?'

'Eight, including the missing girl.'

'Are any of the others students?'

'She's the only one.' Edwards glanced uneasily at Longman, who was now standing at the bookcase examining the titles of some of the video cassettes.

'Do you know what year Miss Sanderson was in at the university?'

'She said she was in her first year. She looked older than that, though.'

'Oh? How much older?'

Edwards pursed his lips. 'Not that much older. I mean, actually, she looked young enough, to someone my age, anyway.' He gave a matey chuckle which descended to a leer. 'She just seemed a bit more mature than an eighteen- or nineteen-year-old. But a real looker, you know?'

'I understand she moved in only on Monday. How and when was that arranged?'

Longman ceased prowling and joined Simon on the sofa, where he began studying one of the magazines, its front cover depicting a paramilitary clutching a gun.

'I advertise in the *Evening Star*.' It was the Westwich city paper. 'When she rang up she said she'd seen my ad. She came over to see the room last week, on Friday, and paid a deposit there and then.'

'Did she say anything about where she was living last term? Why she left?'

'Students sometimes don't want to pay a retainer over the holidays. I supposed it was something like that. She did say she lived in a house in London with her sister.'

'And did you see her in the company of anyone else in the short time she was here?'

'No. Hardly saw her at all. She collected the keys from me on Monday at about half past two and that was the last time I saw her to speak to.'

'And you saw and heard nothing tonight to make you think there was anything wrong?'

'Not until that sister of hers rang. If it hadn't been for her kicking up a fuss, nobody might have noticed anything was wrong for a while yet. Not anyone here, anyway.'

They all contemplated the likely truth of that statement in silence.

'Give the sergeant here the names of your other tenants, would you, Mr Edwards? Along with information on how long they've been living here.'

Simon already had bad feelings about this case. A murder without a body was everyone's worst nightmare – relatives, the police, anyone involved. She might be lying in a dark garden behind a hedge somewhere nearby. But she had been attacked in her room, and it was unlikely that her attacker would have gone to the trouble of removing her unless he intended disposing of the body so that it wouldn't be found easily. He might have put her in the river. A lot of unidentified bodies appeared a hundred miles or more downstream in the Bristol Channel, devoid by that time of any useful forensic evidence.

And they would have to proceed on the assumption that she was dead. The girl could have been attacked by someone from inside the house or have let someone in, and if they came from

12

outside, it was likely it was someone she knew, because whoever it was would have had to ring her doorbell so that she opened the main door and let them into her room. A chance attacker would be highly unlikely to have gained entrance that way. Simon wondered just how many people who knew Emily knew of her new address.

Then there was the window, by which the man must have left, taking Emily with him, since the key had still been in the lock. But he couldn't have got to her that way unless she had been deep asleep. Very deep. And that was unlikely before nine in the evening – the time the sister had made her first call.

Longman coughed, indicating that his list was completed.

'Mr Edwards,' Simon said. 'Was the light on or off in the room when you gained entry?'

'It was off.'

'And the sister told you she was coming to Westwich tonight?'

'Could be here any time.' Edwards got up and wandered over in the direction of the window as if the check for a new arrival amid the subdued movements overhead.

'How easy is it for an intruder to get into the house? Is the front door kept locked?' Simon asked.

'Yes. They've all got a front-door key and a key to their rooms. In summer the door's sometimes left open, against my rules, but in this weather, at this time of year, it's closed and locked. On a Yale,' he explained.

'And I noticed personal bell plates inside the porch. So if anyone visited Miss Sanderson this evening, no one would necessarily have seen or heard?'

'That's right.'

'Was anyone with you when you opened the door to her room?'

Edwards frowned. 'Yes, Lee was. Richard Lee who took the telephone call. Always complaining about it. But he doesn't have to answer the bloody thing.'

'Thank you for now, Mr Edwards,' Simon said, rising from the low sofa. 'I'd like to look outside the house. Is there a light out there?'

The landlord looked apologetic. 'It's not working.'

13

'We've got plenty of torches,' Simon said. 'By the way, did the young woman have a car, do you know?'

'Didn't see one. And she didn't bring much stuff.' Edwards stood by the door to see them out.

'We'll be searching the house thoroughly, including your own premises. I trust you'll have no objections?'

Edwards held his hands wide, palms upward. 'I have nothing to hide, Chief Inspector. I'd just appreciate it if you'd wait until morning.'

'I should think we could do that. Don't go too far in the next day or so, will you? We'll probably have some more questions to ask.'

'I'll be here,' the little man said.

Longman followed Simon to the back stairs and up to the cooler, cleaner air of the hallway above.

Chapter Three

The fog had dissolved into mere hazy mist as he went back down the steps at the front of the house and turned right along the low wall that divided the pavement from the landlord's basement area. The wall joined the house at a right angle on the outside corner of Emily's room and was bordered by a concrete drive. This led to a garage at the rear of the house, where torchlights carved white gashes in the black interior. One of the lights flashed on to his face, dazzling him.

'Point that thing in the right direction, would you?' he called irritably.

'Sorry, sir,' came a male voice, followed by another voice and a low chuckle.

He ran his own torchlight over the pale surface of the drive, looking for bloodstains or other evidence, but found only congealed oil patches, which he nevertheless avoided stepping on. There were no obvious traces, at least in this inadequate light, of anything on the peeling windowsill, but beneath its overhang, caught in the angle of the wall and the drive, were a few bright broken fragments of what looked like white paint. A thin yellow line of light showed in the opening between the bottom of the sash window and its frame, the window too stiff and old, perhaps, for the intruder to have closed it firmly behind him. Simon could hear a low murmur of voices from the men and women at work in the room inside.

The drive sloped upwards away from the road. At its lowest point in relation to the ground, the windowsill was only about four feet high, an easy height from which to escape from the room inside, even if burdened by a dead weight. In fact, if the assailant had draped the body over the sill while he jumped out, it would have been simple to lift her on to his shoulders and perhaps deposit her in the boot of a nearby car. The road was only a few feet away, the drive immediately beneath, if the attacker had had the nerve to park the car here.

He turned to study the immediate surroundings. The nearest streetlamp was twenty yards or so away to his right as he faced outwards from the house, its light partially obscured by the bare branches of a tree in front of the house next door. The wall of the neighbouring house towered above, the width of only two driveways away, silhouetted blackly against the misty light and separated from where he was standing by a six-feet-high wooden fence. He could see no lights on in the property from where he was standing, perhaps surprising considering the police activity. By torchlight he could make out two windows on the first floor, an identical pair above those and another high up in the angle of the roof. The lights had been off inside Emily's room and any activity where he was standing would have been invisible unless some light was shed from one or more of those windows.

As he returned to the steps at the front of the house, a car pulled up, double-parking beside a police vehicle, and a young man got out quickly from the driver's seat and ran round the car towards him.

'What's happening? Have you found her? Where's Emily?' He looked wildly from Simon to the open door of the house, as if in hope of her appearance.

A young woman had by now got out of the car and was standing as if holding back, afraid of what she might hear.

'You must be Emily's sister,' Simon said.

She nodded and took an uncertain step forwards, Simon looked questioningly at her companion.

'I'm Mark Whittaker, Emily's boyfriend,' he said impatiently. 'What's going on, for God's sake?'

Simon gestured up the steps. 'Let's go inside and talk, shall we? Give your keys to the constable there, he'll park your car for you.'

The young woman came slowly, unwillingly, into the house and paused outside Emily's door, looking large-eyed at the activity inside the room.

'There?' She mouthed the word at Simon.

The two followed him quietly to the chill, bare room that Edwards had made available to them at the rear of the house. It contained a narrow divan, a few oddly matched chairs and a table, apparently rejects from even the low standards of Edwards's furnishings. Simon placed three chairs around the table and they sat, looking at him with a fixed intensity.

The sister was probably in her late twenties, fair hair cropped short, her face bare of make-up. She was tall enough to wear with style her long, dark-green raincoat with a voluminous cape. Her blue eyes held his as if willing him to say nothing that she couldn't bear to hear.

He began by introducing himself. 'And your name is Charlotte, Emily's sister?' She nodded, lips compressed.

'Mrs – ?' Simon asked her, her gloved hands giving no clue.

'Miss Sanderson. The same as Emily.'

'Well?' Whittaker said, folding his arms and thrusting his head forward at Simon.

'We don't know any more, really, than what you were told on the telephone,' Simon said, directing his words at Charlotte. 'We're doing a search and questioning the other tenants but so far we've not found her. Nobody we've spoken to has heard or seen anything suspicious. But it's very early in the investigation.'

'Suspicious!' The young man got up and paced over to the uncurtained window. 'There's blood all over her room, isn't there? Isn't that suspicious enough for you?'

His eyes held by the blue eyes in that pale, still face, Simon said, 'Of course. We'll be treating the case as seriously as a suspected murder.' He didn't think he had much choice, given the circumstances.

She caught her breath at that, as if her heart had missed a sudden beat, and shuddered. 'You're sure, then?' she asked in a low voice.

'We can't be absolutely sure of anything yet. But we'll be treating it that seriously,' he said again, conscious of the inadequacy of anything he might say. 'It means that we'll be doing everything we can, with as much manpower as is available.'

'Could he...' She hesitated. 'Could he have kidnapped her, just taken her somewhere alive?'

'It's possible,' Simon said gently. But unlikely, he thought.

17

'In which case we'll probably hear something.'

She nodded and looked down at her gloved hands, clasped tightly in front of her on the table.

'I need to ask you some questions about Emily,' Simon said. 'We know almost nothing about her. She'd only just moved here, I understand.'

Whittaker moved from his position by the window and flung himself down on the bed. 'What do you want to know?' he said, bitterness biting into every word. 'That she was young, beautiful, intelligent, with everything to look forward to and live for? And if I can get my hands on the bastard that did this...' He ran them instead through stylishly cut hair, looking at Simon defiantly.

Simon stared back. The young man was strongly built, around the same age as Charlotte, and dressed casually. Simon thought he probably worked out regularly. His startling good looks were saved from effeminacy by a firm jaw and narrow lips, pulled more tightly thin by his present expression. His anger and fear were understandable, though harder to deal with than the woman's shocked passivity. On the other hand, boyfriends had to be eliminated from such inquiries as these.

'How long did it take you to drive here tonight, Mr Whittaker?' Simon asked.

'Why?'

'If you're going to question every question I put to you, it's going to slow down our inquiries more than necessary.' Simon folded his arms and leaned back in his chair.

'It was about two and a half hours, wasn't it, Mark?' Charlotte intervened.

'Quick, considering it was such a foggy night,' Simon said neutrally.

'Careful, Charlotte, he'll be doing us for speeding,' Whittaker said.

'Don't be silly, Mark.' She said to Simon, 'It wasn't foggy until we got near Westwich. Even then it wasn't too bad. But I did ask Mark to drive fast. You can understand that, surely?'

Simon nodded. 'Emily's in her first year at the university, I believe?'

'Yes. She was reading psychology.'

Simon's thoughts flashed to Jessie, lying in soapsuds in a

18

different world. She had probably known Emily.

'I understand that your sister had only just moved here. Where was she living last term? And why did she move?'

'She was sharing a house with a couple of other girls. From what she said, they were a bit intrusive. She said she wanted more privacy. I don't think she intended staying in this place.' She looked around the dismal room. 'It was just until she had more time to find somewhere she really liked.' The young woman spoke very evenly, as if making an effort to breathe normally.

'And she came down last week from London and found this accommodation? Did she come here because she knew anyone here?'

'No. At least I don't think so. She just saw the advertisement in the local paper.'

'She lives with you in London when she's not in Westwich?'

Charlotte nodded. 'We've got a house in Ealing.'

'And do your parents know what's happened?' Simon asked.

'Our parents are dead, Chief Inspector. A car accident.'

'I'm sorry,' Simon murmured conventionally. 'Any other relations?'

She shook her head slightly. 'Just Emily and me.' Her voice was expressionless.

'For how long?' he asked as gently as he could.

'Four years.'

Her quiet desolation, her dignity, touched him. He wished he could comfort and reassure. But his job was to deal with the worst scenario and there could be no softening of questions and procedures.

'You had an arrangement to telephone her at nine o'clock, I'm told.'

'Yes. We arranged that I'd ring to see that she'd settled in all right, that she hadn't forgotten to bring anything.' Her voice caught for a moment and she cleared her throat. 'She wasn't in. The man who answered the phone went and knocked on her door and came back and said there was no answer to his knock, so I said I'd try again at half past nine.'

'And when he could again get no reply,' Simon said, 'I understand you asked him to fetch the landlord. Why were you so concerned?'

There was an exclamation from Mark. 'How can you ask that, after what's happened?'

'Don't, Mark, please,' she murmured, and he got up abruptly and went once more to the black, blank window.

'I mean only that you had no other particular reason to be troubled about Emily – she wasn't in any difficulty?' Simon asked her.

Her eyes glanced over to Mark. 'No. Nothing that made me telephone because I was worried about her, if that's what you mean. We kept in touch, Chief Inspector, now that there are only the two of us. She said she would be here for my call at nine and so she would have been unless something was wrong. Even then I waited another half an hour before I made any fuss. That half-hour might have been important.' She spoke quietly. Her calm seemed unnatural. It was as if she was denying the possibility of her sister's death.

'And then you telephoned Mr Whittaker. What time was that?'

'What the hell does that matter, for God's sake!' the young man shouted.

'It must have been about twenty to ten,' she said, ignoring Whittaker. 'I telephoned him straight away after the landlord had told me what had happened and asked him to pick me up and drive down here with me. I'm not keen on driving unless I have to. Besides, I was glad of the company.'

'Does your sister have a car, Miss Sanderson?'

'No. She uses mine sometimes.'

'But she doesn't have it in Westwich at the moment?'

'No. Mine's in London. Why?'

'I wondered how and when she moved her things from where she was living before.'

She raised her eyebrows. 'Does it matter?'

Simon shrugged and waited.

She sighed. 'Emily moved her things out last week and brought them home in my car. She didn't take much with her when she went down by train on Monday. Just enough to be going on with, she said. It was one of the reasons we arranged I'd call, as I said, to check whether she needed anything. I would have brought it down this weekend.'

'Term doesn't start until Wednesday,' Simon said, looking at

20

his watch. 'Today, in fact.'

She pulled off a glove and rubbed her forehead. 'She liked to be in plenty of time for things,' she said tiredly.

Simon noticed her use of the past tense, so carefully avoided by the three of them.

'Are you staying in Westwich tonight?' he asked. 'I can arrange somewhere for you to stay if you'd prefer that.'

'Yes. Thank you. I'd rather be here nearby somewhere.'

'I'll stay too,' Mark said, coming over and putting a hand on her shoulder.

'I should like to talk to you both again tomorrow,' Simon said. 'Oh, and do you have a recent photograph of your sister?'

'I brought one,' she said, fumbling with a large black shoulder bag that she'd placed on the table. She held out a colour photograph in a plastic envelope. 'It was taken on holiday last summer.'

Simon studied the picture. It was not very sharp, not ideal for publicity purposes, but he could see that she was strikingly beautiful, with long blonde hair and a joyful smile. Slender and long-legged, she was standing with one foot on a stile, wearing shorts, a haversack on her back, a distant view behind her. The features held some resemblance to Charlotte's: the perfect oval face, the eyes. But Charlotte was like a muted version of her younger sister, shadow to her sunlight. She was lovely, but not with the kind of looks that made you stare, unlike Emily.

Charlotte was watching his face. 'She's beautiful, isn't she?' she said, and he felt as if, in giving him Emily's picture, she was somehow entrusting her to his care, impressing him with her importance.

'Yes, she is,' he said, standing up. 'I'll go and find DC Jones. She'll arrange somewhere for you to stay tonight.'

Chapter Four

After only a few hours' sleep, Simon stood looking out at a dark, drizzly morning from the french windows of his first-floor flat with a mug of coffee in his hand. Lights showed behind closed curtains here and there in houses in the Georgian square, but most of the inhabitants appeared to have wisely put off the moment of facing the day. He looked around his bedroom, clothes flung off untidily in heaps on chairs and floor, and felt thoroughly depressed. He'd lived here now for over five years, and though he loved the square and its odd mix of flat dwellers and house dwellers of all ages and backgrounds, he felt a strong dissatisfaction with the place he called home. It lacked a warmth that had nothing to do with heating. He supposed it was because he wasn't there very much, the demands of his job being what they were. And, if he was honest, he preferred to be at Jessie's small cottage whenever he had the time and she was willing.

In fact, the way things were going, he was practically living there. And she didn't seem to mind. On the occasions when she wanted her own space, she said so simply and directly. The way things worked out, it didn't happen very often and their arrangement seemed satisfactory enough. But it didn't satisfy him really, he admitted to himself. And he didn't know what would. He had known Jessie for nearly three years, ever since that rainy night in a pub car park when he'd helped her start her car, and they'd never talked of marriage, never even mentioned it. It had begun to look as if they were avoiding it. Perhaps, he thought, neither of them wanted to disturb something that was good as it was. Yet there was always this urge that most humans seemed to feel to move onwards, to make resolutions, to affirm, refusing to just let things be. And he couldn't see Jessie as a policeman's wife. He liked to keep her separate from that part of his life. But he realised now, gazing out into the slowly lightening gloom, that he did want her for *his* wife. He wanted a stable, warm centre to his life, and only she could provide it. The trouble was – he smiled ruefully to himself – he wasn't at all sure that she had the same need to him. He wished he was curled up warmly in bed with her at the cottage right at that moment so that he could talk about it with her. But the urgency wouldn't be there then; he'd feel safe, as usual, in his tenancy there.

He picked up the phone, eager to talk to her, even if not on the subject that occupied his thoughts. A young girl was missing, probably dead, and Jessie might have known her.

'Chris?' Her voice always sounded as if she was still in bed.

'I didn't wake you, did I?'

'It's the first day of term,' she reminded him. 'And I have to arrange to get a lift in.'

'Sorry about that.' He felt almost shy of her after his recent thoughts, as if they had changed something between them. Perhaps they had, he thought, with a sudden, sinking fear of the unknown.

'What happened last night? Is the girl definitely missing? The student?'

'Yes. I wondered if you might know her. Her name's Emily Sanderson.'

'Oh, God! Yes, I do, quite well. She was in one of my tutorial groups last term. And some seminars. Lovely girl. What's happened exactly?'

He told her the circumstances. 'What was she like, Jess?'

'If you're asking me if she's the kind of girl that might attract trouble ...?'

'Anything you can tell me,' he said.

'Then you'll have to talk to me properly. I can't discuss her over the phone.' Relenting, she added, 'I would say, though, that she was an innocent.'

'Is that the opinion of a professional psychologist?'

'I'm not talking to a professional psychologist. You wouldn't appreciate jargon.'

'Wouldn't understand it, you mean,' he said, a bit miffed.

'She wasn't a case, Chris,' she said reasonably. 'I don't go around assessing everyone's psychological profile, you know. She seemed a fairly normal, happy girl in most respects, as far as I can recall. Certainly not an obvious troublemaker. I'm so sorry this has happened. Do you think she's dead?'

'Personally, I shouldn't think there's much chance she's alive, given what evidence we've got. We'll be more sure when the forensic checks are done. Jess, did she have many friends?'

'I used to see her in the general company of other students, but I can't remember there being any special friend. She was twenty-four, a bit older than most of the other students in her year, and they can feel the difference when their contemporaries have mostly only just left school.'

'Yes, I suppose so,' he said, thinking back to the lofty sophistication of himself at that great age. '"I was so much older then. I'm younger than that now."'

'Policemen quoting Dylan, no less. Is the New Age upon us at last?'

'Fat chance. Jess, did she have any men friends that you know of?'

'I can't say I ever saw her with any particular male ...' she said slowly. 'Chris, I've got to get on. I really must. Look, can you see me later?'

He thought for a moment. 'I suspect I'll be having words with the university authorities some time today, so I'll be on campus. I'll try and get hold of you.'

'Any time,' she laughed, and rang off.

Superintendent Bradley was waiting inside the porch at number 25, hands in his overcoat pockets, stamping his feet and blowing out his plump cheeks, sending puffs of steam at the offending drizzle outside.

He eyed Simon with his usual disfavour as the chief inspector approached him, pointedly taking in his long, brown overcoat and fringed paisley scarf. Clothes had never been a form of communication that Simon understood, and he hated shopping for them. Despite his dislike of uniforms, wearing one earlier in his career had been a relief to him in freeing him from the necessity of having to think about what to put on.

'Come on, come on,' Bradley said irritably, turning away

24

from the door, trundling his great weight to the small room that had been put at their disposal. It had filled up with the usual police paraphernalia and computer terminals in the few hours since Simon had last been there.

Bradley chose to stand, massively, close to the door, causing a general obstruction.

'I've had a few words with the boys while I was waiting for you,' he said pointedly. 'The boys' was a common term of reference used by Bradley for any personnel of any sex currently under his jurisdiction. Simon assumed that at this juncture he was referring to the scene-of-crime officers.

'They reckon she was attacked while she was moving, put up some form of defence – from the blood evidence. Most of the blood is likely to have been on the rug that was taken along with the body.'

Simon nodded. So much had been fairly obvious.

'Evidence suggests that she was removed via the window. And whoever did it made some efforts to wipe the place clean. Obviously they haven't finished looking for prints yet. But all the obvious, immediate places, anyway.'

Simon looked pensively out of the grimy window.

'Well?' Bradley said. 'Someone she knew, or an intruder?'

'Unless she was deep asleep,' Simon said cautiously, 'it doesn't seem likely it was an intruder coming through her window, anyway.'

'Yes?' Bradley waited.

Simon spoke carefully. 'It was either someone from inside this house – in which case they could have knocked on her door – or someone she let in through the front door. Someone who rang the bell for her room. If it had been someone she didn't know or didn't want to talk to, she'd have had time to kick up a row between the front door and the door to her room.'

Bradley nodded. He liked things spelled out clearly. 'Ergo, someone she knew. And she'd moved here only the day before. So who, among her acquaintances, knew she was living here?'

'I shall have to ask, shan't I, sir?'

'Do that. And what about the other tenants? Anything likely there?'

'I couldn't say. I haven't had a chance to see the interview reports yet. I think we're going to be looking for someone with a vehicle of some sort, if her body doesn't turn up in the vicinity. Though that'll depend on alibis, I suppose.'

'Often difficult to establish at night, except with the help of wives and girlfriends,' Bradley said pseudo-sympathetically. 'Why do you think he took the body with him?'

'The obvious answer to that is forensic evidence, isn't it?' Simon said. 'Seminal fluids after a sexual attack, perhaps.'

'I understand she was a good-looking girl.'

'Not that looks necessarily mean much to rapists.'

'May not have been a rapist. If it was someone she knew, they may have had a row, you know, afterwards. Of course we mustn't forget that it may be a kidnapping.'

'In which case we'll be hearing of it,' Simon said. 'Kidnappers usually plan their attack so as not to do that much damage with a knife or whatever, though, if they're intending to hold on to their victims.'

'It may have been a knife. The bloodstains suggest that, I'll grant you. Speaking of which, you'll have to get a DNA check done, see if we can distinguish any traces of blood from her attacker. I understand her sister arrived last night?'

'Yes, sir. DC Jones has made arrangements for that. And I'll be seeing them later this morning.'

'Them?'

'The boyfriend, Emily's boyfriend, came with the sister – Charlotte. They both live in London.'

'Boyfriend, eh? Well, I trust you'll be checking on him?'

'I'm sure we shall, sir.'

'And you'd better get out to the university and let them know what's going on. And keep them informed of any investigations that involve them, questioning students, staff and the like. I've already spoken to the vice chancellor. He said for you to contact Hugh Smith, the administrator, and refer to him. He'll keep the VC informed.'

'Yes, sir, I'll defer to Mr Smith. I'll see him today.'

Bradley frowned at him, the folds of his face merging comically. 'Yes, well, sooner rather than later, eh?'

'As soon as I've got one or two things out of the way here, sir. I'd like to be as fully informed as possible before I speak to Mr Smith.'

The superintendent grunted 'I suppose you'll be speaking to your lady friend at the university, too. The girl was a psychology student, I understand.'

'Dr Thurrow was one of her tutors last term.'

'Ah, well, I can tell you won't be losing any time following up that particular line of inquiry.'

Bradley always became more emphatically sardonic on those rare occasions when Jessie came into a conversation. Her spectre seemed to arouse all Bradley's male-chauvinist prejudices. Although it might be mere misogyny, Simon considered, eyeing Bradley. Or just fear of the unknown, of which misogyny was probably a manifestation. Bradley had not so far, the police force being as it was, had to deal with too many clever women on their own terms.

'Anything else, sir?'

'I expect I'll think of something.' Bradley turned to the door and then abruptly back to Simon. 'I have already. Make damn sure you get this building searched thoroughly. I don't want any bodies turning up under floorboards.'

'We'll be starting the search today,' Simon promised.

'You hear about the mugging in Acacia Road earlier on yesterday evening?'

'No?'

'Young lad got beaten up. Uniform branch had only just gone when we arrived.'

'They haven't caught anyone, I suppose?'

'Not a chance,' Bradley said. 'But you'd better make sure that *you* do.'

'Of course. No problem.'

'And keep me informed. I don't want you upsetting the university authorities, going off at half cock in some wild direction or other.'

'The murder of a young woman is always upsetting, though, isn't it, sir? Particularly to the relatives.'

'Of course it is,' Bradley snapped. 'But it doesn't give you carte blanche for riding roughshod over everyone concerned.'

'Gentle probing is more my style, sir.'

Bradley knew himself often to have been the victim of Simon's deceptive mildness. 'Good policing isn't about style,' the superintendent said sarcastically. 'It's about method, organisation and orderliness. Of which,' he said, eyeing Simon's dishevelled appearance anew, 'you could do with a little personally.'

Conceding that Bradley probably did have a point there, Simon, for once, said nothing.

'You're treating it as suspected murder straight off?' Bradley eyed him coldly.

'I can't think of how else to treat it, given the evidence so far.' Simon gave his reasons. 'Unless, of course, we hear from the person who's taken her. But I don't think we will.'

Bradley grunted a kind of assent. 'Too much damage done, by the look of it. Well, you'd better get on,' he said, rotating his bulk back into the hallway. 'God knows you've got plenty to get on with.'

Simon followed him out and watched him stomp self-importantly from the premises. Longman was merging from a doorway on the left of the hall, opposite Emily's room.

Simon called to him and the sergeant approached, looking as clear-eyed as usual, for all the world as if he'd had a full night's sleep.

'Anything emerged that I should know about – from the other tenants, for instance?' Simon asked.

'The room next to hers was unoccupied. Apparently the tenant is away for the week. The room opposite that one on the other side of the hall is occupied by a Mr Baber. He went out to meet some friends for a drink at about eight last night and came home at gone eleven. Says he didn't see or hear anything unusual. And none of the tenants upstairs have said anything of interest so far. The only one that claims to have seen her on the relevant night is Richard Lee, room opposite. I've just been talking to him. He was the one who answered the phone to the sister. Says he spoke to the missing girl earlier in the evening.'

'I'll see him now.'

Simon tapped perfunctorily at the open door of Lee's room and went in. DC Rogers, a large and potent presence, was there, sitting in a low vinyl armchair opposite a thin youth with an incipient beard who was reclining palely on the sofa opposite him.

Rogers got up with visible effort. 'Mr Lee, sir. He spoke to

the – to Miss Sanderson yesterday evening, before she disappeared.'

'But not afterwards, I assume?'

'Er, no, sir.' Rogers's colour rose in his already florid
cheeks.

Simon sat in the chair Rogers had vacated. 'I'm Detective
Chief Inspector Simon, Mr Lee. What can you tell me about
Emily?'

'Nothing much,' the yough said sullenly. 'I've already
talked to at least two lots of your people.'

'Bear with me,' Simon said. 'I always like to get my information direct whenever I can. You spoke to her, I
understand?'

Richard Lee sighed. 'She came and knocked on my door at
half past seven last night. Wanted some change for the phone,
that's all.'

'And?'

'I gave her a twenty-pence piece. She only had coppers.'

'Did she make any remark about who she was calling?'

'No.'

'So she was presumably making a local call.'

Lee shrugged. 'I didn't ask.'

'But that was all she wanted, was it? I mean, she didn't ask
for more silver and that was all you had?'

'She asked for a ten- or twenty-pence piece,' Lee said with
emphasis.

'And did you hear her make the call? The phone's just
outside your room, I see.'

'I could hear her say a few words. Didn't hear what they
were. I don't think she was talking for long. I heard the phone
ping after just a short while.'

'You could hear all right, then? You weren't watching television or listening to music?'

'I was watching *Coronation Street*, actually. But it's a soap
opera, not an opera.'

'Did she say anything else when she came to ask for change
for the phone?'

'Introduced herself, like. Said she'd just moved in across
the hall. I had noticed,' Lee said significantly. 'Not every day
someone looking like that moves into this dump.'

29

'You'd never seen her before, then?'

'Nah. Not till she moved here. I'd have remembered.'

'Did you notice what she was wearing when she came to your room last night, Mr Lee?'

Lee screwed up his nose and contemplated. 'She was wearing a short black skirt, black tights or maybe leggings, and boots ... one of them high-neck jumpers, a light colour, and a short jacket – it was a dark mixture, but I can't remember the exact colour. Sort of textured. Stylish, she was.'

'And how did she seem? Worried or tense?'

'No, I wouldn't say that. She was concered about being able to make her phone call, but that was all. She was friendly. Nice.'

'Mr Lee, did you hear anyone going to her room after you'd spoken to her?'

'No, I can't say I did. You see—' Lee seemed to have decided to be as helpful as he could – 'people come and go all the time in a place like this. Door opens out there and you hear it but it don't really register, if you know what I mean. Now there wasn't much to-ing and fro-ing last night – Tuesday's early in the week for that.'

'But you didn't hear any disturbance, or notice anything unusual, between half past seven, when you say she came to get some change, and nine o'clock, when you knocked on her door?'

Lee shook his head, then leaned back on the sofa, stretching his scrawny frame.

'And when Miss Sanderson, her sister, phoned—'

'That's the trouble with being in this room. I mean, it's handy being by the front door an' all, but I'm always answering the bleedin' phone for people. I ignore it sometimes.'

'But you didn't last night. As I was saying, when you went first to knock on Emily's door—'

'Nice name, Emily.'

'Mr Lee, did you notice anything at that time that made you think she was not in her room at nine o'clock?'

'Well, she didn't answer, did she?' Lee wrapped his thin arms around the back of his head and frowned at Simon.

'Could you tell whether there was a light on in her room?'

'I didn't look through the keyhole, if that's what you mean.'

30

'No sound, like music, radio? You couldn't see a light under the door, for instance?'

'Nothing. And I didn't look. Don't s'pose it would have shown, would it, with the light on in the hall as well? Look, I wasn't expecting there to be anything wrong, was I? I mean, it's happened plenty of times, me answering the phone and knocking on people's doors. I never had no dead bodies or nothing to deal with. Anyway –' he folded his arms firmly across his chest – 'It's the last time *I* answer the phone for anyone in this bleedin' place.'

'I can imagine it must be a nuisance,' Simon said. 'Tell me, how are you so sure about the time she came to your door?'

Lee looked at him pityingly. 'I told you, I was watching *Coronation Street*. I had just switched on the telly ready for the start when she knocked on the door. When I closed the door after giving her the change, it had just started. I remem-beer that I wasn't too annoyed because she hadn't made me miss any. D'you want me to explain about how I know what time it was when I answered the phone to her sister, as well?' Lee asked sarcastically.

'I'm sure she can do that herself. So she rang again, you say, at nine thirty and you tried the door again. Then, when you didn't have any success, she asked you to fetch the land-lord?'

'Yeah, yeah,' Lee said yawning.

'Well, thank you, Mr Lee.' Simon got up. 'You've been very helpful. DC Rogers here will be taking your details and questioning you about your movements last night.'

'I thought 'im and that other bloke had already done that. You goin' to start again, eh?' Lee smiled amiably up at Rogers.

'Oh, Mr Lee,' Simon turned back from the door. 'Do you own a car or vehicle of any sort?'

'Why's that? D'you think I took the dead body away in it, or something?' Lee laughed and shook his head. 'Wish I did. Difficult to afford one, you see, when you're living on income support.'

'Some people seem to manage it,' Rogers commented, and flushed again as both Simon and Lee regarded him.

'Does that bother you, Constable?' Lee said sweetly.

31

Rogers didn't answer.

'We'll leave it at that for the time being then, Mr Lee,' Simon said. 'But don't go too far away. We'll no doubt need to speak to you again.'

'That'll be very entertaining,' the youth said.

'Little faggot,' Rogers muttered as they left the room.

'You said something, Rogers?' Simon eyed the big DC coldly.

'Nothing, sir. But I bet he'd fit some kind of psychological profile.'

'He's probably completely harmless.'

'On the spot, though, sir. And a bit of a weirdo, if you ask me.'

'I didn't, Rogers. Was he in his room all last night?'

'Says he was.'

'Well, if he hasn't got access to a car, and the body's not in his room, he's unlikely to be guilty of this particular crime.'

'He's puny, anyway,' said Rogers, who wasn't.

'Detective Chief Inspector Simon!' Amanda Brakespeare, the biologist, emerged from Emily's room and approached him.

'Yes?'

'I've spoken briefly to your Superintendent Bradley this morning, as perhaps you know.' She peered at him questioningly through her spectacles.

Simon nodded.

'It will take us a little while to collect the necessary samples of blood for the processes of elimination. Have you arranged for a specimen to be taken from a relation of the victim?'

'It's being done.'

'Good. There's not a great deal of blood,' she said consideringly. She pointed at the wall above the gas fire. 'The shape of the blood spots there suggests that the victim was moving in the direction of the door when she was struck. Arterial, typical zigzag pattern.' She frowned thoughtfully. 'The blood on the chair – ' she pointed to the chair which Edwards had found in his way on getting into the room – 'may have originated from it falling on the missing rug into the blood that was already on the rug itself. That's speculation, of course, at the moment,' she said, peering up at Simon, 'but we've found

32

traces of fibres which may come from the rug itself.'

'The chair was in the way of the door when the landlord got in,' Simon said.

She indicated a brownish stain on the carpet by the door. 'Just there, then. It must have been pushed out of the way, mustn't it, when the intruder took the rug?'

Simon nodded agreement. 'So it seems likely to have been a quick struggle?'

'Ye-es,' she said, drawing out the word. 'We found one or two drops of blood over by the bed, but from the evidence, most of it must have been shed on the rug. You probably noticed the more or less straight-edged stain over there –' she pointed again to the area near the fireplace – 'which suggests that a larger amount of blood at that point fell near the edge of the rug and, when the rug was removed, left an outline mark. There's no seepage, though. Has the landlord given you any useful description of the rug?'

'He could describe it only as a brown one, as I recall.'

'Probably wouldn't have been too bulky, if, as it seems, the attacker rolled or wrapped the body in it,' the biologist commented. 'And the attacker would probably have had a lot of blood on him.'

'Yes, I'm sure you're right.' Simon smiled encouragingly at her intent face. She obviously went beyond her remit in her enthusiasm for her job. 'So you think it looks like a serious, even deadly attack?'

'Without knowing the amount of blood spilled?' She shrugged. 'But I would say it looks like it,' she said briskly, catching the smile. 'I'll let you know if anything interesting turns up.'

'Thanks, Amanda.'

She turned away and went back into Emily's room. Simon's eyes followed her abstractedly.

'Sir?' Longman came up to him. 'DC Jones said, do you want the sister and boyfriend back here when they're finished?'

Simon looked at his watch. 'I'm going out to the university for a short while. Ask her to get them lunch and take them to my office for about twelve thirty.'

'Right. Sir?' Longman hurried after Simon. 'The word

processor in her room. Shall I take a look at it now?'

Longman had been in computers before he entered the police force. His preference for a more people-centred job hadn't vanquished his interest, and whenever computers figured in an investigation, it was usually Longman who volunteered to deal with them.

'If they've finished with it, yes, by all means. Though you'll probably only find a few psychology essays.' Simon paused on his way again. 'I wonder who she was making that call to last night?'

Chapter Five

The university had been built in the last thirty years or so in the vast grounds of an old country estate. It was an attractive campus, owing much to the parkland undulating with many old trees. The institution had gradually expanded southwards and now also owned some fine older buildings in the city itself, as well as some recent ones, jarring in their flagrant funtionalism. The old manor house had been pulled down at the start but the splendid stable block, lending itself with its simple structure to modern alterations, housed, as it had from the beginning, the main administrative offices of the university. A pale sun, beginning to break through the low drizzle at last, flattered the colours in the lovely old bricks.

Simon, entering the wide glass doors framed in the original arched entranceway, requested an audience with Hugh Smith. After he had shown his credentials to the young man at the reception, and the young man had put through a muted call to the higher echelons, Simon observed a gentle fluttering of quiet comment and glances in his direction from the people working in the open-plan office area. He sat down on a cheap plastic chair, resigned to the requisite pause before being admitted to the presence of those in high authority, and was surprised by the speedy approach of the receptionist.

'Mr Smith says, will you go up straight away.' The young man gave directions and Simon found his own way to the spacious offices of the university administrator on the first floor.

He was seated at a large desk placed at right angles to the arched window at the front of the building and commanding an excellent view over his domain. Hugh Smith was a large man, sparse grey hair under iron control, immaculately dressed in a dark-blue suit with waistcoat and snowy shirt with old school tie. His clothes proclaimed a successful professional man in every respect. Simon could always interpret the conventional when it came to sartorial matters.

'Come in, my boy,' Smith intoned in perfect public-school accents, rising and coming the considerable distance around his desk to shake Simon's hand. 'Would you like a sherry?' He detached his right hand to wave it, white and perfectly manicured, towards a well-stocked drinks table.

'Too late for me, I'm afraid.'

'Hmm? Oh, I see, I suppose you've been up all night. And a bit early for me, really. You're a graduate, I'm told. Oxbridge?'

Simon shook his head.

'Ah, redbrick.'

'Concrete, actually.'

'Ha! Yes, some of them are, aren't they? Can look better than they sound, though. Content that counts, of course. Dreaming spires and all that are wonderful but the universities aren't really interested in producing poets and aesthetes these days, I'm afraid.' Smith displayed his white hand again. 'Come and sit down, my boy.'

It wasn't totally unpleasing to be called 'my boy' in one's thirties, at least by someone who was too amiable to be patronising, though there was surely no more than ten years' distance in age between them. Yet Simon, with his unruly hair and regrettable overcoat, did feel a generation apart from the older man. Smith was one of those people who are born to be middle-aged, Simon thought. He sat.

Smith became instantly businesslike as he resumed his own seat.

'So. Has the girl been found yet, Chief Inspector?'

Simon gave a brief account of what little had so far been discovered.

'Very difficult for all concerned when the body doesn't turn up,' Smith observed. 'Very difficult. Puts you in the invidious position of half desiring what you really don't want. Where did you say she was living?'

36

Simon gave him the address.

Hugh Smith opened a folder from a tray on his orderly desk. 'According to our records she was living at quite a different address last term, sharing with two other women students. I wonder why she moved to an establishment like that?'

'You know of it?'

Smith inclined his head and pursed his lips. 'We have had a little trouble with Mr Edwards in the past. Although he might interpret things differently. It is not an accommodation address that we recommend to our students.'

'And why is that?' Simon asked.

'We've had accusations and counteraccusations, but, to put it simply, some women students who have stayed there objected to his approaches, shall we say. he, in turn, objected to their loose morals in having friends of the opposite sex staying in their rooms overnight.'

'That happens all the time, I imagine,' Simon said. 'Students of the opposite sex, I mean.'

'Oh, yes. But even in this day and age it is not something we, with a responsibility towards the young people in our care, can publicly condone. And there is also the matter of publicity. In fact, if we are to be frank, there is first and foremost the matter of publicity. That it goes on, everyone knows and understands, but when a person such as Mr Edwards threatens to arouse the prurient interest of the town population by starting a campaign in the local press about student morals threatening the fabric of our society, I'm afraid we, the university authorities, are forced to, ah, pour gallons of oil on the choppy waters.'

'So the female students were told to keep quiet about Edwards's behaviour and quietly remove themselves from the premises?'

'Yes,' Smith sighed, then looked sharply at Simon. 'I suppose I shouldn't ask, and it makes one shudder to think of it, but is it possible that he is involved in some way in what has happened to Miss Sanderson?'

'All I can say is that we'll be closely investigating anyone who might remotely be involved.'

'I wonder why she went there,' Smith said again.

'Perhaps it was more a matter of going away from her other place,' Simon suggested.

Smith frowned. 'There may have been some disagreement. First-year students are supposed to confirm the suitability of their accommodation through the university authorities. We have an accommodation office for that purpose. In fact, they're still generally required to stay in hall or be in digs in their first year. But as Miss Sanderson was a mature student, we agreed to her sharing a house with a couple of second-year students.'

'You're impressively well informed about those in your care,' Simon said.

Smith smiled self-deprecatingly. 'Oh, I checked with Mrs Tolsen, our accommodation officer, first thing.'

'I shall of course be visiting the two students she shared with,' Simon said, and asked Smith for their address. He read it out in precise, clipped accents.

'Thank you. We'll keep you informed generally.'

'It sounds craven, I know,' Smith began hesitantly. 'It *is* craven but, when something like this happens, we are concerned about the publicity ...'

'Bad for the image and all that?' Simon couldn't suppress a touch of impatience. He had anticipated something of the sort since his talk with Bradley.

'Yes, well, such considerations probably seem despicable to someone doing a job such as yours. I can understand your lack of sympathy, but we are all trying to do the jobs we find ourselves in—'

'I do understand,' Simon said. 'But, as you say, we all have to do our jobs as best we can. I'll try to introduce as little controversy as possible.' He stood up and took off his overcoat. The room was getting increasingly warm as the sun moved in front of the large window.

'What I would appreciate, at this point,' he said, making himself comfortable again on his nicely upholstered chair, 'is any information you can give me on Emily Sanderson's brief life at the University of Westwich.'

Hugh Smith opened the brown folder. Simon could see a passport-sized photograph of the girl in the top right-hand corner.

'The photograph would be useful,' he said to Smith. It was much clearer than the one that Charlotte had given him.

Smith hesitated and then removed a paperclip and pushed the small picture across the desk.

'You'll return it soon, I hope. I hope,' he sighed, 'that we shall still have a use for it in the future.'

Simon put the picture inside his wallet. 'Might I have a look at her file?' he asked.

A white hand was placed firmly over it. 'We'd rather not, if you don't mind. Not unless it seems absolutely necessary. You see, we claim student information to be confidential – it's a sensitive issue. I'm sure I can tell you anything you want to know without, er, actually handing it over, if you understand me.'

'Oh yes, I do understand,' Simon said. It was to be a matter of the letter, if not the spirit, of the law. Getting nasty with someone like Smith wasn't going to achieve anything.

'So.' Smith straightened up. 'What can I tell you?' he asked, consulting the file and placing gold half-moon glasses on the rim of his nose. 'She was twenty-four, had been working at a publishers in London, Hyde Books, since she left secretarial school three years ago. It was an advanced secre-tarial course,' he said, peering at Simon over his glasses, 'and she already had three good A levels. She worked for the publishers as a secretary and receptionist. She made a late application here. Didn't begin the procedure the previous autumn, just applied here. As a mature candidate she was given extra consideration.'

'What made her decide to do a degree in psychology?' Simon asked. 'I imagine you have her application details there.'

'Yes, I did look through them before you arrived,' Smith murmured, flicking through the pages and pausing at the appropriate place. 'The usual things about wanting to extend herself more, her developing interest in the subject, wide reading and so on.'

'Did her employers give her a good reference?'

Smith turned a page. 'Yes,' he said slowly. 'Yes, they did.' His eyes were rapidly scanning the rest of the page.

'What other referees did she give?' Simon asked, intrigued

by the other man's transparent interest in what he was reading.

There was a small frown crinkling Smith's smooth brow. 'Well, it seems she knew our Dr Peter Dawson, of whom you have no doubt heard. Oh, of course,' he said, brow clearing, 'Hyde Books are his publishers. That must be why – Peter did a little recruitment on behalf of the university, I suppose. If she talked to him about degrees in psychology and he encouraged her to apply, she would naturally want to mention the connection on her application form.' Smith frowned again, though, and peered anew at the sheet of paper.

'And was she a good student, an able one?' Simon asked.

'No trouble at all, as far as I can gather from her tutor's reports. Intelligent, interested, diligent.'

'She had a pastoral tutor as well, did she?'

'Yes, indeed.' Smith riffled through a few more pages. 'But she doesn't seem to have seen him since the beginning of her first term. Nothing much there, just the confirmation that she is in satisfactory accommodation. It's mainly an "I am here if you need me" sort of consultation at that point.'

'And she didn't consult him again with any worries or difficulties?'

'No, apparently not. But she can't have been too happy with the two girls she was sharing with. She should have waited for help over that. If only she had,' Smith mourned.

It might have made no difference, Simon thought. He said, 'Yes, her haste might seem a bit odd.'

'Chief Inspector –' Smith stood the file on end and shook the papers into place – 'I really don't think there's anything else I can help you with. This meeting has been mostly a matter of you and I making contact and establishing the need for, ah, discretion, if possible. But it's the first day of term, as you probably realise, and a very busy time for those of us in administration. Students will be beginning to register at around ten o'clock, so—'

'I can contact you another time if there's anything I want to ask or convey,' Simon finished for him, getting to his feet and pulling on his overcoat. 'I'll want to talk to some members of staff and students, of course.'

'Yes, just keep me informed, would you? I'm so sorry, I

don't mean to be abrupt,' Smith murmured contritely as he saw Simon to the door and waited courteously as he watched Simon go down the wide staircase.

The large entrance area was transformed by flocks of students, all, it seemed, exclaiming loudly and greeting each other, swamping the administrative staff, who seemed to be having a hard job administering to them. Simon pushed through the throng and went out into the tranquil sunshine, tempted to walk through the pleasant campus to see Jessie in the psychology department on the edge of town. He retrieved his car instead, with some difficulty, from the midst of students' erratically parked vehicles and drove slowly along the circular road that ringed the campus.

He had never visited Jessie in her room at the university before. He parked in the same car park that he had used the previous night and entered the same door, only to be told that Dr Thurrow was two buildings away along a covered way and up two flights of stairs.

There were few people around in this attractive corner of the campus. Term was only just beginning to stir. A black-bird, high in the bare branches of a tree near the entrance, seduced by the unseasonably warm sunshine, sang loudly in anticipation of spring.

'You look tired, poor love,' Jessie said as he entered her room. 'Have some caffeine.' She went over to the machine on a side unit.

'You don't,' he said appreciatively. She was wearing a warm brick-red jacket with a colourful scarf and a short matching skirt revealing more than usual of her very fine legs. Her wild chestnut-tinted hair spilled down her back, catching the sunlight that poured into the room.

'Did you get in all right this morning?' he asked.

'No problem. Sid whisked me here in half the time it would usually have taken me.'

He stood at the window for a moment looking at the view, conscious of the pleasure of now being able to picture her at work. There was an extensive pond below her window, busy with ducks and other ornamental wildfowl he couldn't have named, framed on one side by willows and surrounded by lawns where the ducks hadn't paddled them to bare mud.

41

She handed him a steaming mug of black coffee. 'I suppose you've been to see Hugh?' she asked as he sank into a low chair. 'The authorities won't be relishing the publicity, I imagine.'

'I'm afraid that won't be my first consideration,' Simon said.

'Of course not.'

'Apparently Peter Dawson was one of her referees when she applied to the university.'

'Mmm. Yes, she worked for his publishers, didn't she?'

'Mmm.' Simon mimicked.

'He must have inspired her,' Jessie said lightly.

'No doubt. Real charmer, isn't he? Jess, have you had any thoughts about Emily since I spoke to you? Anything you think might be relevant in any way?'

Jessie hesitated.

'You said she was an innocent,' Simon prompted. 'What did you mean exactly?'

'That was a bit off the top of my head,' Jessie said.

'That's not necessarily unreliable. As you, a psychologist, must surely recognise,' Simon said, mock seriously.

'I don't like being put on the spot about this. There's a lot at stake.'

'How do you mean?'

'Oh, someone who's presumably been murdered ...' Jessie said evasively.

'Come on, Jess. Did you mean she was naive?'

'In a way, I suppose. Let me think.' She folded her arms and paused.

'You feel you didn't really know her well enough to comment?' Simon prompted.

Jessie glanced at him and frowned. 'I spent quite a few hours in her company in a teaching context, and I saw her in social situations as well. She was a member of the Arts Club, for instance. I used to see her there. And in the university bars, socialising like everyone else.'

'And?'

'Well, I'd say she didn't seem to have any real conscious-ness of her effect on other people. I mean, it was partly her looks – she seemed unaware of the impact she made because

42

of them, she had no conceit about being so beautiful. And she was very beautiful. It wasn't just flesh and bones; she sort of shone, if you know what I mean?' She looked to Simon for affirmation.

'I think so,' he said, remembering the photograph Charlotte had given him.

'But at the same time, she was dangerous,' Jessie said abruptly.

'Oh? In what way?'

'Look, I'm still only basing this on a fairly limited experience of the girl ... ' Jessie hesitated and came to sit in front of Simon, one hip perched on her desk.

'Go on.' Simon took a mouthful of coffee and leaned back.

'She lacked awareness,' Jessie said. 'She thought everyone was like her, thought like her, and always looked bewildered if she was disagreed with. She lacked empathy. But she needed to be liked. No, perhaps that's not quite right. She would put herself out to charm and then, unaware that she had aroused intense attraction rather than mere liking, she would leave the person – usually a male – absolutely flat. What to them had been a powerful experience was just, well, everyday to her.'

'A bit of a teaser?'

Jessie shook her head emphatically. 'No. She wasn't like that at all. She was naive, if anything. For her, intense admiration seemed to hold the same value as friendly liking does for others. Her parameters were different. It occurred to me that she felt, perhaps unconsciously, she didn't exist except through the other person's image of her.'

'Isn't there some philosophical argument for that anyway?' Simon said.

'Not only philosophical. But this was a bit different. She needed to constantly have reflected back this image of herself. But she did it in such a way that it embraced the other person too. A form of projection, in a way. She made the other person feel that they were wonderful as well, and then she sort of left them flat, as I said. Her actions belied all the emotional excitement that she engendered. It wasn't followed up.' Jessie went over to the machine and poured herself a mug of coffee. 'I wondered,' she said thoughtfully as she perched again, 'what she would do if she ever failed to charm.'

'Her parents are dead,' Simon said. 'She has just one sister. The sister is lovely, but in a different way – quite a different character, too, I'd say. Was all this with Emily a sort of pathological need to be loved?' As usual, he felt awkward using half-baked psychology with Jessie.

'Most patterns of behaviour begin early in life. When did the parents die, do you know?'

'About four years ago, I think her sister said.' Simon set his empty mug on the desk beside her. 'What made her dangerous, then? Was it this lack of awareness?'

'Yes, partly. She didn't separate people from her own consciousness, lacked any objectivity. Oh, I'm not expressing this very well.' Jessie sighed and placed her mug beside Simon's. 'It was a childlike quality. She had the ego of a child, and that can be dangerous in children, let alone young women.'

Her phone buzzed and she went around the desk to answer it. 'It's Geoff Longman.' She handed the phone across to him.

'I guessed you'd be there. I tried Mr Smith's office first, though.' Longman sounded eager.

'Well, what is it, Geoff? Have they found her?'

'No. I just thought you'd like to know what I found on her word processor.'

'Yes?'

'There's a letter dated the twelfth, this last Monday, written to someone called Peter.'

'What does it say?'

'She tells him that she's moved to this new address and that he's got to come and see her the following evening at eight. That it's important she sees him.'

'Would it convey any greater meaning if you read it to me?'

'Not really, sir.'

'Anything else there?'

'Nothing personal, no. Essays, like you said.'

'Thanks, Geoff. I'll see you at HQ in about an hour.' Simon put the phone down gently.

'She wrote a letter to a Peter, asking him, or telling him, to come to her new address on Tuesday – last night – at eight.'

'I heard,' Jessie said. Longman's voice on the telephone

44

was notorious for its volume. She got up and went to sit on the other side of her desk.

'I'm wondering if it was Peter Dawson she was writing to. It's not a common name in the younger generation.'

'You'll no doubt be following it up along those lines,' Jessie said. 'And I'm afraid you're going to enjoy doing it.' The ease between them had disappeared.

'He wasn't there at your start-of-term get-together last night when it happened. He came in at the same time as I did – at about a quarter to nine.'

'Of course he was there.'

'But at what time? Was he in earlier? What time did he leave? He told me he'd had to go out for a while. I wonder why?'

'I can't say I noticed.' Jessie sounded indifferent.

'Are you aware of any relationship between Peter Dawson and Emily Sanderson?'

'Look, Chris, I'm not one of your interviewees at the police station, so don't cross-examine me,' Jessie said coldly. She seemed to have created more than a physical barrier by placing herself behind her desk.

'Oh, of course, he's a friend of yours, isn't he? I shall have to be very careful about treading on sensitive toes.'

'What's the matter with you, Chris? I'm seeing another side to you, and I'm not sure I like it.'

'It's called being a policeman. I'm sorry if it offends your sensibilities.' He didn't want this. He was miserable at the tension that had sprung up between them so quickly. He remembered his thoughts earlier that morning, looking out at the drizzle in St Anthony's Square, and had an uneasy feeling that some kind of rite of passage was going to be required before the subject of his thoughts then could ever be broached with Jessie.

'Jess, I'm sorry. This has got to be gone through. A girl's missing, probably dead. Personal feelings tend not to count for much—'

'So I see. I appreciate your difficulties but don't, please, lay them at my door. Just because you and I know each other isn't going to give you any special access, you know.' She went over and poured herself another mug of coffee, not offering him one, and stood, glass jug in hand, waving it in his direction. 'Don't expect me to pry on colleagues, spy on them for you.'

'Know each other! Is that what you call it?'

She managed a smile. 'In the biblical sense at least.'

He wanted to challenge her, to ask, What about love, friendship? But the words remained unspoken. She was right in a way. Their relationship had nothing to do with it. Or rather, just how much or how little their relationship had to do with anything, they were about to find out.

'Have I asked you to pry on colleagues?' he protested.

'You asked me about Peter Dawson and whether he had any relationship with Emily Sanderson. You asked me if or when he left the party last night,' she reminded him.

'And it's a question I shall be asking him and other people who were there. You were there, so I asked you.'

'And I still think you're presuming on our relationship.'

'And would it be presumptuous if I ask you if you could name any particular friends the girl had?'

'I suppose not.' She sipped her coffee, apparently unmoved. 'Well?'

'She didn't have any particular friends that I noticed.'

'Well, that's extremely helpful. Thanks very much, Dr Thurrow.' He stood up awkwardly, extricating his long frame from the low chair with none of the dignity he would have liked to have summoned.

'Don't be childish, Chris.'

There was a tap on the door and it opened immediately, admitting Hermione, red hair aflame in the sunny room. Sensing the mood there, she asked, concerned, 'Have I butted in at a wrong moment?'

'No.' They both spoke at the same time and Hermione looked from one to the other, brows raised.

'Shall I come back later?' she asked Jessie.

'No,' Simon answered for her. 'I was just leaving.'

Hermione came further into the room. 'I'm sorry to hear it,' she said gently. 'Are you here about Emily Sanderson?'

'You've heard already, then?' Simon spoke more irritably than he meant to.

'It's all round the department,' Hermione said.

46

Simon glanced at Jessie.

'Don't look at me,' she warned.

'Oh? I can't even do that now?'

'Don't be childish,' she said again.

Simon, colour slightly raised, looked mutely from one woman to the other, the one mutinous, the other puzzled but sympathetic.

'I'll see you, then,' he said, making for the door.

Hermione moved to let him pass. 'If there's anything I can help with ... ' she said hesitantly.

'Thank you. I'd be grateful if someone would,' he said and went out of the door without looking back.

Chapter Six

In Simon's room at headquarters Charlotte Sanderson was
waiting with Longman in attendance. She had taken off her
long raincoat and was wearing a light-coloured, loosely cut
top over a linen skirt. It draped down to a pair of shapely
ankles. She looked more slender, more frail even, than she
had last night.

'Where's Mr Whittaker?' Simon asked, pulling off his overcoat and frowning at Longman.

'He went out for some cigarettes,' Charlotte answered. 'He
won't be long.'

'I want to talk to you on your own anyway,' Simon said to
her. 'Geoff, find him somewhere else to sit when he comes
back, until I'm ready for him.'

'Yes, sir.' Longman eyed Simon sidelong, aware of his
edginess. Never one to pass an opportunity to dig a little, he
added, 'Dr Thurrow all right, sir?'

Simon narrowed his eyes at him. 'Blooming, thank you,
Sergeant.'

'Just wondered.'

'Let's get on, shall we?' Simon said. He spread some blank
sheets of paper on his desk and picked up a pen. 'Miss
Sanderson—'

'Call me Charlotte,' she said quietly. 'It seems less intimi-
dating.'

He looked at her in surprise. 'I'm sorry. I had no idea that I
was. You had the blood test done?'

'Yes.'

'Good. Miss Sanderson, Charlotte, there are several questions I didn't have the opportunity to ask you last night—'

'There's something I have to tell you,' she interrupted,

seeking his eyes. Then she lowered her own and fumbled in her bag, producing a packet of cigarettes. 'Do you mind?' she asked. 'I don't smoke much, I've more or less given up, but—'

'Difficult to do when you're under stress,' Simon said. 'I know what it's like. God knows what would happen to the crime rate if we banned smoking in police stations.' He pushed an ashtray across his desk towards her.

'Thank you.' She lit up and took a deep drag on the cigarette.

'You were saying?' Simon prompted.

She blew smoke at the ceiling. 'I think I have to tell you this. I just don't want it to be general knowledge.'

'That depends,' he began.

'She was pregnant, Chief Inspector.'

'Oh?' He glanced at Longman, who raised his neatly trimmed eyebrows. 'How many months?'

'It will be about four months now.'

'When did she tell you this?'

'Not until just before she returned to Westwich. I could tell there was something –' she hesitated – 'not wrong, but different. She wasn't her usual self. There wasn't any morning sickness or anything, or if there was she kept it well hidden.'

'Was it Mark Whittaker's?'

'No, she said it wasn't. That's why I didn't want to say anything about it last night, with Mark there.'

'Did she say who the father was?'

'She wouldn't tell me. And I don't have any idea.' She drew on her cigarette again. 'Emily didn't talk much about her time here at the university. She wasn't much of a talker about herself anyway. She was a very private person and I think she sometimes thought I could be a bit overprotective.' Charlotte bit her lip and stared at the tip of her cigarette.

'You were close, though, you said last night.'

'Oh, we were. Supportive of each other.'

And yet the girl had obviously not told her sister as soon as she knew she was pregnant.

'How long had she known she was pregnant, Charlotte?'

'She said she confirmed it at the end of last term. She saw someone at the university medical practice.'

49

'Why didn't she tell you sooner? I mean, her only relative, who is so supportive of her?' He couldn't keep the doubt from his words.

She bowed her head. 'I don't know,' she said in a muffled voice, then looked up at him, her eyes wet. 'I don't know,' she repeated.

'Did she say whether the father knew?'

'He knew, she said.'

'And she planned to keep the baby?'

'Oh, yes. She talked about creches at the university. The baby was due in June, at the end of her first year. She said it all fitted in quite well, considering. She was very practical in some ways.'

Given a *fait accompli*, perhaps, Simon thought. 'And was she expecting the father to be involved in all this, acknowledge the baby, help care for it?'

'She seemed very confident about it. It was only when I questioned her more closely that she got a bit upset and told me not to interfere – that it was none of my business.' She took another draw on the cigarette and looked miserably towards the window.

'She was obviously being defensive,' Simon said.

'Yes,' she whispered and got out a handkerchief. 'It just makes it even worse, the fact that she was expecting a baby.'

Whittaker abruptly came through the door without knocking, brushing aside the young policeman who had attempted to restrain him. He immediately went to Charlotte's side, concern on his face at her distress.

Simon indicated to Longman to move him somewhere else. They could hear the young man's loud questions for some moments as he was escorted down the corridor. Then everything was quiet again.

The interruption seemed to have helped her to calm down a little. She stubbed out her cigarette and swallowed with an effort, waiting for him to speak.

'Charlotte, did Emily ever speak to you of someone called Peter?'

She fixed her large blue eyes on his but seemed to look somewhere far beyond them. 'Not recently anyway. It's possible, but – I can't think straight. She may have done.'

'She made a telephone call last night at seven thirty. Is it possible that it was to you, perhaps to let you know that she wouldn't be in when you called?'

She shook her head. 'No. It couldn't have been me she rang.'

'We think it was probably a local call, anyway. She asked one of the tenants for some small change,' Simon said. 'Charlotte, Emily was working for a publisher in London before she came to the university here. Did she talk to you about her decision to leave her job?'

'A bit. I think she was afraid I would think it a bad idea. She enjoyed her job with Hyde Books – she'd been happy there.'

'And did you express any disapproval?'

'No, I didn't. I would have had no right to. Emily was very bright. I could understand that she wanted to stretch herself.' Charlotte looked at him intently. 'Is all this of any importance, Chief Inspector? I mean, what are you doing about finding her?'

'Everything we can think of is being done at a practical level. What I'm trying to do is find out as much as I can about your sister. We can't tell yet what may be relevant,' Simon said. 'By answering our questions you'll be giving us the best help you can.'

She rubbed her hands together as if she was cold and stared at him emptily again.

'And you can't recall her mentioning a Peter in connection with work?'

She paused in the act of lighting another cigarette. 'Of course. Someone who used her publisher. Yes. She pointed him out to me on television once.' She smiled apologetically. 'I remember now. It was him that she talked to about doing a degree here. What's his name?' She searched her mind, frowning. 'Dawson. He's quite well known, isn't he? I should have remembered, sorry.'

Longman tapped briefly on the door and came in, resuming his seat against the wall and picking up his notebook again.

'What is it you do?' Simon asked her.

'My job, you mean? I have a computer consultancy. I work from home,' she said. 'So is this the Peter you were asking

51

about? Why did you ask if she knew a Peter?'

'She wrote a note to a Peter the day before she disappeared. It's on her PC. We certainly don't know that it was to Dr Dawson, so I'll have to ask you to be discreet – if the press ask you any questions, for example.'

'The press?' She looked anxious.

'They're already beginning to build up in the road she lived in,' Simon said.

'I won't be talking to them,' she said emphatically. 'I hate the way they prey on other people's misfortunes.'

'They can occasionally be useful in cases like this,' Simon said, though he shared her sentiments.

'I'm sorry,' she said. 'Please don't send them in my direction.' She took another lungful of cigarette smoke and blew it out again almost immediately. 'So you know what the note said?'

He told her.

'It sounds as if you need to find this Peter, then,' she said. She leaned forward in her seat, stubbing out her second cigarette and frowning. 'Chief Inspector, if this Peter is the one she met in London, the one who's on TV, who teaches at the university here, I hope you won't be treating him any more carefully than you would anyone else.'

'We have to treat everyone carefully, Charlotte, even if we don't always want to.'

'I suppose so,' she said. Her brief show of assertion had vanished. 'Oh, God! I hope you can find her, Chief Inspector. And find her alive.'

'I can only promise again that we'll do all we can. You're exhausted,' he said. 'Hadn't you better go home? We'll keep you informed, I promise you.'

She sighed. 'It feels like deserting her. But I suppose there's nothing I can do here. I didn't bring any personal things, it's true. I need a change of clothes. And Mark will have to get back to work – so will I, at some point. There's a pile of stuff waiting for me.'

'How long has Emily known Mark Whittaker?' Simon asked.

'A couple of years. He works for Hyde Books. She's only been going out with him for about a year, though.'

'And did you think it was serious, the relationship?'

'I suppose so – on Mark's side, anyway. And Emily seemed keen on him, though it was obvious she didn't want to settle down yet. But I think Mark wanted to.'

'So he'd be pretty upset to find that Emily was pregnant by another man?'

Her eyes widened as she caught the possible implication. 'No! I mean – yes. But he didn't know, Chief Inspector.'

'I'll need to talk to him, you understand. Just as I'll be talking to anyone who knew Emily well.' Simon got up and went to the window, looking down at the movement of police vehicles along the busy road. 'Go and get some coffee or something now while I speak to Mark and then you can both get back to London.'

She still seemed reluctant to go, a slight furrow in her smooth brow. As Longman escorted her out, she looked back at Simon again, catching his eyes, impressing on him her need, his responsibility.

He leaned back and put his feet on his desk. The pregnancy raised certain avenues of thought. It wasn't much of a motive for murder in this day and age, except in certain situations, in certain lives. With someone whose career it might damage, someone with a responsibility towards young people, someone going places – like Peter Dawson. It wouldn't do him any good, poised for the post of professor of psychology. And any scandal probably wouldn't help his media career, either.

Simon would have to talk to Dawson soon. But before he did so, he wanted to be as well informed as possible, so he would talk to others first.

Longman came into the room, bringing two plastic cups of coffee.

'Whittaker said he'd be along in a minute,' he said. 'He's having a word with Charlotte.'

Simon said nothing, still absorbed in his thoughts.

'She got upset again,' Longman added.

'She seems pretty fragile, yes,' Simon said. He dragged his feet off the desk and sat up, pulling the coffee towards him, then pushing it away.

'So we wonder who the father was?' Longman said.

'Maybe those girls she was sharing with will have some

53

ideas. I'll try and see them today.' He passed across the details that Smith had given him. 'See if you can contact them, find out when they'll be in.'

'The fact that she was pregnant could be a motive,' he went on. 'For some people.' He didn't mention Dawson for the moment. 'And the character of the victim—' He paused.

'Must be considered in a murder case,' Longman finished for him.

'Yes. She was a very attractive girl, not just in looks. Apparently she used to fascinate people rather easily and not follow it up, if you know what I mean.'

Longman nodded wisely.

'But it was unconsciously done, I'm told,' Simon said, struggling to recall Jessie's rather more elaborate rendition.

'A bit of a dangerous way to behave,' Longman said. 'Especially with looks like hers.'

Longman had chosen the same word as Jessie: dangerous. Simon repeated the word. 'So it's possible that she was attacked by someone who didn't understand her casual need to make people love her.'

'And he'd take the body, we assume, because of possible forensic evidence from a sexual attack,' Longman said, always happier when he could connect to facts in an investigation. 'And if she was pregnant, that gives us yet another motive for removing the body. DNA testing of the baby.'

'It would tell us who the father was,' Simon agreed.

'And it's possible that the same person could have both motives.'

Simon tapped a pencil and considered. 'It's possible. But the pregnancy suggests an ongoing relationship. Yes, not necessarily,' he said, as Longman looked questioning, 'but she was, what, four months pregnant? A sexual attack as a result of what he interpreted as a come-on by someone who had known her for at least several months is less likely than from someone less close to her.'

'But by no means unlikely,' Longman insisted. 'Rejected lovers are some of the worst offenders.'

When he had thought about Dawson as a possible suspect, Simon realised that he had automatically assumed that it would be Dawson who did any rejecting, casting off. He couldn't envisage the man allowing himself to be caught up emotionally by anyone – not enough to drive him to murder. The only motive he could attribute to him would be self-protection. And he was assuming an awful lot on the basis that Dawson's name was Peter, that she had written to a Peter, that she knew Dawson from her London days.

'What about this Peter she sent the letter to?' Longman said. 'Shouldn't we be looking for him?'

Still conscious of his prejudice when it came to Peter Dawson, Simon again made no mention of his Christian name. 'Yes,' he said. 'Make sure you pass it on to the others so that they can ask around among Emily's friends and acquaintances.'

Longman made a careful note.

Simon said, 'Smith tells me that Edwards the landlord used to make advances to female students who stayed there. The university doesn't recommend the address.'

'Not surprised. His video collection showed a taste for the exotic.'

'Whittaker is taking his time,' Simon said, looking at his watch.

'He's just making a statement,' Longman said drily.

'Hmm?'

'Not the written kind, sir. You know – asserting himself, not at our beck and call, all that stuff.'

Simon felt irritated. The row with Jessie that morning had already affected his mood, and the thought of another wrestle with Whittaker did nothing to improve it. 'You speak to him Geoff. We can't hang about like this. I'll see those girls myself, after I've called in at Acacia Road.'

'Not redolent of bloody murder, is it, Acacia Road?' Longman said.

Simon was already pulling on his overcoat. 'What? Oh, in the annals of crime, you mean? Like Rillington Crescent and Cromwell Street. I expect they sounded innocent enough once.'

'There's something in names, though. They each have a different vibration, did you know that? Makes you wonder, doesn't it?'

Simon picked up his old paisley scarf. 'You know, Geoff,

for a computer expert, you've got some oddly romantic tendencies.'

'I call it being open-minded. What do you want from Whittaker?'

'The usual stuff. How long he's been involved with her, did he come to Westwich to see her often, his movements that evening.' Simon paused at the door. 'Ask him if he had much to do with a Dr Dawson who publishes with his company.'

'The one from the university that's on the telly?'

'That's the one. And find out where Whittaker was last night before Charlotte rang him and got him to bring her to Westwich.'

'He'll be calling his solicitor. I know the type,' Longman said heavily, taking Simon's seat behind the desk.

'Don't get comfortable. Go and get him.'

Chapter Seven

Sinclair Road, where Emily Sanderson had spent her first term at university, was on the south side of town, an anonymous monotony of tidy Edwardian semidetached houses amid other identical streets in this part of the city. Simon parked his car in one of the few available spaces and looked for number 60. The houses all seemed to be named similarly – Fern Villa, Primrose Villa, Rose Villa. He was amused to see that the house next door to number 60 had been renamed Aston Villa, the new nameplate hung over the original, the renaming probably done by its occupants rather than its owner. Number 60 showed no hint of student occupation. Clean white net curtains hung at polished windows, the paintwork shone and even the small front garden area was free of weeds between the coloured tiles which framed a dead-looking shrub.

The heavy iron door knocker resounded with a satisfying thud. After a short delay the door opened on smooth hinges and a young women with a severe haircut and plain round face looked up at him. 'Are you Detective Chief Inspector Simon?' she asked.

He had spoken to her or her companion on the telephone less than fifteen minutes before. 'That's right,' he said.

She waited, blocking with her sturdy body any move he might make to enter. 'Well? Aren't you going to show me your identification?'

'Of course. Sorry.' He reached inside his pocket and held out the plastic wallet, opening it in front of her face.

Startling him, she made a grab for it and examined the photograph, scanning his face and swiftly reading through the text before handing it back to him. 'You can't be too careful,' she said. 'Besides, you're not quite my idea of a policeman.' Her tone was disapproving. She stood back and allowed him into the hallway, leading him into a room at the front of the house where another young woman was seated doing some tapestry work beside a lighted gas fire.

'This is Celia,' the plump young woman announced, 'and I'm Harriet.'

'Do sit down,' Celia said, indicating with a tapestry needle the chair opposite her. She had mousy hair which hung fine and straight to her narrow shoulders.

The room was warm after the chill sunshine outside, but Simon hesitated to make himself so much at home as to take off his overcoat. 'I'll sit over here, if that's all right,' he said, choosing an upright chair beside the highly polished dining table against the wall.

Harriet plumped her rotund little body into the seat he had disdained and demanded, 'Well? We've been puzzling, haven't we, Celia, but we can't think of any way in which we've transgressed the law – at least recently.'

Celia gave a snuffle of agreement.

'I'm physics, by the way, and Celia's chemistry,' Harriet offered.

Simon said, 'It's about Emily Sanderson that I've come to see you.'

'But she doesn't live here any more,' Harriet said. 'Left without a word.'

Simon was beginning to see why that might have been.

'Anyway, what's she done?' Harriet asked.

'Harriet!' Celia admonished and cast a sideways glance at Simon.

He explained the circumstances that had brought him to their door and watched their faces as they looked meaningfully at each other. There was mild shock, he supposed, but no sorrow that he could see.

'We're terribly sorry to hear about it, of course, but how do you think we can help you?' Celia ventured, her needle hovering above her stitched canvas. Simon couldn't make out the design clearly but it looked disconcertingly like a row of cabbages.

58

'You say she left without a word. Did she give you no notification at all that she was moving?'

'Not a word, except for a ten-pound note left on the kitchen table with a scribble saying she hoped it covered any remaining bills,' Harriet said.

'And did it?' Simon couldn't resist asking.

'I suppose so,' Harriet said grudgingly. 'We'd settled most of the quarterly bills at the end of last term. And she'd paid her rent. But no notice given so that we could get someone else in.'

'I don't think we shall. Do you, Harriet?' Celia said quietly.

'Shouldn't think so,' Harriet agreed, but was not to be distracted from her grievances. 'I don't want to speak ill of the dead and all that but I didn't like the sneaky way she did it, coming here while she thought we were both away. I actually saw her driving off. She saw me arriving at the door and had the cheek to wave and smile. And she didn't even have the decency to stop.'

'This was last week, was it?' Simon asked.

They both nodded. 'Wednesday of last week,' Harriet said.

'So you had no indication from her at the end of last term that she was thinking of moving out?'

'None at all,' Harriet said emphatically.

'Did Emily have any particular friends that you know of?' Simon asked.

'She didn't bring any here, if that's what you mean. And our paths didn't cross at the university much, being in differing departments.'

'There was her boyfriend that time, Harriet,' Celia reminded her.

'Oh, that! Yes, early last term. He came down from London and stayed overnight in her room.' She sounded as if she disapproved.

They were incredible, these two, Simon thought.

'I'm engaged to a priest,' Harriet explained comfortably.

A resolutely celibate one, Simon thought.

'The boyfriend from London – was that Mark Whittaker?'

They both nodded.

'Did Emily have any other boyfriends, as far as you know?'

They glanced at each other.

'We thought she did,' Harriet said. 'She used to go out quite regularly and come in late.'

'Perhaps she had meetings with some society or other,' Simon suggested.

Harriet shook her head and smiled knowingly. 'Those were nights when she always took particular care over her appearance. Went out looking like something off a catwalk, didn't she, Cee?'

Celia pursed her lips and nodded agreement, stabbing her creation expertly.

Envy, malice and jealousy in these two was likely to distort every action of Emily's, Simon thought, but ploughed on.

'Did you never mention where she was going, who she might be seeing?'

'We asked her once, didn't we?' Harriet again looked to Celia for confirmation. 'We said something like, "Your boyfriend will be getting jealous, Emily," and she went a bit pink. But she didn't deny it.'

Pink with rage perhaps, Simon thought.

'So it's just supposition on your part?' he said.

'No, I don't think so,' Harriet said stoutly. 'We did think, didn't we, that it was someone she maybe didn't want to talk about.' Celia counted with her needle and nodded as she stabbed again. 'We thought it might be one of the lecturers, or a married man.'

'Or both,' Celia added.

'Why should you think that?' Simon wished the information came from a more objective source. But they were not stupid, these two. They had other failings, but he recognised the sort of prurient interest that could unerringly identify any falls from grace in their fellow mortals.

'Well, we were talking over breakfast one morning about sexual harassment,' Harriet began.

Simon repressed a smile.

'It's a big issue in student affairs, as it is anywhere else. And as usual the harassment comes most often from men in positions of authority – the lecturers, in other words.'

'Do male students ever complain about women lecturers?' Simon asked, smiling.

'It's no laughing matter,' Harriet said, like one who bent

under such impositions daily.

'I'm very incorrect politically,' Simon apologised.

'I don't doubt. Being a policeman probably doesn't help,' she said, fairly accurately. 'Anyway, the university authorities have to take it very seriously these days. So, as I was saying,' she went on without taking breath, 'we were discussing this, and I said that I thought there should be an absolute ban on male staff fraternising with female students. Emily got quite indignant about it and said I was being ridiculous.'

'Well, it's not totally unreasonable to disagree with the statement,' Simon suggested. He was rather enjoying himself.

'You don't know what you're talking about,' Harriet said rudely. She went on, 'Anyway, I said something like, was she afraid it might cramp her style? And she said yes, it certainly would. And Celia said – didn't you – "You don't mean you're involved with one, do you?" And she said, "Engrossingly so", or something equally over the top. But whenever we referred to it again, she wouldn't be drawn. So we never found out who it was.'

It wasn't necessarily a statement of fact, Emily's response to Celia's challenge, but it was perhaps indicative. He had doubts that two such as these could have discovered much about a character like Emily. Even her gentle sister had had difficulty.

'She never mentioned a friend called Peter, I suppose?'

They both paused and shook their heads.

'Did Emily ever mention her life before she came to Westwich?' he asked them.

'She said there was just herself and her sister,' Harriet said. 'And she mentioned that she had been working for a publisher in London. Made us feel quite provincial, didn't she, Cee?'

Celia winced. 'It didn't worry me. I couldn't bear to live in London.'

'And that's all you learned about her?' Simon asked, not hiding his disbelief that they could know so little of someone they had shared their living accommodation with for months.

'Huh! Even that we only found out by asking,' Harriet said.

Making a last attempt at eliciting anything useful, Simon tried a more open question. 'What else can you tell me about her that you perhaps worked out for yourselves, or observed?'

They looked at each other, raising eyebrows. Celia said, 'Well, she was quite disciplined, wasn't she?'

'With her work, you mean?' Harriet said, 'Yes, I'll give her that. She seemed to do a lot of reading and made the odd comment about taking an essay in. She never seemed to have any worries about deadlines, no burning the midnight oil.'

'Anything else?'

'She was obviously popular with the opposite sex,' Harriet said. 'We had a lot of visits from the men next door, asking to borrow sugar and tea and things. Quite a nuisance. They're students at the university too,' she added.

The boys from Aston Villa, presumably.

Thinking of the pregnancy, Simon wondered whether the two girls had noticed any signs of it. 'And did she seem well to you at the end of last term? Not depressed or ill or anything?'

'That's a curious question.' Harriet put her head on one side and regarded him thoughtfully. 'I mean, it's not as if she's committed suicide, is it? What do you think, Cee?'

'She always looked very well,' Celia said cautiously. 'If anything, I thought she was a bit hyper, you know, quite lively.'

'Yes, you're right. She was a bit excitable,' Harriet agreed.

'In what way?' Simon asked.

'Difficult to say,' Harriet mused. 'Cat that's got the cream, that sort of thing.'

'Yes. Pleased with herself.' Celia chimed in.

As likely to be a bit of classic projection on their part, Simon thought – the eagerness in humankind to be irritably conscious of faults in others that were more accurately their own. He'd had enough of this complacent pair and their petty spitefulness.

'I wonder if I might look at her room, if you wouldn't mind?' he asked.

Harriet raised herself and went to the door. 'Come on, then,' she said.

She went ahead of him up the stairs, and his eyes were gripped by the gyrations of her round bottom in black leggings. There were two bedrooms at the front of the house, overlooking the street, and a bathroom and a smaller bedroom

62

at the back. Harriet opened the door of the latter and stood aside.

'She left it tidy enough, I suppose,' she said grudgingly.

The room was immaculate, with no sign of occupation left there, no tags of old posters on the walls, no dust and no detritus. It was only about seven feet by eight, with a small wardrobe, a chest of drawers and an old-fashioned wood-framed bed. The only personal touch in the room was a colourful old patchwork bedspread.

'That's attractive,' Simon said to Harriet's watching eyes. 'Does in belong to the house?'

'No. Emily left it behind. It was a parting gift, I suppose, an apology for leaving as she did.'

'She left nothing else?'

'Nothing.'

Simon looked quickly through the chest of drawers and wardrobe, empty as Harriet had stated, took one more swift look around the room and returned to the landing. 'If you think of anything else that might be helpful,' he said without concealing the irony, 'let me know, won't you?' He handed Harriet his card.

'I'll see you out,' she said, hurrying ahead of him.

He put his head in through the sitting-room door as he passed and repeated the request to Celia. She was still placidly stitching.

'Yes, of course we will, Chief Inspector. We do hope you find her soon.' She spoke coolly, as if Emily had been merely mislaid.

Harriet escorted him from the premises.

Driving back to headquarters, Simon thought over the little he had been able to glean from those two odd young women. There certainly seemed no mystery about why Emily had felt the need to get away, but the place she had moved to hardly lifted the spirits. Why hadn't she waited until the beginning of term and consulted the university's accommodation officer? After all, she had lasted at Sinclair Road for a whole term. Why the sudden rush? The new address to be sure gave her more privacy than she had had before – no one knew her at Acacia Road, there were no students from the university there; in fact, it was a blacklisted address. Maybe the anonymity was an attraction. So that she could meet a lover there? The one that Harriet and Celia had believed in. Peter Dawson, perhaps? He fitted with what Simon had learned so far. In addition now to the letter she had written, he had the suggestion from her former housemates that she was having a relationship with one of the lecturers at the university. Whichever way he looked at it, an investigation of Dawson's activities on the night in question was justified. He wanted to make it as justified as possible, though.

He found Longman in the canteen having a belated lunch and joined him.

'They've both gone back to London, sir,' Longman mumbled, his mouth full of bacon and eggs.

'What did Whittaker have to say for himself?'

'As little as possible. Said he was fully aware that the police were always interested in the boyfriend when anything like this happened so we should take care in questioning him if there was any chance of regarding him in the light of a suspect.'

'Sounds as if he said quite a lot.' Simon grinned.

'Huh! Talked a lot and said little, if you know what I mean. I think you should have spoken to him.'

'And so I shall. I'll be going to London to talk to the publishers that Emily worked for. I'll see him then.'

'Well, good luck.' Longman took another large mouthful, aware that his meals for the next few days might be erratic and occasional.

'Did he say what he was doing on Tuesday night?'

'Said he got home about six thirty, had a meal and listened to some music. He's an opera buff, he said. He was still doing that when Charlotte Sanderson rang him to tell him the bad news.'

'Did you ask him about Dr Dawson?'

'Yes. He seemed curious about me asking. So I improvised a bit and said I was an admirer of Dawson's and had heard that Hydes were his publishers and what did he think of him?'

'Which probably made him more curious than ever,' Simon said.

'Well, you asked me to ask him about the man. You didn't say why,' Longman pointed out. 'Anyway, I tried to keep it as low-key as possible, not knowing what it was all about. I said that of course we knew that Dr Dawson was an acquaintance of Emily's and that he had encouraged her to come to Westwich to do a degree in psychology and we would be asking him for his advice about her, so I wanted to know a bit more about what Dawson was like, him being so important and all.'

'By which time you had presumably reinforced any ideas Whittaker had about our interest in Dawson, but at least lulled his own fears. Well done, Geoff.'

'What interest in Dawson, sir? Have I missed something?' Longman held a forkful of food in midair, pointing it at Simon.

Simon improvised only slightly mendaciously. 'No, Geoff, not at all. It's just a line of thought, inquiry possibly. Dawson's Christian name is Peter and that, with the fact that he knew Emily fairly well, means we shall need to speak to him. So what did Whittaker have to say about him?'

'You think he might be the Peter that Emily was meeting that night? Why didn't you say?' Longman eyed him critically.

'You haven't answered my question yet.'

'Not a lot,' Longman said after a pause. 'I got the impression that he didn't like the bloke much. But I may be wrong. He said that he didn't have much to do with him directly, not being one of his editors.'

'Did he say whether Emily had had much to do with Dawson?'

'Well, I might have asked him if I'd known the direction your thoughts were taking, sir.'

'They're not taking any particular line.' Simon was wary of indicating too keen an interest in Dawson at this stage. 'Several, rather, so you'd better eat up and we'll get back on the job.' Simon had finished his meagre portion of sandwiches already.

DI Bob Monkton, whom Simon had left in charge at Acacia Road, came into the canteen at that moment, waved to Simon and weaved his way through the tables towards them. DC Rhiannon Jones entered a few moments afterwards and followed him.

'Bob. Any news?' Simon leaned back in his chair.

'I suppose no news is news of a kind in a case like this,' Monkton replied in his usual morose manner. His dark, cadaverous looks were not relieved by the black leather coat he had taken to wearing. 'We're still doing a thorough search of the house,' he added, 'and they're still out checking the area. They've found what they think are rug fibres caught on the bottom of the lower sash window, but we didn't need those to tell us that she was taken out through the window, did we?'

'Have you notified the river authorities to keep a lookout?' Simon asked.

'Yes. Already done.'

'Sir?' Rhiannon provided a welcome contrast to Monkton in tone as well as appearance. The young detective constable was as bright as she looked, choosing, since she had come out of uniform, to wear clothes that were as far removed from dark blue as she felt she could get away with. It had given her a harder job in dealing with the rampant sexism of her male colleagues, but deal with it she did. The gentle lilt of the Welsh Valleys had beguiled more than a few policemen into believing that her heart was as soft as her voice. In fact her tongue gave utterance to such harsh putdowns that even Simon winced at times, sympathetic as he was to her situation.

'Yes, DC Jones?' Simon had discovered that Rhiannon disliked being called by her first name while male colleagues of her rank were called by their title or surname. She would prefer not to be called simply Jones, but apart from that wanted no discrimination, preferential or otherwise. Simon for his part had never felt comfortable with the militaristic element of police work and the rigid authority structure, although intellectually he could see the point of it, and he tried to avoid using formal titles with his colleagues. Even so, he employed them more often than he liked to admit, to shut people up when the need arose.

'Sir, I've made a list of people at the house who've got vehicles. It's not a very long one, I'm afraid.'

'That sounds like good rather than bad news.' Simon smiled. 'It should help cut down on people we need to eliminate.'

'Well, yes, it does, sir. The ones with vehicles all seem to have good alibis for the time we're interested in.'

'Even better,' Simon said cheerfully. 'We'll go through what we've got at the next meeting, shall we?' He turned to Monkton. 'Meanwhile you'd better coordinate checks on these alibis, Bob.'

'Right.' Monkton turned away, Rhiannon following, his expression as grim as ever. Simon would have liked one day to be the bearer of really good news to the man, just to see what he looked like when he was happy. Apart from funeral director, it was hard to think of another job in which his face would not look entirely out of place.

'Geoff, I'm going to make a phone call before we go back to Acacia Road. Wait for me in the car, will you?'

Simon put through a call to the university. Hermione's distinctive voice came on the line.

'Chief Inspector Simon. This is a pleasure.'

'I'm glad to hear it,' he said, conscious that this conversation would probably be reported back to Jessie. 'I wonder if you feel able to answer some questions for me? I don't want to make the questions official at the moment, but it would help me as a general guide, if you wouldn't mind.'

'Are these questions that Jessica didn't want to answer this morning?' her tone was amused rather than accusing.

'We didn't really get that far.'

'Well, go ahead and I'll see whether I feel that the seal of the confessional binds my lips.'

The analogy was inappropriate enough to raise his hopes.

'I'd prefer it if it would bind them as far as this conversation goes, anyway,' he said.

'Anything you say, Chris. Are you sure you wouldn't rather come and see me to talk about this?' Her voice was innocent of the kind of meaning she had given it the night before, but he was wary.

'Love to. But things are pretty busy.'

'What's it about, then? I didn't really know the missing girl. She wasn't one of my students last term.'

Simon decided to plunge ahead. 'It's about the get-together the psychology department had last night. Did anyone leave early, and if so, can you remember when?'

There was a pause, then Hermione said, 'Well, you know

67

that Peter Dawson was absent for a while. I saw him come in with you when you arrived.'

'What time did he go out?'

There was another pause before she replied. 'Oh, well, since I can't stand the bastard, what the hell? He left shortly before the meeting came to an end. Just after half past seven, I would think.'

'Did he give any explanation of why he left?'

'Dr Dawson follows the maxim of never explaining and never apologising. But I assumed it had something to do with the telephone call.'

Simon swallowed. 'What time was the telephone call?'

'That was at half past seven. I looked at my watch. I do dislike departmental meetings and I was looking forward to a drink.'

He asked cautiously, 'Have you any idea who the call was from?'

''Fraid not. He didn't look terribly pleased about it, though. It was actually Dawson who answered the phone, so I'm afraid you're going to have to ask him.'

So be it. Circumstances were sufficient now to warrant it. In an effort to distract from the impression of too much interest in Dawson, Simon returned to his original question.

'Thanks, that may be helpful. Did anyone else leave early?'

'Chris, are you seriously suspecting members of the psychology department of being involved in this murder?'

'It might seem like it, I suppose,' Simon said lightly. 'But it's not like that. There are other, circumstantial things that need to be put into the chronology, that's all.'

'I'd never have suspected you of peddling gobbledegook, Chris. You disappoint me.' He heard her laugh.

'Anyone else, Hermione?' he repeated. 'I really appreciate this.'

'How much, though, I wonder? Let me think. The meeting finished at about quarter to eight and everyone stayed for at least one round. After that, the evening became a bit of a haze. Oh, Phillip Beardsley left early. I remember because I offered him a drink and he said no, thanks, he was off.' She paused. 'What is all this about? I've got nothing against Phillip, even if he is a bit of a wimp.'

Simon had no desire to be put in that same category, but he couldn't manage more than a feeble repetition of what he had said before. 'I hope you understand, we're just checking the whereabouts of anyone who knew Emily. Anyway, thanks, Hermione.'

'You're welcome. And let me know any time you want some advice on how to handle women. A quiet drink somewhere, perhaps?'

It was how to handle Hermione that most preoccupied him at this moment. 'Aren't you and Jessica supposed to be friends?' he asked.

'Sure we are. She knows me well.' Hermione chuckled. 'I could tell her I've offered you some therapy.'

'I'd rather you didn't,' he said.

'Well, get in touch with her and make up, why don't you?'

'I'll do that,' he promised, and rang off.

Chapter Eight

'Chief Inspector! Perhaps you would update me on your meeting last night?'

Simon, passing Bradley's office, had hoped to escape unnoticed and get on his way to London. He had been surprised by the superintendent's absence from the meeting the night before, but had hoped, obviously vainly, that the man was letting up a little on the close scrutiny he seemed to pay in particular to Simon's duties. Without disguising his reluctance, he followed Bradley through the door of his office.

The superintendent lowered himself slowly into his office chair, his weight causing it to creak protestingly. Simon thought the man was looking unwell. His flabby jowls looked as grey as his hair and his eyes were baggy and red-rimmed. He picked up a cup of coffee and drew out a packet of biscuits from his desk drawer.

Simon stood by the window in the hope of signalling he was in a hurry. The day had started grey again but with a chill wind which might blow away some of the cloud and bring a return of yesterday's sunshine. He watched people in the car park below step from the warmth of their cars and then clutch the collars of their coats as they dashed for the steps of the well-heated building.

'Well? Any progress?' Bradley asked.

'It's a bit early to say yet, sir.'

'Do me a favour, will you, son, and just give me some crystallised thoughts on the case.'

Bradley's manner lacked its usual ebullience. Simon wondered just how unwell the man might be. He himself didn't feel much in the mood for the fencing that usually went on between the two of them. He relaxed a little and took a seat.

'No sign of the girl yet, or you would have heard. The search is still going on for the body and the rug that the body was probably wrapped in. As far as we know, she wasn't seen after half past seven, when she made a local phone call. We've turned up no one so far who admits to having heard or seen anything suspicious, either in the house or the neighbourhood. So there's nothing very interesting in terms of evidence.'

'What about the letter the girl's supposed to have written?'

Simon often wondered why these audiences with Bradley were considered necessary. He always seemed to know most of what was going on.

'I was coming to that.' Simon explained the contents and source.

'So who's this Peter?'

'The only Peter she knew that we're aware of was a Dr Peter Dawson, from the university, whom she met first when she worked for his publishers.'

'*The* Dr Dawson?'

'The same.'

Bradley blew out his cheeks. 'Not necessarily him, though, eh?'

Simon felt it might be politic at this stage to give Bradley the several reasons why it might indeed be him.

'Don't got jumping to conclusions too soon, my boy. You know what you're like when you get an idea in your head. Bull at a gate.'

Another piece of classic projection, Simon thought. Ever since Jessie had mentioned the concept, he seemed to be finding it everywhere. He didn't protest the point, though, because on the subject of Dawson he was aware that his own prejudice might indeed sway his judgement.

'I've warned you, we don't want to go upsetting the university authorities without any need. And I suspect he's one of their blue-eyed boys.' Bradley struggled forward in his chair and thumped his desk to emphasise his point. 'Have you spoken to Dawson yet?'

'No. I'll have to at some point, but I want to get as much background as I can before I do so. That's one of the reasons I'm going to London to speak to people at Hyde Books, the publishers she worked for.'

71

'You've cleared it with the Met, all this gallivanting?'

Simon still had good contacts there from his earlier experience in the police force. He nodded.

'What about the boyfriend? Have you checked him out?'

'Mark Whittaker? It's being done. He says he was at home that evening, alone.'

'Oh, yes?' Bradley cocked a quizzical eyebrow.

'There were very poor driving conditions that night. He'd have taken a while to get to Westwich and back. And there was the body to get rid of during that time, unless he still had it in the boot when he brought the sister to Westwich. Anyway, I'll be seeing him again today. He works for the publishers.'

Bradley nodded. 'Anything else you should have told me?'

'We've learned from the sister that Emily was pregnant, about four months.'

'Thank you for mentioning that small detail, Chief Inspector.'

'Sorry. Thought you might have heard, sir.'

Bradley frowned. 'I don't want to have to rely on other sources when I've got you under my command, Chief Inspector.' Bradley, unlike Simon, was very comfortable with pulling rank.

'Who's the father?'

'We don't know.'

'Did she?'

'According to her sister, yes. She just wasn't telling yet,' Simon said. He gave the gist of what Charlotte had told him.

'And the pregnancy could be a motive for hiding the body,' Bradley remarked.

'And for murder, if it threatened the status of a lover,' Simon added.

'Bringing you back to Dr Dawson.' Bradley sighed. 'Well, I take your point. You'd better get on. But tread softly, my boy.'

As meetings with Bradley went, Simon reflected, driving out of the car park, that one hadn't been so bad. Maybe the old fellow, nearing retirement, really was unwell. Calling Simon by anything but his name, which, being also a Christian name, might sound a touch too friendly, was usual with

Bradley. His prejudice against graduate entrants like Simon went deep and would take more effort to eradicate than Simon could be bothered to muster. Office politics irritated and bored him.

Simon had not mentioned to Bradley the comments that Harriet and Celia had made about Emily's state of mind at the end of the previous term, 'like the cat that had the cream', as Harriet had put it, when she was presumably already aware that she was pregnant or suspected it. At that time Emily must have been confident that news of the pregnancy would be received well by the father of her child. But there was a lot of presuming, or assuming, in that. Perhaps her doctor would know something about Emily's expectations of the father.

Simon switched the wiper blades on as a blast of heavy rain hit the car on the new road to the motorway link. He glanced at the clock, intending to time his journey, driving as fast as he could within reason. Fiddling with the radio to find a station giving road as well as weather conditions, he caught instead the tail end of a report on the missing student Emily Sanderson. He had managed so far to keep his own person at a distance from the news reporters, Bradley always preferred to assume that public role.

They had decided against any formal television appeal at this stage, given Charlotte's obvious reluctance to be involved, but he wondered whether the decision had been entirely wise. Most of the tabloids had led with the story on the front page that morning and the city newspaper had already begun a campaign on the subject of violence in our town and what the police weren't doing about it. It was a recurrent theme these days, he thought irritably, realising he was threatening to turn into the sort of copper he never intended to be.

He tuned into a station broadcasting music. Billie Holiday was singing 'My One and Only Love'. He switched it off. The song was one he could remember being played one night at one of his and Jessie's favourite restaurants, which specialised in his kind of music. It had been a good night, ending happily. Like many others.

He refused to think about Jessie. She had been unfair and her behaviour had hurt. Conscious of what had been on his

73

mind that very morning, he had felt even more humiliated.

A car flashed its headlights behind him. He was in the outside lane and couldn't even recall driving on to the motorway. He moved over, noting sourly that the other driver was accelerating past at over ninety miles an hour. Thick spray was flung back at him. He turned his wipers up to maximum speed and put his foot down hard.

It took him two hours to reach the outskirts of London and another half-hour to find Hyde Books off Holborn.

It was an old-established firm, still on the same premises where William Hyde had founded it over a hundred years before, although walls had been removed to widen the reception area to the width of the narrow Victorian building and there was much plate glass. Emily's replacement, a young and beautiful Asian girl, received him graciously and asked him to take a seat.

He examined the display of the company's publications while he waited. It included a variety of both fiction and nonfiction with several well-known authors among them, including of course Peter Dawson. Simon took down what appeared to be his latest book, *Morality and the Millennium*, and browsed through it. It was popular rather than academic in style, with plenty of pictures and subheadings. The book was co-written by Phillip Beardsley, though his name was less prominent on the cover. Simon recalled that Hermione had mentioned his having left early on Tuesday night. Someone else who must have known Emily.

'Mrs Marsden can see you now.' The receptionist had approached quietly and startled him. 'I will show you the way.' He put the book back and followed her to an office on the first floor.

Julia Marsden looked both at home and at ease. She wore a royal-blue suit, loose-fitting and comfortable, and low shoes which she kicked off as she sat down after greeting him. Her greying brown hair was straight and cut to ear level. It looked as if she had already run her hands through it several times that day. Her eyes were brown, seeming, from the number of smile lines radiating from them, to be permanently lit with amusement. The only make-up she wore was bright-red lipstick, of which just enough remained to leave a clear outline to a wide and generous mouth. She put down her cigarette in an overflowing ashtray and asked if he'd like coffee.

He looked around, interested, as she made fresh drinks for them both from a small espresso machine on an oak table in front of the high, narrow window. The walls were lined with bookshelves filled with the firm's own publications, and almost every other surface, including the floor, was covered with piles of manuscripts. Julia Marsden's solid, Victorian desk was relatively clear, holding in- and out-trays, three or four stacks of paper and the inevitable computer terminal.

'I'm terribly sorry to hear about Emily,' she said as she handed him his coffee in a small bone-china mug. Her voice was pure Roedean. 'Though I'm not terribly clear about how I can be of any help. After all, she left here almost six months ago.'

'I'm really trying to get to know more about the girl. It can help in investigations if you have a clear insight into the personality of some victims of crime,' he said.

'For every murderer, there's a murderee? I can't remember who said that, can you? Is that the idea you subscribe to?' She looked at him, eyebrow raised.

'I think that's an entirely different meaning.'

'But is it true, do you think?' She lit a cigarette but didn't take her eyes off him.

'I'd hate to think so. But some victims, I suppose, do something to attract harm to themselves. With the majority I should have thought it was much more random.'

'And what about Emily? If you want to find out about her personality, then surely you are looking at ways in which she might have attracted what seems to be considerable harm done to her.'

He had a feeling that he wouldn't win in any verbal sparring with Julia Marsden. 'Yes. Of course I'm looking at those. They've to do with what is commonly referred to as motive.'

She gave him an unexpected broad grin. 'Keep your shirt on. I don't get many policemen in my clutches. So what are your questions?'

Simon smiled back. 'Would you just tell me to begin with exactly what Emily did here, what her job was?'

'A nice, open question,' she said, screwing up her eyes

against the cigarette smoke. 'As you probably know, she was a receptionist, saw visitors in, answered the telephone, all the usual duties, and she did letters and things for some of the editors. She was a very attractive girl, with a welcoming manner and plenty of tact. We were sorry she was leaving but expected that she might come back here in a different capacity.'

'Oh?'

'We thought she was editorial material. She needed to develop her potential and all that, and we felt it was a good move for her to go to university. She was grossly underused in the work she was doing officially.'

'And what was she doing unofficially?' Simon asked.

'She was quick and capable and her job didn't keep her sufficiently occupied, so she got into the habit of lifting a few things from the slush pile – the unsolicited manuscripts – and reading them, passing on her comments to the editorial staff. Her opinions were often helpful, and some of the editors started handing manuscripts over to her as a matter of course. She was really interested in the whole business of what we publish and why.'

'Was it only the slush pile that she looked at?' Simon asked, thinking of Dawson.

Julia looked surprised. 'I don't know. Probably not. She was an avid reader and after she got involved with Mark, I imagine he gave her a fairly free rein.'

'You publish Peter Dawson, don't you?' Simon said. 'It was he, was it, who suggested that Emily go to Westwich University to do a degree in psychology?'

She gave him a thoughtful look. 'I imagine so,' she said. 'Certainly he liked her company, and he probably was the reason for her selecting Westwich.'

'Did she spend time with him, then, that you know of?'

'Of course. It's not unheard of for attractive young receptionists to be invited to lunch by authors. I saw her with the pair of them a few times.' She drank the remains of her coffee and offered him another.

'He shook his head. 'No, thanks. You said "the pair of them". Who was with Dawson? Whittaker?'

She gave a throaty chuckle. 'No. Peter Dawson has done a

76

couple of books with a colleague, Phillip Beardsley. They used to take her to lunch together.'

It seemed more innocent, less suggestive of an intimate relationship if Beardsley was there too.

'Do you think that Emily may have had a more involved relationship with either of those two?' he asked.

'Motive, Chief Inspector? I wouldn't know. Peter Dawson has a certain notoriety with women. I don't suppose he would pass up an opportunity if it was offered. Phillip is quieter, a bit of a dark horse. And Emily was rather impressionable. She was young enough to be easily seduced by someone as well known as Peter, and I don't think he's among the most scrupulous of men. But I'm merely speculating, because I don't know.'

'You don't like Dawson,' Simon commented.

'Do you?' She went on without expecting a reply, 'Dawson is something of a phenomenon. Top media don, darling expert pundit, ego the size of Buckingham Palace. And, of course, unusually for most of these dons, he's got the looks. That's what swung it for him most of all, not so much his grey matter. But you don't get where he's got without a degree of cynicism, it seems to me. And I come from a generation where academic credibility is more reliably earned than poncing about on television and radio, reducing complex subjects to neat sound bytes.'

Simon was wondering whether her dislike of Dawson was, even so, more personal than philosophical, when she added forthrightly, 'We were at Oxford together. He was a bastard even in those days.'

'But it hasn't stopped you publishing his books,' Simon said, immediately regretting the naivety of the remark.

'We're as much tarts in publishing as in the other media, Chief Inspector. We go where the money is.' She stretched her arms above her head and gave a broad yawn. 'Some publishing houses more than others, perhaps, but only just.' She pointed to a framed painting of an austere Victorian gentleman, which hung inconspicuously above the doorway. 'My great-grandfather. He wouldn't just turn in his grave, he'd be digging his way out.'

Which was all very interesting in its way, but veering somewhat from the track. Simon thought that if Julia Marsden could have dished him any real dirt on Dawson, she would have done so.

'Is Mark Whittaker in his office, do you know?' he asked. 'I'd like to have a word with him.'

'He's taking it very badly,' she said. 'I suggested he had a few days off but he says he's better off working, keeping his mind off it. So, yes, I think you'll find him in. Do you want me to ring through?'

She saw him to the door in stockinged feet. 'Go gently on the boy, Chief Inspector. He was very fond of Emily.' She directed him up a narrow flight of stairs. 'Straight in front of you when you reach the next floor.'

Mark Whittaker shared a large office with several other people. He looked up, noticing Simon as soon as he arrived at the open doorway, and waved him over. The room was more identifiably part of the twentieth century, being furnished with modern office equipment, but piles of manuscripts were everywhere, as in Julia Marsden's room.

Conversation lulled as he made his way to Mark's desk by the window and Simon was conscious of being watched by most of the room's occupants. He took a seat beside the young man's desk as Mark asked eagerly for any news.

'Nothing, I'm afraid,' Simon said.

'Why are you here, then?'

Simon explained that he had been talking to Julia Marsden.

'I still don't see why,' Whittaker said. He looked drawn and pale, with dark smudges under his eyes, and his manner lacked the aggression he had shown the last time Simon had spoken to him.

'I'm finding out about Emily's connections and background.'

Whittaker glanced around the room, aware, as Simon was, of the fact that others were overhearing them.

'Look, shall we go somewhere else?' he said in a low voice. 'There's a bar not far away.'

'If you like.'

Whittaker led the way out and Simon followed him down to street level, where the young man spoke to the receptionist before preceding Simon again into the street.

'This way,' he said, and they walked without speaking the hundred yards or so to a small bar in a narrow side street.

They sat with a beer each in a cubicle at the back of the gloomy bar. Whittaker got out cigarettes and lit one, taking a deep lungful.

'I needed that,' he said. 'So, did Julia have anything useful to tell you?'

'Possibly. I'm never quite sure what's useful until things start to come together. But it helps to find out as much as I can.'

'You don't seem to be proceeding on the assumption that it was some random attack then, or someone from inside that house she was living in?'

'The police don't always "proceed", despite popular conceptions.' Simon smiled. 'Sometimes, like me, they go around in circles until they find a point that seems to lead somewhere.'

'And this is just part of the circle, not particularly leading anywhere?'

'I don't know yet.' Simon took a sip of beer. It tasted acid and flat.

'Well, what did you want to see me about? I assume I'm a significant part of your spheroid picture.'

'It must be hard, knowing that you may be suspected of harming someone you cared for,' Simon said, 'if you've done no such thing.'

'It is. It's—' Whittaker paused for a word, 'enraging, if you'd really like to know what it feels like.'

'I understand. But in a paradoxical sort of way, though the police seem like your enemy, they are also your friend – because they're interested only in finding out who's harmed that person you care for. So if you're not responsible for what's happened to Emily, the best way to help her is to help us.'

'And forget about all those wrongful convictions the police are so famous for these days? Wrap the case up and forget about justice.' Whittaker smiled back disbelievingly 'Nice try, Chief Inspector.'

'We really do like to be able to eliminate people from our inquiries, you know. It makes life so much simpler,' Simon said.

79

'There's not much you can do about me, is there? I was home and alone when Emily disappeared and there's nothing I can do to prove it.'

'Charlotte rang you at nine forty, is that right?'

Whittaker nodded.

'And you got home at what time?'

'I've already told your sergeant, about six thirty. I had a quick drink in here, but I doubt if anyone would remember. I left work at half past five. And, as you are no doubt aware, if I had driven like a maniac, rushed in on Emily, done some ghastly deed and driven back even faster, disposing of her body on the way, I could just about have done it.'

'The timing's tight, I agree,' Simon said mildly. 'And I'm not really here to question you again on where you were or weren't that night.'

'What, you mean you're not here to harass me?' Whittaker took a long mouthful of beer and wiped the back of his hand across his mouth.

'Just to ask a few general questions, since I was in the area,' Simon agreed.

'Get on with it then.'

Simon pushed his almost full glass of beer aside. The bar was beginning to fill up with lunchtime trade and the noise level was rising. 'How well did Emily know Peter Dawson?'

Whittaker took another drag on his cigarette.

'And if you don't ask me why for every question I ask you, we'll get out of here a lot quicker,' Simon said.

'All right.' Whittaker grinned briefly. 'As far as I know, she knew him through work. He used to take her out to lunch sometimes when he was in London, not always when he was visiting his publisher, and usually with his sidekick Beardsley. Dawson's the type to want an attractive girl at his side, but as far as I know that's all there was to it. I've no idea if she saw more of him after she went to Westwich. You'd better ask him that. But she never said anything to me about him, other than the occasional remark about lunch.' He drained his beer glass.

It was the most detailed answer Whittaker had given, and entirely lacking in any curiosity about the motive for the question. If there was anything between Dawson and Emily, Simon would have thought that Whittaker would have sensed it. The

80

apparent indifference of his reply was unexpected.

'When did you last see Emily?' Simon asked.

Whittaker ostentatiously rolled his eyes towards the ceiling as he gave thought. 'It must have been December the twenty-first,' he said.

'That's quite a long time not to have seen your girlfriend. Why so long?'

'She was away over Christmas with her sister. Didn't Charlotte tell you? They always go away from London at Christmas. They rent a cottage on the Welsh coast. Family tradition. Emily didn't want to let Charlotte down.'

'She didn't want to go, then?'

'Oh, I wouldn't put it as strongly as that. But since there were just the two of them, and Charlotte's on her own, Emily didn't like to desert her and go off jollifying with me over Christmas and New Year.'

'And you didn't see her after she got back?'

Whittaker shook his head and sighed. 'One way and another, no. Not that there was much time between then and her going back to Westwich. They didn't return until around the eighth and I was away myself for a few days, so we missed each other. Charlotte prefers the sea in winter, so she makes it her main vacation. This time Emily was able to stay with her the whole time because she didn't have to come back to work.'

'How did Emily seem when you last saw her?'

The crowd in the bar nudged closer and someone backed into Whittaker's shoulder. 'Do you want another drink?' Whitaker asked.

'No thanks. Have mine.' Simon pushed his still brimming glass towards Whittaker. 'How did Emily seem?' he repeated.

Whittaker pulled an unhappy face. 'She was all right, I suppose. Seemed to be glad, actually, to be going away. The fact is, we had a row.'

'Because she wouldn't be staying in London?'

'Partly, I suppose. She seemed to feel so responsible towards Charlotte.'

'Understandable, perhaps,' Simon said. 'After losing their parents, and there just being the two of them.'

'It's not quite that simple,' Whittaker said, drinking down

81

half of Simon's glass in a mouthful. 'She felt guilty about her.'

'Why was that?'

Whittaker sighed and lit yet another cigarette. 'It's nothing, really. It's not relevant anyway.'

Simon waited.

'Emily caused the break-up of Charlotte's marriage.'

'How?' Simon asked.

'Stupid question,' Whittaker muttered.

'Deliberately?' Simon asked.

'No, I don't think so,' Whittaker admitted. 'If what Emily told me was true, and it probably was, it was just that Oliver fell for her and fell out of love with his wife.'

'I didn't realise Charlotte had been married,' Simon said.

'She changed back to her maiden name after she and Oliver split up. They're divorced now,' Whittaker said. 'You see, after the accident when the parents died, Charlotte insisted that they all live together in the parental home. That was when the trouble started.'

Simon recalled what Jessie had said about Emily's need to attach people to herself. Her usual need might have been exaggerated by the desire to be accepted by Charlotte's husband, who might otherwise have regarded her as an intruder. And, as usual, Emily had gone too far.

'Emily didn't have an affair with him then?'

'*Affair*,' Whittaker mocked. 'You mean did she sleep with him?'

'Well? Did she?'

'She said she didn't. Anyway, Charlotte's behaviour seems to support that. There wasn't any question of Emily being the one who had to move out. Oliver was trying it on with her, you see.'

'What does he do?'

'Who? Oliver Harwood? He works in a drugs clinic off Tottenham Court Road, near the university. Counsels addicts. Dismal sort of job.'

Whittaker had finished the last of Simon's beer and was flicking the glass with his nails. 'I'd like to get some lunch now, if you don't mind,' he said.

'Thanks for your time,' Simon said. 'I'll keep in touch.'

82

'I'm sure you will, Chief Inspector.' Whittaker grinned at him and got up to push his way through the press of bodies.

A young man leaned over the table. 'Have you finished with these glasses?' he asked accusingly. Simon went in search of a sandwich from somewhere less popular and more congenial.

Chapter Nine

There were snowdrops growing under the birch tree in the front garden of the house in Ealing. The house was mid-Victorian, detached, with a brass knocker glowing on the dark-blue front door in the fitful sunlight. She came quickly in answer to the single tap he made with the knocker, blinking in the light, glasses pulled down from the rim of her nose.

'You've got news?' she asked breathlessly.

He wished he had telephoned her before arriving. 'No. It's just that I was in London, and thought I'd come and see how you were.'

'Oh. I see.' She stood back, holding on to the door. 'Well, come in.'

She showed him into a room at the front of the house. It was comfortable and lived-in, with two sofas with bright covers and a lovely Turkish rug between them and in front of the fireplace. On the walls were several framed paintings, colourful abstracts.

Charlotte removed her glasses and placed them on a table near the door.

'I hope I haven't interrupted your work,' Simon said.

'Oh, I'm not managing to do much. Can't concentrate. Would you like a drink of something? Coffee? Or would you like tea? Ceylon? Earl Grey? China? Or would you prefer Indian?'

'Indian will be fine.'

The paintings looked less abstract when he examined them properly. He could now see unexpected figures in landscapes of cliffs or beaches, always with the sea there somewhere, but no sunlight or shadow. Their atmosphere was melancholy but they were impressive.

She returned with a tray laden with two pots of tea and placed it on a low table, her back towards him.

'These are good,' he said, gesturing at the paintings. 'Who did them?'

She sat down on the sofa and set out cups and saucers. She was wearing a short skirt today, revealing legs every bit as good as Emily's in the photograph. The loose top was a rich shade of blue, emphasising the blueness of her eyes but also the blue smudges beneath them. When she finished with the tray she leaned back on the sofa, looking at him as if she had forgotten, or not noticed, what he had said. He stared back, waiting for her to answer. Then she said, 'I did.'

'They're very good.'

'Thank you.' She smiled. 'My father used to paint, too. I've got his pictures in the room I use as an office. His are different, more realistic. We used always to take our painting things when we stayed in Wales, in Pembrokeshire.'

'You were there over Christmas and New Year, Mark tells me.'

'You've been to see Mark?'

'Just.'

'How is he? He telephoned me last night. He was terribly upset.'

Simon wondered if offloading the fact on a grieving sister was any help to her. 'He seemed calm enough today, but I don't think he's too keen on revealing anything to the police, even the extent of his misery. Thinks we might use it against him.'

She began pouring the tea, China for her, dark Indian for him. 'He can be a bit defensive, can Mark. I can assure you it's not a sign of guilt. I know you're bound to consider him a suspect but truly, I assure you, it's just not possible.' She handed him his cup and saucer and he sat down for the first time, opposite her.

'You're quite sure he knew nothing of the fact that Emily was pregnant?'

'You didn't ask him about it, did you?' she said, concerned.

'No.' Simon realised that perhaps he should have done.

'I'm quite sure he didn't know. Mark isn't the type to hide things. It's all pretty much out in the open with him. If he'd known, I would have known.'

85

'How do you think he would have reacted?'

She raised slender shoulders, holding her cup halfway to her lips. 'He'd have been upset, of course.'

Simon said, 'I've brought a list of the things of Emily's left in her room. I wonder if you'd take a look at it when you can, to see if there's anything you think might be missing.'

He took the sheet of paper from his overcoat pocket and passed it across the low table to her. She glanced at it and placed it beside her.

'Unusual, a computer expert who's also an artist,' he said.

'Oh, it gives me a sort of balance,' she said. 'Don't they say that they come from different parts of the brain, the logical and creative?'

'Do you enjoy the painting more?'

'Yes,' she said. 'But it doesn't pay the bills. And besides, I prefer not to mix love and money.'

'Did your father paint for a living?' Simon asked.

'No. He was a literary agent.'

'With a love of literature. Hence the names, I suppose?'

She blinked. 'Charlotte and Emily, you mean?'

'But no Anne or Branwell?'

'I think my parents might have drawn the line at Branwell,' she said. 'Yes, my father loved the Brontës. He took us to Haworth several times.' She sighed. 'But all that's over.'

Simon felt he had been inept to stir up memories. Her loneliness troubled him. 'I hope you've got some friends around,' he said, 'to come and keep you company.'

'Oh, I'm coping,' she said. 'I have company if I feel I need it.' She offered him another cup of tea.

'How long have you lived here?' Simon asked, accepting the refilled cup.

'It was the family home. Our parents left it to us. There are lots of memories here.' She looked around the room vaguely, resting her cup and saucer on her knees.

Whittaker had said that Charlotte had wanted the three of them to be together after the accident. So it looked as if it had been Charlotte and Harwood who had moved in on Emily rather than the other way round.

'Would you like to see Emily's room while you're here?' she asked.

'It's got to be done,' he said, conscious that he should have brought Longman to help.

'I've had a good look already. Emily was so private about her personal life, I thought perhaps there'd be something I wasn't aware of. But I didn't find anything – no letters from strange men or anything like that. You didn't find anything at Westwich?'

He shook his head. 'Only that letter on the word processor that I told you about.'

'Have you found out any more about that? Who the Peter was? Was it the one from the university? Did you ask about him at the publishers?'

'She used to go to lunch with him sometimes when he was in London, according to Mark. But I haven't had the opportunity to speak to Peter Dawson yet.'

'Mark told me, when we were driving back to London yesterday, that she certainly knew him quite well. I thought relations between university staff and students were rather frowned on. Isn't he married?'

'Yes, he is. And it is a bit of a delicate area. Female students are alert to harassment from male members of staff, and relationships between staff and students are under scrutiny more as a result. We haven't found any direct evidence of anything significant between him and Emily yet.'

'I expect you have to tread a bit carefully, don't you, with the university?' she said sympathetically.

He was pleased at the understanding. She could have been angry that Dawson hadn't been questioned yet, that city politics were allowed to influence how the police did their job sometimes. 'Something like that,' he said.

'It would be a bit of a coincidence if there was another Peter in her life, one nobody else was aware of.' Her voice had tensed and she was frowning.

He owed her a truthful response, but feared to mislead her. He cleared his throat. 'I'll be talking to Dawson about Emily, probably tomorrow. And you really mustn't be afraid that we won't follow every possible lead, I promise you.'

She searched his face with her large blue eyes and nodded as if satisfied. 'And what about the telephone call? Have you found out who she was telephoning that night? Can you trace the call?'

'I'm afraid not. If all calls were itemised, we could, but they're not yet.'

'I thought they were now,' she said.

'Only those over a certain number of units, but it must have been a local call.'

'I see. Perhaps it was to Peter Dawson, do you think?' She crossed her long legs and wrapped her arms around them, keeping her eyes on his.

'I'll be asking that,' he said.

He would have preferred to tell her that it looked likely, but was afraid to say too much. She was surely owed as much information as the police could give her, but not if it was only speculative still. That was always a problem in investigations: the victim's family's right to know versus the rights of the suspected criminal. Simon had always taken a liberal stand-point, conscious of the insidiousness with which the powers of authority could undermine civil rights. But civilians in this context fell into at least two groups and the rights of the offender tended to be more closely defended than the rights of those offended against.

She stirred, uncrossed her legs again and stood up. 'Emily's room then? As I said, I didn't find anything—' Her emotions surfaced at last. She fumbled with the cups and saucers on the tray. 'I'll just take these to the kitchen.'

He was standing waiting for her when she came back. He felt awkward, like a bird of ill omen clouding the bright sitting room, a dabbler in dark deeds, possessor of dark knowledge. He felt inappropriate in her life, in this pleasant, innocent family home.

Her eyes looked red-rimmed, but she smiled up at him. 'I'm glad it's you who's investigating all this,' she said. 'I haven't had anything much to do with the police, but you seem –' she hesitated – 'kinder, more sensitive than I expected a police-man to be.' She turned away slightly. 'That probably sounds a bit silly. But it does help.'

After the moments of self-doubt, he was grateful for her reassurance, but embarrassed, too, that her image of him was in some ways illusory.

'Shall we, then?' he said, puting his hand to the door, close to her head.

88

She went ahead, up the thickly carpeted staircase, and led him to a room overlooking the front of the house.

'This is her room' she said, going forward and staring out of the window, as if detaching herself.

It was as tidy and unlived-in as the one in Sinclair Road, though this room had had an identity conferred on it by its absent occupant. One wall was lined with books, a history of a life's reading, from A. A. Milne through C. S. Lewis and Arthur Ransome to C. G. Jung and a collection of other psychology books, including one or two by Peter Dawson, he noticed. He took one down and looked inside the flyleaf. There was an inscription which read, 'To Emily with love, Peter Dawson.' Which could mean something, or nothing at all. He replaced it and looked at the rest of the room. A chair by the window was piled high with a collection of teddy bears, and there was a desk, free of papers or books, in an alcove.

'I should look through her things,' he said awkwardly to Charlotte's back. 'You might have missed something.'

He thought she nodded. 'Perhaps you'd like to go and look through the list I gave you,' he suggested gently.

She put out a hand to one of the teddy bears, rubbing one of its ears, and he heard her sniff. He stood helplessly, but when he saw her shoulders give a shake he pulled out a handkerchief, examining it to make sure it was clean, and went over to her. As he held it out, she turned and leaned on his shoulder and began to cry in great sobbing gulps. After a moment he thrust the handkerchief into her hands and put his arms around her. They stood there for what seemed a long time, the sounds her sobs slowly fading into heaving breaths.

'I'm so sorry,' she finally said, standing back and looking down, not meeting his eyes.

'It's all right,' he said, a hand still on her shoulder.

'It's being in her room, I think.' She blew her nose. 'I can cope better if I'm working. It distracts me. I tell myself she'll come back, but she won't, will she? She'll never come back, I know it.'

'I don't know,' he said quietly.

She looked up at him, eyes huge with tears. 'I'll do what you suggested,' she said huskily. 'I'll look through that list for you.' His hand fell from her shoulder as she moved quickly to the door. 'Take what time you need,' she said. 'It's nice to have someone in the house.'

'You should have someone with you,' he said again, but she had gone. He turned back to the room and began the job of examining all its contents.

It was over an hour later that he went back to the sitting room. It was already getting dark and she had lit the gas fire and drawn the curtains.

'I've made some more tea,' she said brightly. 'Will you have some?' She held up a china teapot.

'Thanks.' He sat down again opposite her.

'Did you find anything of any help?' she asked.

He had searched through books looking for hidden correspondence and through all the cupboards and drawers in the room. It was a distasteful business, intrusive even in times like this, when it was to aid a victim of crime rather than convict a felon. Emily had been organised in her private life, everything appeared to be in its place. If she had something she had not wanted found, she would have been efficient about that, too.

'Nothing that seems relevant at the moment, anyway,' he said. 'How about you and that list?'

'I can't think of anything of hers that seems to be missing,' she said, 'though I suppose something may occur to me. I mean, you don't carry an inventory of your sister's possessions in your head.'

'No,' he agreed, watching her as she sat on the rug in front of the fire. She had brushed her hair and golden glints glowed in the soft light.

'There was one thing, though,' she said, turning her head and looking up at him. She picked up the list, squinting at it slightly in the low lighting. 'It just struck me as a bit odd. She disliked the colour so much. And I've never seen her wear it. It was the beige scarf.'

Simon recalled seeing it. 'It was a cashmere one,' he said.

'But not Emily's. She never wore beige,' Charlotte said with certainty. 'Where was it in the room?'

'It was near her coat, lying on the floor.'

'It could be her attacker's.'

'Could be. There'll be forensic checks done on it anyway.'

90

He finished his tea. He was feeling hungry and it was time he left.

'Nothing else on the list that should or shouldn't have been there?' he asked, placing cup and saucer on the low table.

'I'll let you know if I think of anything,' she said. 'I suppose you'll have to be going.' Her face was sad and watchful again.

He reached for his overcoat. 'I'm afraid I must,' he said.

She got up and saw him to the front door. 'Keep in touch, won't you? Let me know what's happening?'

'I will. And please try to get some company in. You shouldn't be on your own.'

She put out her hand to his and squeezed it. 'Thank you,' she said, and closed the door slowly behind him. The light from the hallway narrowed across his path and disappeared and he was in a dimly lit road with the moon rising.

Chapter Ten

'Sir!' Longman rumbled along the corridor in pursuit as Simon approached his office at headquarters.

'What is it? Have they found her?' Simon went on into his room and flung off his overcoat.

'No. Not that.' The sergeant sank down on a seat, breathing heavily. 'But we think we've found the rug.'

'Can you give me the whole story, or do I have to extract it slowly?'

Longman wondered what now was disturbing his senior officer's delicate equilibrium. 'It was found downriver, caught on the lower branch of a willow tree,' he began, 'drifting gently with the flow of the current, mermaidlike, borne up by the weeping brook, about a mile beyond the outer limits of this ancient city.'

'We are talking here about a rug rather than a body, are we? I mean, should we find our missing girl in the same watery grave, I should hate to think that your literary sources had been all used up.'

Longman grinned. 'No chance of that. Not now we've joined the theatre club. We're supposed to be going to see *Twelfth Night* at Stratford. Though I doubt I shall be able to make it.'

Longman's wife had recently begun a quest for a social life that involved her husband. They had no children yet to draw Longman home at a sociable hour, so in her usual practical way she was making an effort to remedy things in an agreeable manner. So far Longman was responding well to the project and would occasionally draw Simon into discussions of the plays he had seen – English literature having been Simon's degree subject – with the object of upstaging his wife, as he had happily confessed to Simon recently. He looked enquiringly now at Simon for an answer.

'Your doubt is probably justified. So what's happening with the rug? Did you get Edwards to look at it?'

'We did. It's not a particularly unusual make of rug, but he was pretty sure it was the one we're looking for because there was a burn mark near the middle. Said it would be easier to be sure when the thing was dry but it's gone to forensics for examination.'

'And I suppose there's not much chance of anything useful being found on it after immersion,' Simon said cheerlessly.

'There were what looked like bloodstains.'

'That might confirm that it's the right rug. But we've already got blood. I mean other evidence.' Simon put his feet up on his desk. He was feeling weary. 'Well, it's indicative, I suppose, of where Emily is. But it can take months for a body to emerge from that river and its estuary.'

'We're still searching the city area,' Longman said neutrally, 'building sites and parks, any open ground—'

'And they'll have to carry on. We can't give up on other possibilities. The rug may have been chucked in the river without the body.'

'I suppose so,' Longman said doubtfully. 'So how was your day? See the publishers?'

Simon gave him a rundown of the interviews with Julia Marsden and Mark Whittaker.

'We already knew she knew Dawson from her work at the publishers,' Longman concluded. 'Was there any hint from Mark that he thought something else might have been going on?'

Simon hesitated. 'Not really. I just sensed there was something a bit off about it all but I can't put my finger on what at the moment. Of course, Whittaker has a pretty secure ego – it probably wouldn't occur to him that any girlfriend of his would look in another direction.'

'Or he might not admit it. I always thought that the most egotistical types were actually a big fragile in that department. And,' Longman said with emphasis, 'Whittaker would have plenty of interest in showing no suspicions of Emily's extracurricular activities if he's got anything to do with her disappearance.'

'True. He was cool enough about Charlotte's ex-husband's relationship with Emily.'

'Yet another man in the case of young Emily. Are you going to talk to him, too?' Longman asked.

'I shall do. But I'm more interested in speaking to Peter Dawson at the moment.'

'What about his sidekick, whatsisname?'

'Phillip Beardsley. Him too. He may have something to offer.'

'Oh! I forgot. There was a telephone call for you from Jessie,' Longman said.

'When? Why the hell didn't you say?'

Longman shrugged. 'This afternoon. It's in your in-tray.' He pointed to the overflowing pile which lay, as usual, unregarded by Simon. It had occurred to Longman that Simon should have his in-tray divided into a series of trays graded from 'Absolutely Vital' to 'Someone Else Deal with It'. And Jessie's messages would always come in the first category, Longman thought. He was surprised then to see Simon hesitate with his fingers still hovering over the phone buttons.

'Aren't you going to ring her?' Longman asked.

'Not with you in the room,' Simon said.

Longman made a gesture towards removing himself.

'I'll ring her later,' Simon said, ignoring Longman's shorn but still mobile eyebrows. 'Let's go and talk to Dawson.'

It had turned into another foggy night and there was not much other traffic about. Simon drove slowly along the outer ring road towards the village suburb in which Dawson lived, to the northwest, not far from the university. Much as he had looked forward to this interview with Dawson, he felt a bit apprehensive. Dawson seemed to him to be a man completely sure of himself, while Simon, at that moment, felt anything but.

Still, he assured himself, he had plenty of grounds for asking Dawson to answer some questions now. He couldn't yet prove what the status of the man's relationship with Emily had been, but it was more than likely it had been an intimate one. The man would have a lot to lose if a pregnant Emily decided to make a scandal of their relationship. The tabloids would love to get their hands on it – well-known television pundit, author of *Morality and the Millennium*, no less, sexually exploits young student (and others no doubt). They still might get wind of it.

Longman, who had been humming a tune from *I Puritane*, broke off from his mournful notes as they left the outer city limits. 'You've met this Dawson before, I suppose? Him being in the same department as Jessie.'

'Briefly, once,' Simon said.

'What d'you think of him?'

'I didn't really see enough of him to form an opinion,' Simon lied. 'What's your impression of him? You say you've seen him on television.'

'Not quite the same thing, is it? I mean, people are different in the flesh. As for what he talks about on the telly, I think some of it's a load of rubbish. I mean, what experience does he have? Like most of these experts, they waffle on about their solutions to social or personal problems that they're totally removed from in their ivory towers. Julie won't let me watch 'em these days – she says she can't stand me arguing with the television.'

Simon smiled at the image. 'I know what you mean. But you should enjoy confronting an expert with a personal problem of his own, then.'

'We don't know that for sure, do we? Dawson may have had a perfectly innocent relationship with Emily Sanderson.'

'Things are suggestive enough,' Simon said shortly. 'I want to know who phoned him that night. I can't believe that it's just coincidence that he received a call at the same time that Emily made one. And there's the letter, too.'

'This is the turning.' Longman pointed.

Dawson's house was in a cul-de-sac at the edge of the village. The houses had open grass in front, divided only by drives leading to double garages. Simon pulled up on the wide front drive behind two other cars that were parked there. Dismayed, he recognised the one immediately in front of him as Jessie's Peugeot.

Longman, unaware of Simon's discomfort, strode towards the front door and rang the bell with vigour. Simon waited behind him in the shadows. A bright light came on, exposing him, as Peter Dawson flung wide the door.

'Chief Inspector!' he exclaimed, ignoring the sergeant's stolid presence. 'Am I to be of assistance to you in your investigations, or have you just come in search of your significant other?'

Longman gave Simon a quick look before facing Dawson again. 'It's you we're looking for, sir,' he said agreeably. 'May we come in?'

Dawson, with an amused smile, showed them both into a large room designed to define its owners as cultured, with abundant taste and money. In front of the blazing log fire Jessie was standing, a glass of red wine in hand.

'Chris!' she exclaimed. 'I tried to phone you.'

Simon couldn't begin to speculate on what she was doing there, apparently alone with Dawson; he just felt an illogical sense of betrayal. He noticed that she was still wearing her coat and wondered if she had just arrived or was just leaving.

'Yes, I heard,' he said.

Dawson was watching, still with a smile on his face. Longman had gone to warm himself by the fire, ostentatiously ignoring the general atmosphere.

'Can I get you both something warming?' Dawson asked smoothly, looking from Simon to Longman. 'Or is that against police ethics?'

He appeared relaxed and entirely untroubled by the night-time visit from police officers. Dressed casually in a baggy, collarless shirt with loose trousers and his hair tousled, he looked much younger than his years. Simon understood that the offer of a drink was not a hospitable gesture but made to put him at a disadvantage.

'Thanks. What have you got?' he asked, and saw Dawson raise an eyebrow at Jessie.

'You, Jess?' Dawson asked her familiarly.

She shook her head. 'I must be going. No, thanks.' She had turned to stared at the fire and kept her gaze riveted there.

'Make mine a beer,' Longman said cheerfully, and was ignored as Dawson reeled off a list of drinks for Simon.

'A beer, please,' Simon said, rejecting the more exotic offers. 'You do have beer, do you?'

'But of course.' Dawson left the room in soft-soled shoes, making a muted flopping sound on the parquet floor.

Jessie continued to stare at the fire and Longman began an overt inspection of the room's furnishings. It took him to the end of the large room and out of earshot for the moment.

'Social call?' Simon asked Jessie, going to stand by her side.

She gave him a swift, angry glance. 'He had some books that I needed for tomorrow. What's your excuse?'

'Mine's strictly business.'

'Haven't you any other suspects to harass, or is it just coincidence that you're here at this time?' She twirled her wine glass in her hands.

'What! You surely don't think I followed you here, do you?' he hissed at her.

She gave him a long look and then shrugged. 'No of course not. But I think you've got a fixation about Peter.'

'Where's his wife?' Simon asked unreasonably.

Jessie gave an exclamation of disgust and tossed off the last of her red wine. 'Give me a call when you can begin to talk sense, will you?' She picked up her bag and a couple of books that were lying on a table near the fire.

'You're not going yet, are you, Jess?' Dawson was returning with a tray of drinks. It irritated Simon, as the other man must have known it would, to hear him address Jessie so familiarly. Dawson put the tray on a low table and turned to put a delaying hand on Jessie's shoulder. 'Don't you want to stay and see your boyfriend in action? He's going to give me the third degree, judging by the expression on his face.' It was all said with a tolerant smile, but everything he said and did seemed malicious.

Simon had a strong urge to smack the smile off his face but instead managed to say, with a degree of apparent good humour, 'Yes, why don't you? Then you'll be able to make a proper judgement of police methods. And after all, you knew Emily. You may be able to make some helpful suggestions.'

Jessie, still with Dawson's hand on her shoulder, said, 'Thanks for the offer, but I'll give it a miss, if you don't mind. I really do have some work to do.'

Dawson shrugged and let his hand fall to her elbow. 'I'll see you out then,' he said.

'There's no need,' she said. 'Really, Peter.' But he followed her anyway, and Simon heard the murmur of voices in the hallway as Dawson sought to prolong the goodbye.

Longman had been watching for the last couple of minutes

with an appearance of absorbed interest. He came to stand beside Simon now, as if in support.

'Smooth bugger, isn't he?' he said, pulling a face at Simon.

'Isn't he just?' Simon stared at the hypnotic fire, feeling the sting of warmth prick his eyes.

They heard the door close after Jessie and Dawson returned, bringing a rush of cold night air with him.

'You're welcome to sit down, or do you feel more powerful standing up?' he asked, throwing himself comfortably on one of the plump, white sofas. 'And do help yourselves to beer, please.'

Longman picked up a bottle and opened it, pouring a glass. He offered it to Simon, who gestured it away and sat down in a beautifully upholstered Victorian armchair.

'I assume that you're here to talk to me about our missing student?' Dawson said, leaning forward and resting his elbows on his knees.

'That's right,' Simon said. 'You knew her, I understand, before she came to the university here.'

'Yes. From Hyde Books,' Dawson agreed. 'But I wasn't one of her tutors here.'

'You received a telephone call at seven thirty on Tuesday night at the university. Who was the call from, Dr Dawson?'

'My wife,' Dawson said, a shade too swiftly, Simon thought.

'And where is your wife?' Simon asked.

'She's out at the moment. But she will be able to confirm this. Why do you ask, anyway?' He sounded innocently interested.

'Why did your wife call you from a meeting at that time? You did leave the meeting shortly afterwards, didn't you?'

'You obviously have your sources, Chief Inspector. I can't believe that the lovely Jessica has turned police snoop. I wonder who you have been talking to,' Dawson sneered.

'I shall interview the whole of the psychology department if necessary to get to the truth of what happened that evening. Would you answer the question, please, Dr Dawson,' Simon said evenly.

'She was having trouble with our youngest, a bit of a hyper-active child. Rachel doesn't seem able to handle him at times, so she asked me to come home and settle him down for the night.'

'Half past seven is a little early by modern standards. How

old is the child?' Simon asked with tolerant disbelief.

'He's eight and we are traditional parents, Chief Inspector. He, in particular, needs rest and quiet so that he doesn't become overstimulated.'

'You have other children?' Simon asked, having difficulty in picturing Dawson in the role of paterfamilias.

'A girl, from my first marriage. She's seventeen and lives with her mother,' Dawson said. 'Would you like more details of my family history?'

'Not at the moment, thanks.'

There was a sound of the front door opening and closing.

Dawson called out, 'Rachel, darling, we're in here.'

The woman who entered the room, cheeks flushed from the cold night, looked younger than Dawson but not the sophisticated figure that Simon had pictured. Her hair was brown, shiny and straight and she had a tip-tilted nose. Her dark eyes glanced from face to face as she said, 'Hello, darling. I didn't know we were expecting visitors.' She went over and dropped a kiss on the top of Dawson's head. 'Has Ben been all right?'

'Fine,' Dawson said, getting up and solicitously taking her long overcoat from her. 'These are policemen, Rachel. They're here to ask what I know about Emily, the missing student.' He introduced her to Simon and remembered at last to acknowledge Longman by asking his name.

She looked at them without smiling and studied their faces. 'What sort of help do you think my husband can give you?' she asked directly.

'The Chief Inspector here was asking who telephoned me on Tuesday night at the university, darling. I explained you were having trouble with Ben,' Dawson pre-empted Simon.

'Why did you want to know that?' she asked. Simon detected a trace of a northern accent in her voice.

'Emily Sanderson was making a call at that time. We wondered if it might have been to your husband, Mrs Dawson,' Simon answered.

'Well, it wasn't,' she said, taking off her scarf and going to stand in front of the fire to warm her hands. 'Why should you think it was?'

'She wrote a letter to him the day before. She was trying to get in touch with him,' Simon said, watching what he could of her face. Her eyelids gave the faintest flicker and she turned to her husband.

'Did she, Peter?' she asked.

'It's the first I've heard of it, if she did,' Dawson said emphatically. 'Just where did you get that from, Chief Inspector Simon?'

Longman cleared his throat. 'There was a copy of it on her word processor.'

'Really? Whatever did it say?' Dawson was making an effort, but for the first time Simon could hear a note of uncertainty in his voice. Dawson's wife was watching him expressionlessly.

'She asked you to meet her at her new address on the following night, the night she disappeared, the night you left the meeting at the university and didn't return until nearly nine o'clock,' Simon said.

'I didn't receive it,' Dawson said shortly. 'And I can't imagine why she would send such a letter. And if she did, why she should phone me. Or why she should phone me at all.' He was beginning to bluster a little.

His wife said coolly, 'Darling, I could do with a cup of coffee. Would you mind making it? I'm absolutely exhausted.' To emphasise her point, she sank down on the sofa and looked up at him appealingly.

'Anyone else?' he asked. Simon asked for coffee too. Longman hopefully drained his glass but was ignored.

'We had our first meeting of the Drama Society tonight,' she said to Simon. 'A lot of discussion about what play to put on next.'

'Exhausting,' Simon agreed.

'What did you decide on?' Longman asked.

'We haven't quite. It seems to be a toss up between *The Seagull* and *Faust*.'

'I saw *Faust* at the Royal last year. Very good it was. The seven deadly sins and all that. They seem a bit outdated now, don't you think?' Longman asked.

'Don't you mean *Dr Faustus*? Did the Royal do it? I wasn't aware. Oh, well, I suppose it could be Chekhov.'

'No, not the City Royal. This was in Cardiff,' Longman said.

'You are a culture vulture, Sergeant,' she said drily.

'And you, Mrs Dawson?' Simon felt stung to the defence of his amiable friend.

'I, too,' she said sweetly. With a change of expression, she asked, 'Look, Inspector, why are you asking my husband all these questions? Surely you don't suspect him of being involved in the girl's disappearance? I thought it was a prowling attacker, or someone like that.'

'We don't believe it was anyone like that, Mrs Dawson. Tell me, what time did your husband leave after settling your son for the night?'

She cast a swift glance towards the door. Sounds of crockery being handled came from the rear of the house.

'Let me see,' she pondered, examining her fine-boned hands, then looked up swiftly at him, her eyes reflecting the flickering fire. 'You know, I'm not sure you should be questioning us here like this without the presence of a solicitor.'

'You're welcome to telephone for legal representation if you think you need it.'

'I don't like the implications of that remark, Chief Inspector,' she said.

'If you think that replying to my question may compromise your husband, Mrs Dawson, I suggest that you do telephone your solicitor.'

'It's not that at all,' she said. 'It's more the principle of the thing.'

'What time was it, then?'

She pushed her silky hair behind an ear and sighed. 'I suppose it must have been about eight, eight fifteen. I don't know, I wasn't watching the clock.'

Dawson came back, carrying two mugs of coffee, and handed them to his wife and Simon respectively, then poured himself a whisky.

'You seem to have taken quite a while to get back to the university after your visit home. We have about half an hour unaccounted for,' Simon said, sure that even if Dawson had coached his wife about his activities that Tuesday night, he had forgotten to put a precise time limit on them. The psychology department couldn't be much more than a mile from Dawson's house, he estimated.

101

Dawson raised eyebrows at his wife as he lifted his glass to his lips. 'What have you been saying, darling? The inspector seems to be a little confused.'

Simon repeated what Rachel Dawson had said. 'So you seem to have taken rather a long time getting back to the university,' he repeated.

'It was a foggy night, Chief Inspector, and my wife has no sense of time, do you, darling?'

'Terribly vague,' she agreed.

'To get back to the letter that Emily Sanderson wrote to you,' Simon said.

'I didn't receive any such letter,' Dawson said firmly.

'Did you know that Emily was pregnant?' Simon asked him abruptly, trying to keep his eyes on both Dawson and his wife at the same time.

Dawson took another gulp of whisky. 'No. Why should I know that?'

Rachel Dawson, after a slight start, was watching her husband expressionlessly. 'Do you think we should call our solicitor, darling?' she said.

'There's no need for that,' Dawson said irritably. He picked up a carved box and extracted a cigarette. 'Only my second today,' he announced and lit up, blowing the smoke roofwards.

'I'd no idea the poor girl was pregnant,' he repeated. 'Her boyfriend, I suppose. What was his name? Mark. I met him at Hyde Books.'

'You used to take Emily to lunch when you were in London, I understand,' Simon said.

'That's right,' Dawson said, glancing briefly at his wife. 'With Phillip Beardsley, who I did my last book with. She had become very interested in psychology and liked to talk to us about it.'

'When did you last see Emily, Dr Dawson?'

Dawson scratched his chin, glass in hand. 'I suppose I saw her some time towards the end of last term. Not to talk to, though.'

This was getting nowhere. Without some more concrete evidence than Simon had at present, there was no chance that he was going to get Dawson to admit to anything that would implicate him in more than a benign interest in Emily's academic prospects.

'I wonder if I might speak to you alone, Dr Dawson,' Simon said.

'Why do you need to do that, Inspector?' Rachel Dawson asked. 'Do you think you'll be able to browbeat him more successfully without me present?'

The thought of being able to browbeat Dawson was attractive but it was an unlikely prospect. Dawson cocked an eyebrow at Simon as if reading his thoughts and smiled down at his wife. 'Let's indulge him, shall we, darling? I promise I'll call you if he gets too menacing.'

She shrugged and went over to the fire to feed it some more logs from the basket. 'I'll prepare us some supper,' she said. 'I imagine the policemen won't be very much longer, will you?' she challenged Simon.

'That depends on your husband to some extent,' Simon said.

She cast a quick glance over her shoulder at Dawson as she left the room. He refilled his glass with another inch or so of whisky and returned to the sofa. 'What is it you can't ask in my wife's presence, Chief Inspector?' he asked. 'This is all a complete waste of time, you know. I haven't harmed Emily and I have no wish for her to be hurt.'

'I'm glad to hear it. In that case you will understand that by answering our questions you'll be doing your best to help her,' Simon said. 'So was Emily's letter sent to you at the university?'

'I've told you. I didn't receive any letter from her.'

'And on Tuesday night you left the meeting or party to come home to settle your son to bed.'

'That's right.'

Simon tried a more direct approach. 'Try if you can to look at it from our point of view. We know you had a relationship – of some sort – with Emily Sanderson. She wrote a letter to a Peter, asking him to meet her at her new address on the evening she died. She made a telephone call to someone locally at seven thirty that same evening. You received a telephone call from someone at that time.'

Simon paused. There was no reaction so far from Dawson. 'So you must understand, Dr Dawson, that there is some rationale behind our questioning of you.'

Dawson studied the whisky in his glass before looking up

from it at Simon. 'I think what I understand is that you seem to be making a very serious accusation,' he said calmly. 'And you should tread very carefully unless you have any real evidence rather than merely prejudice and vindictiveness.'

It was obvious that Dawson was right. Without proper evidence, Simon would never get Dawson to concede the smallest point. He said, 'I'm just doing my job. You don't get any special treatment.' Even to his own ears it sounded petty.

'Oh, really? Forgive me if I think that's exactly what I am getting,' Dawson said.

'Well, you would, wouldn't you?' Simon managed to smile down at him as he got up. 'We'll see ourselves out, shall we?'

'If you wish.' Dawson leaned back on the sofa in apparent ease, whisky glass in hand.

Longman got up and headed for the door, where Simon joined him.

'There's one thing I've forgotten to ask about.' Simon turned back, doorknob in hand.

Dawson sighed. 'What now?'

'You wouldn't happen to have misplaced a beige cashmere scarf, by any chance?'

He saw Dawson frown. 'I don't think so. Why?'

'You do own one, then?'

There was a pause while Dawson contemplated the fire. 'I do own one, yes.'

'Would you show it to me, please?'

'It's probably in my car,' Dawson snapped. 'Do I have to go out to it on a cold night just to satisfy some whim of yours, Chief Inspector?'

'You can bring it in to police headquarters if you prefer.'

'Perhaps I will,' Dawson muttered. 'It will give me the opportunity of having a word with your superior officer.'

'I'm sure he'd like that,' Simon said, aware that that was true.

'Look, Inspector,' Dawson said, with an effort at cordiality, 'I'm terribly sorry about what's happened to Emily. She was a lovely girl, with a good future in front of her. But I did not go to that house and kill her that night. It's far more likely that she was attacked by some lunatic, surely?'

'As I'm sure you are aware, most murderers are husbands

104

or lovers, Dr Dawson.' Simon said. 'Enjoy your supper, and do thank Mrs Dawson for us, won't you?' He turned and left the room, joining Longman, who was waiting by the front door.

A full moon shone in the western sky, sparkling in the frost that covered the car. Longman sprayed front and back windscreens and joined Simon inside. They sat breathing visible warm breaths in the bright light for a moment before Simon started the car and manoeuvred around the one Mrs Dawson had parked close behind.

'What was that about the scarf?' Longman asked as they reached the outer ring road.

'I called in to see Charlotte. Gave her the list. She doesn't think the scarf was Emily's, so it may have belonged to the attacker.'

'Dawson could go and buy a new one,' Longman said.

Simon laughed, relieved the interview was over. 'It won't help him if there are traces of him on the one we've got – like hairs, for example.'

'What if there aren't, though?' Longman asked doubtfully.

'He won't be sure of that, will he? No, the scarf's his.'

'If it is, it's pretty damning evidence, then.'

'Yes.' But it occurred to Simon at that moment that the scarf Emily might have borrowed and kept it from some earlier encounter. Like everything else to do with Dawson, it was suggestive, but it wouldn't prove anything.

'I'm wondering if she told her doctor anything about the father – who he was,' Longman said.

'I'll ask tomorrow. I'm ready for an early night.'

'She's a patronising bitch, isn't she?' Longman said.

'Mrs Dawson? Nobody can patronise you without your consent,' Simon paraphrased. 'But with some people it's difficult to evade it. She wasn't quite what I expected. I thought he'd either be married to a mouse or a vamp – and she's neither.'

'She strikes me as a fairly strong character,' Longman agreed. 'In fact, I'd say she was the boss around there.'

'Mmm.' Simon changed gear at a roundabout. 'So if Dawson was having an affair with Emily—'

'If? Are there any doubts then? You sounded so sure.'

105

'I am. That was just a manner of speech. If she knew about the affair with Emily, or any others that Dawson feeds his ego with, how do you think a woman like that would react?'

'Get pretty angry about it, I should think.'

'I'm not so sure. She's the stoical sort, and she wouldn't allow his affairs to be too important in the scheme of things. What she would do would be to assert the strengths of her marriage, home, child. To give importance to his other women would implicitly diminish her own significance – and I don't think she's that sort of woman. By treating them as of no account, she conveys that value to him and keeps her marriage more secure.'

'Maybe,' Longman said. 'I've come across women like that. They're generally the ones with intact marriages. On the other hand, she might, like any other woman, wonder whether such a marriage was worth preserving.'

'Alternatively, if someone posed a real threat, like a young, beautiful girl who was carrying her husband's child, she might take strong action to protect herself and her own child. Or just be motivated by old-fashioned jealousy,' Simon said. 'If that letter arrived at Dawson's home address rather than the university, she had an obvious opportunity to find out about the meeting that Emily planned.'

'In which case, maybe she got there before he did. We'd better do a check with the neighbours and see if she went out that night.'

'And check on Dawson's movements at the same time. Find out if anyone did notice his car at home that evening.'

There was silence for a while as they drove smoothly along the well-surfaced ring road. Then Longman said, 'I wonder if the others have come up with any other Peter of Emily's acquaintance.'

Simon felt a spasm of irritation. 'It's not a popular name these days. They won't find anyone.'

Longman didn't bother to argue.

The phone bleeped in the ensuing silence. Simon picked it up. It was Monkton.

'They've found another student dead. Name of Peter Rudley.'

Chapter Eleven

With characteristic abruptness Monkton had rung off without offering any additional information. When Simon phoned headquarters he was unable to track the inspector down, but finally managed to elicit from others a few details of the 'incident', including the address.

Longman, throughout these frustrated questionings and in the minutes following, refrained from commenting. The new destination was not far out of their way, being a short distance from the southern perimeter of the university campus in one of several streets of tall terraced houses largely given over to student population. There was already a number of marked and unmarked cars parked untidily in Walman Street when Simon added his own car to their ranks.

The young police constable at the door pointed. 'At the top of the first flight of stairs, sir.'

It would have been obvious enough without his directions. The door was open and Simon could see a few people inside the room as he rose from a view of their legs and feet to a more level image. Monkton, for a start, was there.

'Who's supposed to be in charge?' Simon asked him abruptly.

Monkton shrugged laconically. 'Me, for the want of the appropriate person, at present. There was no one else available when the call came in and when I got the name Peter, and the fact that he was from the university, I thought I'd get out here, see if there was any connection with the case we're on.'

'Very quick-witted,' Simon said drily.

Monkton cleared his throat. 'Anyway, DCI Cameron's on his way, should be here any time now.'

Simon could see McAllan, the police surgeon, rising to his

feet through the doorway of an inside room. From where Simon stood on the landing, he became aware of white faces, blenched by the stark lighting in the stairwell, peering anxiously by ones and twos from doorways on this and the upper floor. They were mostly male, but with the occasional female held protectively inside an arm.

One young man stood awkwardly alone just inside the door of the flat, his thin body crouched in an attitude of one who has received a painful knock, one hand rubbing the palm of the other slowly, his eyes fixed on the activity in what appeared to be the bedroom.

'The young lad who found him.' Monkton gestured briefly.

At that moment McAllan came out of the bedroom, carrying his bag and looking as grim as he usually did. He was a tall man, taller than Simon's six foot four, and carried himself with dignity, intensified by the splendid head of grey hair and equally splendid beard. To Simon he had the appearance of an eminent Victorian, and McAllan's manner did nothing to diminish the illusion.

Without acknowledging Simon, he approached the young man by the door and, laying a large hand on his shoulder, drew him further into the room.

Monkton, catching Simon's expression, compressed his lips in what passed for a smile. He knew as well as Simon that it was not really the police surgeon's place to question a witness, or whatever, particularly outside the presence of a senior officer.

Simon, conscious of all the watching faces and the general shambles, jerked his head at the inspector and entered the room, drawing the door close to behind them. Longman, almost forgotten, stepped speedily between the narrowing gap between door and jamb.

'So. What exactly seems to have happened here?' Simon asked Monkton. 'You were more than cryptic on the phone.'

'Was I? Oh, well, you got here, sir.'

Simon waited, expressionlessly.

'I don't know much more than seems obvious yet myself. That young lad, name's Michael Paxman, telephoned the emergency services about an hour ago. Said he'd just found his mate in there, Peter Rudley, and he thought he was dead. That's it, really.'

Simon took a breath. 'You haven't spoken to Paxman yourself? I mean, does he share the flat with this boy Peter? When did he last see him alive?'

'Oh, yes,' Monkton said calmly. 'He does share it with him, but he said he hadn't seen him since last night – Wednesday night – when they had a bit of a party going on.'

Again Simon waited. He was going to have to do something about Monkton.

'Michael there –' Monkton nodded his head in the young man's direction – 'was with his girlfriend after the party and they both went in to the university together the following morning – this morning. Michael said he didn't get back here until just before he made the phone call to us and he hadn't seen Peter since the party they were all at. In this house.'

'What subject was he reading, Peter Rudley?' Simon asked.

Monkton began to shrug and decided to shake his head instead. 'I haven't asked.'

'Has any questioning of the other students begun yet? I'm assuming they're all students?'

'Hasn't been much time,' Monkton mumbled.

Simon gave up and approached McAllan. The huge Scot appeared to have just ended his own questionings.

'Detective Chief Inspector Simon!' the voice boomed. He always accorded police officers their full title, and his habit of speaking with the loudest volume, rolling his Scottish r's enthusiastically, in or out of the presence of death, had a way of making even experienced officers flinch a little. The fact that his conversation with young Michael had been conducted sotto voce proved that his great frame was capable of gentler exhalations. Simon had always thought him a bit of a poseur, the kind of personality that, having failed to make it to the giddier heights of consultant surgeon, still exhibited the traits more fitting for those prima donnas of the medical fraternity.

'Dr McAllan,' Simon said, quietly, in the hope of inducing an equally low-voiced response. The surgeon did lower his voice a fraction as he drew Simon by his arm away from the other police officers. It was an unusual experience for Simon to be, as it were, manhandled by someone taller than himself. Like many tall men, Simon was inclined to slouch, but McAllan had obviously never felt his own height to be a handicap.

'Drugs,' McAllan said disgustedly. 'It's pretty clear to me the young lad in there mistook his dosage,' he rolled his bright brown eyes in the direction of Paxman – 'it appears there was some partying going on and the lad admits to me there were funny fags and not so funny drugs circulating. What with the drink and all . . . ' He shook his head.

'Any idea what sort of time he died?' Simon asked.

Unlike some police surgeons Simon had known, McAllan was always ready to attempt an answer to this difficult but inevitable question. 'Rigor's still present,' he said. 'It's cold in here, as you can tell for yourself. Between twelve and twenty-four hours, then.' He grinned at Simon's expression and relented. 'Nearer twenty-four; let's say in the early hours of this morning. It's now Thursday at—' he glanced at his watch – 'eleven p.m. Yon lad tells me the party went on until three or four o'clock this morning, but that he was preoccupied with his girlfriend and doesn't remember when he last saw his friend Peter.'

'No question of foul play?' Simon used the term self-consciously, but shied from the only other available word that came to mind. 'Or suicide?'

'Difficult to prove either way, isn't it, when it comes to drug abuse?' McAllan said shrewdly. 'But no.' He pursed his lips. 'I'd say it was another wasteful mistake. Choked on his own vomit, anyway. So sad,' he said, his face mournful. 'But you'll have a clearer idea, perhaps, from the pathologist.'

Simon doubted it. It was more likely that a clearer picture would come from questioning the students in the house, particularly while they were still in shock and therefore less guarded. He wanted to establish whether the death might be linked with the disappearance and probable demise of that other student, Emily Sanderson. It was possible. The young man had died only thirty or so hours after she had gone missing. Suicide out of remorse didn't look likely, though, in view of McAllan's opinion. It all depended on whether this dead Peter had known Emily, and whether he had an alibi for that time on Tuesday night. Simon hoped Cameron wouldn't mind, in the circumstances, his being involved in the questioning.

McAllan patted him heavily on his shoulder and moved over

110

to the door as it opened to admit Cameron himself, another Scot among the many who had heeded Dr Johnson's advice. While McAllan, with a puzzled look over his shoulder at Simon, began a reiteration of his earlier remarks, Simon noticed that Monkton had disappeared with Longman in tow. Too late, he thought, to prevent the flushing of several loos and the disappearance of incriminating substances into the city's sewers.

While he had the chance, Simon steeled himself to go and look at the dead face of Peter Rudley.

He looked very young, very vulnerable. But he was vulnerable no longer, Simon reminded himself, no longer heir to the thousand natural shocks and all the heartaches. Those belonged instead to the boy's parents, wherever they were.

It was a peculiarly undignified way of death, a humiliating form of waste for any human being. The young man lay on the floor beside his bed, from which he appeared to have rolled in his last heaving effort at removing the poison from his system, face down in the yellowish, congealed contents of his stomach. Fair-haired, fair-faced, intelligent yet ultimately stupid. But was he anything worse? Simon was sure, on seeing the boy's face, that he was not here looking at Emily Sanderson's attacker.

Cameron was still talking to McAllan as Simon took a seat on the sofa beside Michael Paxman. The boy was staring sickly at the floor between his feet.

Simon was conscious of how little time was his alone. 'I'm sorry to question you now, but I'm afraid I'll have to,' he began gently.

The young man lifted red-rimmed eyes to his own and sniffed. 'Yes?' he said, and his voice was a croak.

'What subject was Peter reading?'

Paxman frowned and looked vague. 'History, same as me.'

'Second year?'

Paxman nodded at the floor.

'Do you have any idea where Peter was on Tuesday night?'

The boy looked at him vaguely. 'What day is it now?'

'It's Thursday night.' Simon looked at his watch. 'Almost Friday morning. Term started yesterday, Wednesday, if that's any help.'

There was a pause while Paxman studied the floor again.

'We came up together on Tuesday, on the train. He got on at Reading, I came from Paddington. Same train.'

'What time did you get here then? You share this flat, I understand.'

'Five o'clock, about. Dumped our things. Went out for some fish and chips and a drink.'

'You were with him all evening?'

Paxman focused on him again. 'What d'you want to know all this for? What's it got to do with anything?' His eyes filled with tears.

'I'm sorry,' Simon said. 'There's a good reason for my questions. If you could manage to answer them, I'll leave you be.'

Paxman gave him a doubtful look. 'Yes, we were together all evening. Don't you want to know about last night?'

'Not at the moment.' Simon was conscious that Cameron would, any minute now.

'Did either of you know Emily Sanderson?' he asked.

'The student that's disappeared?'

Simon nodded.

'First-year psychology, wasn't she? No. Look, what is all this?' His voice rose high and quavering, recalling the broken notes of puberty, not so very many years behind him. It attracted the attention of Cameron, who finally said his farewells to McAllan and approached them.

'Any particular reason for your presence here, Chief Inspector?' Cameron stood stiffly in front of them as Simon rose to his several inches of advantage over him.

'Can I have a word, Cameron?'

As he made his explanations to the other chief inspector, it was clear to Simon that any connection between this Peter and the object of Emily's letter was pretty unlikely. He brought the interchange to a close as soon as he could and, with a backward nod to Paxman, went to extract Monkton and Longman from whatever they were involved in.

Cameron, finally mollified, had agreed to let Simon know, should any possible connection with his own case emerge, unlikely as it seemed. Monkton and Longman had managed to talk to a few of the other student residents and they too had unearthed nothing that could link Peter Rudley to Emily

112

Sanderson and the attack that had been made on her.

'Rudley's got a steady girlfriend,' Longman said as Simon drove him home. 'She doesn't live in the same house, but she spent the night with him after a few of them met in the pub on Tuesday night. She was there at the party with him, but she went off to her own flat at about midnight after the two of them had a row about him being more than a bit drunk. No mention of drugs, of course.' Longman breathed heavily. 'Might have been that, rather than drink, that they rowed about. Anyway, she hasn't been round here since, as far as the others know.'

'Didn't anyone wonder where he was all day?' Simon asked.

'Apparently not. They were all doing their own thing. I think they assumed he was with his girlfriend.'

'And she assumed that he was with them and that the row was still on,' Simon said. 'Not that it made much difference. He was dead before the party ended, in all likelihood.'

'Why do they do it?' Longman asked the unanswerable.

The rest of the journey was made in silence.

Chapter Twelve

After another night with only a few hours of restless sleep, Simon gave up and got out of bed. He padded to the kitchen in his bare feet and put the kettle on, rubbing one foot over the other, trying to keep his circulation going. It was still dark outside; the silvery light from the old streetlamps shone sleekly on the rigid black branches of the plane trees in the square.

The flat was freezing. He had forgotten to set the timer on the central heating the day before. After fiddling with the dial, he carried a steaming cup of black coffee into the sitting room, pulled on his overcoat that he had left lying on a chair, and sank down on the sofa. The depressing effects of the night before had carried on into the new day. Despite everything else that had happened, Jessie had invaded his consciousness even in the small amount of troubled sleep that he had managed. He realised that Jessie was after all only being true to herself – but wondered if it was her independence that galled him above all, or just her apparently greater loyalty to Dawson than to himself.

His thoughts shifted to Charlotte Sanderson, another independent woman. But his latest memory of her, of her head on his shoulder, was of a woman capable of expressing need. He thought resentfully that Jessie had never needed him like that, never turned to him for comfort. Not that Jessie, thank God, had ever had such cause as Charlotte. He thought of Charlotte alone in that large house, all those who had ever been close to her gone for ever, and wondered if he should telephone her to see how she was. But she would want news of how the investigation was going, would think that that was why he had contacted her, and he had nothing new to give her.

Hands in his overcoat pockets, head lowered, he stared at the empty fireplace, unable to summon the energy to switch on the gas fire. His mind returned to the question of who had killed Emily, of where that vision of brightness might now be mouldering. If it had been Dawson who had removed her body from that dismal room, Simon hadn't properly addressed the question of exactly when and how he had disposed of it. Some time between ten to eight and about ten to nine, when he had met Dawson outside the psychology department, the man would have had to enter the room and murder her, presumably either with the proverbial blunt instrument or with a knife. He would probably have come prepared.

She would have taken a few minutes after he arrived to get to the point – and say what? That she expected him to divorce his wife and marry her? And if he didn't fall into the desired raptures at the prospect, did she then begin to threaten him, and he begin to recognise what a danger she could be to his highly satisfactory career?

All this would perhaps have been followed by pleading on the part of Dawson: he might, urbanely, have advised an abortion and pointed out to her how undesirable a baby would be, interrupting her university course, her future career. Then, pushed, he would have given a reasoned exposition of his own situation, the proposed chair of psychology withdrawn before he had warmed the seat – and so on. From her an emotional reaction, tears turning to anger, from him the sudden and irreversible decision to be done with her and the situation. It would all have taken time. And afterwards there was the business of getting the body away to his car and having to dispose of it.

They had searched the neighbourhood thoroughly and found the rug, and he was sure it was *the* rug, in the river. It was perhaps a mile and a half from Acacia Road to the most likely place where it (and the body?) had been thrown in, and the fog had been very dense. And the drive back to the university – another three miles at least – meant that he could hardly have done it in the time. Simon realised that Emily might still have been lying in the boot of Dawson's car when he had met the man in the departmental car park. If that had been the case, he would have had plenty of time to get rid of the body. But Amanda Brakespeare thought the attacker would have had a lot of blood on him. Unless he had covered up in some way, or was naked ...

The shrill of the telephone startled him. He paused before answering, wondering if it was Jessie. It was far more likely to be one of the several police officers on the case. With a sigh, he reached for the instrument and grunted an acknowledgement.

'Christopher! You *are* in, then. I've been trying to telephone you, but you seem to be all over the place.'

'Don't you read the newspapers, Mother? I'm investigating a murder case. It tends to make inroads into one's social life, you know.'

'No, dear, I didn't know,' she said, he assumed in answer to his question rather than his statement. 'If you're talking about that poor student, I thought that it was Superintendent Bradley who was in charge.'

'Mmm,' Simon said, not inclined to expatiate. 'Did you want something in particular, or is this a sort of social call? A rather early one.' He glanced at his watch. Half past seven already.

'What have you been doing to Jessica? I've just spoken to her. I thought you'd be there, Christopher. You usually are these days.'

'Pressure of work and all that,' he said.

'Nonsense! I've never known that to be the case.' She gave a delicate snort. It was untrue but he wasn't in the mood to argue. Fond as he was of his mother, there were times when he refused to be led into her mental byways.

'Well, dear, what's up?' she said brightly. 'You know how highly I think of Jessica, and I don't like the idea that you've been upsetting her.'

'It wouldn't occur to you that it might be the other way around?' he enquired, then wished he hadn't allowed himself to be drawn.

'No, it wouldn't,' she said bluntly. 'I know your tendency to take umbrage. And you've never had a girlfriend I've liked as well as Jessica. I really hoped this time that you would be thinking of settling down—'

He interrupted her. 'Look, Mother, I don't know what Jess has been saying to you to bring all this on, but it's none of your business. How's the garden?' he asked, hoping to divert her to her consuming passion.

'In January?' She sounded like Lady Bracknell. 'Don't try to change the subject. Jessica sounded most unhappy. I suppose it is none of my business, as you say, but I wish you would telephone her, dear, and make up. Time is passing, you know, and you'll be quite old by the time your children are in their teens if you don't get a move on. And that's a time that you'll really need all your energy and wits, as I well know. Not that you were as difficult as Rose.'

'How is Rose?' he asked, glad to change the subject to his sister.

Her voice relaxed, conceding that she had said what she wanted on the former subject. 'I had a card from her last week. She's in California – with that painter chap I imagine,' she said doubtfully. 'Not much chance of her settling down. And I should so have liked to have grandchildren,' she added regretfully.

This, as he was aware, was the real issue for her.

'She might get the urge – you never know. Turn up on your doorstep with an infant wrapped in a shawl one of these days.'

'It's not the same,' his mother replied, almost sharply. 'There are too many children being born without the benefit of a father in this modern world. Have you not heard from Rose?' she asked abruptly. 'She usually seems to keep in touch with you rather than with us.'

He had heard from Rose fairly recently: a rather disturbed transatlantic telephone call which he had no intention of reiterating to this mother. Rose had been high, euphoric, and had laughed at his brotherly concern when he had asked what she was on. 'Always the copper, Chris! Would you run me in, your own sister? Of course you would,' she had added with a typical switch to depressive-aggressive. He had found it impossible to have a proper conversation with her in that state. He was worried about her, but there was nothing he could do with her so far away.

Before he could come up with a reply, his mother added, 'I'm afraid she may be on drugs, Chris. What do you think?'

The tone of her voice didn't alter but he didn't doubt the deep anxiety that was there. His own experience last night softened his irritable desire to make some comment on the subject of being one's sister's keeper.

It seemed likely now that it was Rose, and not Jessie, who had prompted the call.

'I really wouldn't know, Mother,' he said. Feeling that it was too obviously evasive an answer, he added, 'It's commonplace over there. Everyone experiments a bit. I wouldn't worry. You know Rose and her enthusiasms.'

It sounded feeble, even to his own ears, but he felt exasperated with his sister.

'But you know what she's like,' his mother was saying. 'She never does anything by half measures. Will you talk to her about it if she does ring you? Try to get her to come home for a spell. I'm sure she doesn't eat properly.'

'I'll do what I can,' he said faint-heartedly. 'There's no point in worrying. How's Dad?' he asked.

'Oh, keeping busy. You know your father, can't sit still for five minutes at a time.'

'Unlike you.' As he grew older, he had come to admire the relationship between his parents. When he was younger they had seemed insufferably steady and dull. It hadn't been until Jessie was discussing them one day that he had seen their marriage in a different perspective. She had made some remark about contemplating it with awe, a bit like contemplating Mont Blanc. Or had it been Mount Etna?

'Things are all right, are they? You didn't ring about anything in particular?'

'Yes, everything is fine. I was merely keeping in touch, you know. I rang Jessie's number because you're there such a lot normally—'

'Well, I hope you didn't wake her up,' he interrupted again. 'She cherishes her sleep, you know. So, give my love to Dad, won't you?'

'I didn't wake her. I rang last night.' When Jessie had probably still had a good head of steam. 'All right, dear, I'll stop talking and let you get back to work if that's what you're doing. But try to get in touch with Rose. And you will ring Jessica, won't you?'

Pride forbade him repeating the hint that she tell him just what Jessica had been saying to her, though it would have helped to know. 'I'll be in touch with her, of course I will, but in my own time, Mother.'

She made a disparaging sound. 'Don't let pride allow you to spoil a good thing. Goodbye, dear.'

He replaced the receiver and sat staring at it for a while, wondering whether to ring Jessie or leave it for a bit. He hadn't needed his mother to put the thought into his head. But whenever he started trying out various imaginary beginnings to the conversation, they sounded wrong. He still felt annoyed with her, that was the problem. Still annoyed that she seemed to be defending, supporting, Dawson. And Dawson's smug awareness of Simon's discomfort made things worse. On the other hand, what did it all matter, really, beside the good times they'd shared. He punched the buttons on the phone quickly before he could change his mind.

The phone rang for a long time and he was on the point of putting it down when she answered.

'Jessie?'

'Chris.' The flat and unenthusiastic statement of his name did little to encourage him.

He put pride aside. 'Would an apology help?'

'For what, in particular?'

'Give me a list and I'll tick the appropriate boxes.'

'Total submission, eh?'

'I didn't say I'd tick all of them.'

'Well, in that case ...' she said, but he knew her voice and there was the beginning of a smile in it.

'Perhaps we could get together and negotiate terms?'

'It goes a bit deeper than that, I'm afraid.' The smile, if it was ever there, was gone.

'Tell me,' he said heavily, wishing he had followed his instinct to leave her alone for a while.

'You know I don't like long conversations on the telephone – particular when it's about something personal.'

'You miss my body signals, don't you? Admit it,' he said, and raised a faint chuckle. 'Oh, come on, Jess. It's nothing more than the fact that Dawson gets up my nose. I'm allowed to experience that all too human response now and again, aren't I?'

'Not when it prejudices you in a murder case, you're not. And not when you drag me into the scenario. How dared you behave like that when you met me at Peter's?' She was obviously still very angry and he was on the point of cravenly replacing the receiver.

'Simple jealousy, I imagine,' he blurted, not without a sense of relief.

'No excuse,' she said, but her voice had lost some of its coolness.

'Look, Jess, I really don't know what it is about Dawson that gets under my skin. We should talk about it. When can I come and see you?'

'Mother's orders?'

'That, too. I just want things to be the way they were.'

'You're emotionally lazy, Chris, like most men.'

He let that pass. She wasn't usually prone to sexist remarks.

'I'm getting ready for work,' she said. 'I'll think about it. Maybe I'll ring you.'

With 'maybe' he'd have to be content. The whole conversation, such as it was, had been on her terms. He pulled off his overcoat in rough exasperation and headed for the shower. What the hell did it all matter? All he wanted was to wrap his body warmly around hers and rest content. Why couldn't it be that simple for her too? Why did women have to talk so much, analyse everything?

After his shower, feeling slightly more benign, and conscious of a sense of neglect, he looked up the number that his mother didn't know he had and telephoned his sister in California. There was a lonely beeping in a faraway apartment and no one came to the phone.

Chapter Thirteen

The morning meeting took place in the incident room in Acacia Road. The overcrowding in the room that Edwards had made available to them added to the general confusion of Simon's mind. Several voices were raised and smokers lurked by the doorway, their unwelcome exhalations driven into the room by the draught from the constantly opening front door.

Simon was struggling with the question whether the nicotine vapour was the source of his problems or the answer to them, when saved by a request in Rhiannon Jones's melodious Welsh accent that the offenders clear out or clear the air. 'Besides, it's bad for the computers, sir,' she added, going over to raise the sash window and send a blast of icy air over them all.

'And that's no good for them either,' Monkton was heard to mutter.

By the time they had all settled down, Simon was feeling a little clearer-headed. He gave them a brief account of the events of the night before, and then returned to the subject of their own investigations.

There was no forensic report yet on the rug but there seemed little doubt now that it was the one from Emily's room and it seemed highly likely that her body was somewhere in the river estuary or the Bristol Channel. And that meant it might be a considerable time before they found it.

Watkins, his large ears pink in the cold blast from the window, gave a résumé of the interviews held with tenants of the house and neighbours. 'She was seen by one of the neighbours in the road, walking in the direction of the main North Road at just after ten in the morning.'

This was the time Edwards had seen her go out. North Road was the direction she would have taken for the city centre.

'Another neighbour was walking the dog and saw her again going towards North Road at five thirty in the evening. And one of the tenants in the house saw her going up the steps just ahead of him at twenty past six. That was Jason Turner on the first floor, sir,' he said, closing the file.

'Did he speak to her?' Simon asked.

'He says not. She was a bit ahead of him.'

'None of the immediate neighbours saw anything suspicious?'

'No.' There was a general shaking of heads.

'So we need to find out where she went that afternoon. Was she carrying anything? Did she perhaps visit the university library? Or did she visit a friend? In which case, why haven't they come forward? Surely we've had more reports than that? A striking-looking girl like Emily was bound to be noticed.'

'Yes,' Monkton said. 'We've had the usual sightings from Scotland, Wales and Ireland, Tipperary and Timbuktu, but these were the only ones so far that seemed likely.' He laid out some notes in front of him.

'Oh?'

'There's one report she was seen in the city library in the morning and another that she was in Copperfield's café in the town centre around lunchtime.'

Simon delegated a number of officers to follow these up and continue inquiries. 'Get as much detail as you can, will you?' Simon requested of the room in general, not without some exasperation. 'We have little enough to go on, so when you do get a response, make it a thorough one, for God's sake.'

'Can I shut the window now, sir?' Rogers, the burliest of the team, protested.

'No. Maybe a bit of fresh air will wake you all up.' There was no answering groan – perhaps they were conserving their energy. He gave them an outline of what his own investigations had revealed and reported his interview with Dawson.

'Is this the Peter we're looking for, then?' Monkton said.

'There's no evidence that the dead student knew Emily.'

'But we can't be sure,' Monkton persisted.

'I don't remember suggesting that you stop making enquiries.' Simon's irritation showed.

'So they have an alibi for each other – Dawson and his wife, sir?' This was Rhiannon. 'Doesn't mean much.'

'No, but it doesn't mean they're lying, either,' Simon said with conscious impartiality.

'But who might be covering for whom?' she persisted. 'Suppose the wife did it – jealous, you know. If she intercepted that letter Emily sent, she might have turned up instead of her husband.'

'In that case, where did he go after receiving the call at seven thirty?' Longman objected. 'I can't see them both turning up at the same time and deciding to conspire in killing the girl.'

'Perhaps they already had,' Rhiannon said. 'Decided to conspire, I mean.'

There was a moment's silence while they considered the possibility.

'Well, I want their neighbours questioned about the movements of the two of them on Tuesday night,' Simon said. 'You can close the window now, Rodgers. Come in, you lot, and close the door,' he said to the smokers still huddled in the open doorway.

'And what about this man Beardsley, as well?' Rhiannon spoke again. 'I mean, he seems to have known Emily too.'

'And Whittaker, the boyfriend, don't forget,' Rodgers added sarcastically.

'The local police are checking on him,' Simon stated.

'Talking of false alibis –' Inspector Monkton said – 'our friend Edwards the landlord seems to have been a little bit misleading as to his whereabouts.'

'Oh? And why didn't this appear with Watkins's report?' Simon asked with a touch of annoyance. Monkton was showing an undesirable tendency to keep aloof from teamwork lately. The fact that he unerringly seemed to uncover some useful item of information didn't lessen Simon's objections. He was going to have to have a quiet word with him.

'Only found out last night when I was having a jar with Perfect from uniform branch,' Monkton said easily. 'He's been dealing with that mugging.'

'Well?'

'Well, Perfect said he saw Edwards coming down the road

at twenty past nine and letting himself into his house when he says he was in all night with his mates having a drink and watching some doubtless dodgy videos.'

'From which direction?' Simon asked.

'North Road.' Monkton added quietly, 'I notice Edwards's car's back in his garage this morning.'

'Is it?' Simon hadn't noticed. He'd been late arriving and had hurried into the building without looking around. 'That's something I was going to speak to him about.'

'Where was it that night, I wonder?' Monkton said.

'We all do,' Simon said shortly.

'Sir?' Rhiannon said. 'The body must have been removed in a car. Can't we just get forensic checks run on those belonging to people who might be considered suspects?'

There was a general groan.

'I wish we could, DC Jones,' Simon said. 'But until we have stronger evidence linking any of them to the crime, that's not within our power – as I'm sure you know.'

Undeterred, she persevered. 'But you'd think if a person was innocent, they'd be glad to help, if only to clear themselves from any suspicion.'

'Not when forensic evidence is still as imperfect as it is, young woman,' Monkton said in a manner designed to patronise. 'And human beings as well, come to that.'

'You'd know about the latter, I suppose,' she countered in sweet accents.

There were smiles from all but the inspector as Simon brought the meeting to a close.

'What now?' Longman asked Simon as the room thinned out, the smokers pausing on the threshold to light up again.

'We'll have a word with Edwards and then I want to speak to Emily's doctor. You can find out if the lad who was mugged has regained consciousness yet. Perhaps he saw something or someone.'

Longman nodded. 'After we've talked to Edwards, then. What d'you make of what Monkton said? Maybe we need to be looking a bit closer to home after all?'

Simon didn't answer, leading the way down the back staircase to the malodorous depths of Edwards's living area.

The landlord appeared to have scarcely begun his day. His

hair was standing in spikes and he wore a stained satin dressing gown tied loosely and revealing a hairy stomach above some indecent pyjama bottoms. A half-eaten breakfast of everything fried was on the table under the window with the most sensational tabloid propped open in front of it.

'Sorry to disturb your breakfast, Mr Edwards,' Longman said cheerfully. 'We thought you'd be finished by now.'

Edwards gave an insincere smile and returned to the table. 'I'm not really a morning person, Sergeant.'

'That's what we wanted to talk to you about,' Longman said amiably.

Edwards had turned his back to them as he sat to his meal again and said nothing for a moment while he noisily masticated some more food.

Simon this time took the opportunity to wander around the room, poking about on shelves and generally disrupting the man's digestive juices. As Longman had said, the videos and magazines on the shelves all seemed to cater for low and violent tastes.

'I understand you do some photography, Mr Edwards,' he said over his shoulder. 'Do you video things as well?'

Edwards swallowed audibly. 'What things?'

'You tell me.'

'No,' he answered, 'I don't.'

'So it wasn't your own productions you were showing to your friends the other night? The night Miss Sanderson disappeared?'

Edwards put down his knife and fork noisily and turned to face Simon's back. 'What difference does it make what we were looking at?'

Longman watched him from his own position on the sofa, unable to see anything but the usual bland expression on the man's face.

'None – if that's what you *were* doing.' Simon turned to face him and Edwards's expression changed to one of injured innocence.

'Don't know what you mean.'

'It seems that you didn't tell us the truth about your whereabouts on the night of Emily Sanderson's disappearance. That's extremely serious. At the least it's wasting police time, and at worst it puts you under suspicion of murder.' Simon, as usual, spoke very mildly, and Edwards's bewildered scrutiny of his expression raised a smile on Longman's face.

'Well?' Simon snapped, making Edwards blink and straighten in his chair.

'What have you been told then?' Edwards asked with an attempt at jocularity, getting up and going over to turn up the gas fire. Longman pulled at his collar and made an expression of disgust at Simon. It was already too hot in the room, intensifying the unpleasant odours that pervaded the place.

'I don't have to tell you that, Mr Edwards,' Simon said. 'We're here for you to tell us the truth for a change.'

'I told you – I was here with my mates.' The landlord rose slowly from the fireplace. The short man looked foolish facing Simon in his nightwear. 'Look, d'you mind if I just go and get dressed?'

'Yes, I do,' Simon said, not about to give him time to invent another likely tale. 'Just sit down and answer my questions, if you would. You weren't here with your mates. So where were you?'

'But I was,' Edwards protested with a show of indignation. 'Of course I was here. Who said I wasn't? You know I was. I got that door open for that woman when she phoned, didn't I?'

'Miss Sanderson was, of course, attacked and removed some time earlier than that,' Simon said. 'It's that period of the evening that I'm interested in.'

Edwards raised his eyebrows at Longman, who looked back expressionlessly. He turned a look of bewilderment on Simon.

Simon sighed and gave in. 'You were seen, by a member of the local police, as it happens, coming into the house at twenty past nine that night. Where had you been?'

Edwards was silent for a moment, regarding the grubby carpet. 'I went over to one of my mates,' he said quietly, as if trying out the statement to see how it might sound.

Longman ostentatiously got out his notebook. 'Where and who?' he said.

Edwards hesitated and gave him a name and address.

'Why, when you had visitors, did you go visiting someone else?' Simon asked. 'A bit discourteous, wasn't it?'

'They'd gone by then.'

'I see. So, in fact, you didn't account for the time we asked you to.'

Edwards shot him a quick look, then said, 'I did. They were here and they left just before I went over to Jack's. They were here the time you said.'

'We'll be checking that,' Simon said, with an unpleasant feeling that Edwards's friends would back up his story. 'Tell me, where was your car that night? I see it's back in your garage today.'

'It broke down,' Edwards said cautiously.

'When?'

'That night. In fact, I gave a couple of them a lift into town when they were leaving and when I got to Jack's place it wouldn't start again. So I left it there. Dicky starter motor. I went over today and it got going, no trouble, so I drove it back here,' he said, all injured innocence.

'And how far would that be, the friend's house? How long do you think it would take to walk from there?' Simon addressed Longman, who was still studying his notebook.

The sergeant pursed his lips, considering. 'About twenty minutes or so, I should say.'

'And you were there how long, at Jack's?'

Edwards thought again. 'Not long. I wasn't watching the clock, you understand. Being as how I never expected to have to account for my movements that night.'

'So what time did you leave here? With your friends?' It was obvious to Simon that Edwards had something to hide. But whether it was homemade pornography or something more serious, he wasn't yet sure. He was tempted to leave Longman to question the man and move on to some literally fresher pasture.

'I can't remember,' Edwards was replying sulkily.

'Oh, come on!' Simon exclaimed, his limited patience evaporating. 'OK, it may be that you did have one or two friends in that evening, but unless you can prove otherwise they may have left much earlier, leaving you time to go up to Miss Sanderson's room, wheedle your way in there on some pretext, attack her and take away her body in your car – which is perhaps why the car wasn't here that night. You left the body in it while you decided how to dispose of it.'

'No,' Edwards said blankly.

'Then you go and visit this Jack in some spurious attempt to establish an alibi.'

'No,' Edwards said again.

'Hadn't you better be a bit more helpful then, sir?' Longman said kindly.

'I did have those friends here,' Edwards said, turning anxiously to the sergeant. 'They'll tell you so. She must have been killed while they were here.'

'Perhaps you were all in on it,' Simon suggested. 'Perhaps, given your shared tastes, you all decided to enact some of your combined fantasies? When exactly were they here? And what makes you think she must have been killed during that time?'

Edwards's expression suddenly changed along with the tone of his voice. 'Look, I don't have to listen to this. I don't have to answer any questions unless you decide to arrest me. So cut it out, all right? I've told you as near as I can what happened that evening, and if you'd give me time to think I could probably be more certain of the times.

'Fine,' Simon said abruptly, thankful for an excuse to get out of the stuffy little room. 'I'll leave you with my sergeant and you can get some kind of a statement down. You do realise that, if you were coming and going from the house that evening, as you say you were, what you did or didn't see at those times will be relevant to our inquiry.'

Edwards, trudging sullenly through to the kitchen with his dirty plate, ignored him.

Chapter Fourteen

The university health practice was housed in the main administrative block, with access through its own entrance in a wing of the old stable block. It must have been some estate, Simon thought, to have been serviced by what must surely even then have been an excessively large building for stabling horses and carriages.

As he watched a group of students debouch noisily from the main entrance, he wondered what the shades of that past would have made of the present occupants of their lavish inheritance. Students raised scruffiness to a kind of art form, he thought, entirely unconscious of his own sartorial limitations. They were so studied in every detail of their carelessness that it belied the indifference to conventional form that it was supposed to convey and ended as a convention in itself.

He entered the pristine health centre and encountered a young receptionist. She asked with unexpected officiousness if he was a mature student, and was he registered, because she didn't remember having seen him before. He showed his identification and explained that he had made an appointment to speak to Dr Tremeadow.

She looked embarrassed and apologised. 'Actually, I haven't been here very long and I feel a bit intimidated by all these clever people,' she said naively. 'It's not a bit like an ordinary GP practice.'

Simon smiled. 'Not so much of varicose veins and arthritis, I'd guess.'

She looked serious. 'The worst thing is, they won't accept it when I say they can't have an appointment straight away. They argue, shout at me on the phone and even in here, to my face. I never used to get that sort of thing before.'

Simon, whose health was excellent, had little first-hand experience of doctor's receptionists, but he knew others who had and felt secretly cheered.

'They have problems with bureaucracy, the young,' he said.

She returned to business. 'Doctor is still with one of her patients, but I shouldn't think she'll be long.'

Was it significant, Simon wondered, that the medical profession seemed to be the only one that shared with God the lack of any need for the definite article? He tried out a few others' 'Accountant will see you now', 'Solicitor ... ' He couldn't come up with any other examples of divine eminence among the professions. Not even 'Vicar will see you now.' Or 'Bishop ... ' It seemed a bad sign.

He was aware that the young woman was eyeing him curiously. The whole university was no doubt disturbed by what had happened to Emily and would soon be equally distressed by the news of Peter Rudley's death: he had heard no reference to it on the local radio news on the drive out to the campus, so clearly the police had not yet released the details. He had noticed, in the entrance to the health centre, some new-looking posters on women's self-defence, as well as some colourful, and probably ineffectual, warnings on the dangers of drugs.

University funding seemed not to be lacking in the admin block anyway, he thought, looking around him. The furniture was expensive, as were the curtain fabrics and general decoration. They contrasted dramatically with the basic functionalism of the teaching areas, which looked scuffed and down at heel.

It was a good ten minutes before a young man with dreadlocks emerged from what Simon hoped was Dr Tremeadow's room, during which time the receptionist had given several demonstrations of her ineptitude at dealing with an articulate clientele on behalf of 'Doctor'. Still on the telephone, she waved Simon in the general direction he was meant to go and returned to her altercation. Simon had been given highly privileged treatment with his appointment if the dates the receptionist was offering were any guide.

Dr Tremeadow was a tiny woman somewhere in her thirties. She had shoulder-length straight hair and wore no make-up but, as if in compensation, sported a pair of brightly painted parrots suspended from her earlobes. Her natural good humour was confirmed in her expression as she stood up and held out her hand over her desk.

'You're Jessie's fella, aren't you?' she said, smiling up at him.

'I hope so,' he said, smiling back as he shook her hand.

'Oh, is there some doubt?'

'I hope not.'

She laughed and gestured to the seat in front of her desk, turning immediately to the purpose of his visit.

'Are you getting anywhere with the investigation?' she asked.

'Several places at once.'

'You wanted to ask me about Emily's visit to me during the early part of the Christmas vacation.' She pulled a thin cardboard file towards her and put on a pair of over-large heavy horn-rimmed glasses. 'She came to see me on the fifteenth of December. I didn't see her after that. You know what she wanted to see me about?'

Simon nodded.

'She wanted confirmation that she was pregnant and I was able to tell her that she was. Three months.'

Simon did a brief calculation. 'So the baby was conceived – when? September?'

'That's right.'

So, before she became a student at the university. 'When exactly did she become aware that she was pregnant?' he asked.

'Some young women can be amazingly vague about these things. I don't think she'd known for long. She had forgotten to take the pill on more than one occasion, as far as I can gather.'

'And when you confirmed that she was pregnant, did she say anything about the father of the child?'

'She didn't tell me who he was, if that's what you were hoping for. Of course, if you'd found her body, you could run

131

a DNA test on the foetus, which would take you in the right direction.'

'Well, we don't have the body,' Simon said. 'Did she say anything at all that might be of help? I mean, in cases like this, don't you discuss their relationships with them, their emotional state and so on?'

'That depends. They're all individuals, Chief Inspector. Their behaviour doesn't follow a set pattern.'

'Call me Chris,' he said.

'Thank you,' she said solemnly. 'I'm Liz. Look, I don't really think that I can be a lot of help, nice as it is to meet you. I can only say that Emily didn't seem unduly cast down at the idea of being pregnant. In fact, she seemed rather pleased.' She hesitated, wrinkling her brow. 'You have to understand that I hardly knew Emily. She had only consulted me once before, early on in the term, with a sore throat, and it's impossible on so small an acquaintance to make a judgement on her normal state of mind. That's what makes me hesitate to pass any comments on her psychological state.'

'Don't,' Simon said. 'Whatever comes as an impression to you might be useful. Don't worry that you might mislead me – I'm used to that.'

She gave a brief grin. 'Oh, dear. Right – off the top of my head, she struck me as a bit strange.' She frowned again. 'I mean, her general manner seemed rather distant, but she seemed almost purposefully to brighten up when I confirmed that she was pregnant. Not the sort of reaction students usually give when they hear that news. I know that's a bit vague,' she said apologetically.

'No, it's relevant, I'm sure,' he said thoughtfully, though more to encourage her than from any conviction. 'Anything else?'

'I asked her what her plans were, and she said she hoped I wasn't suggesting an abortion – which of course I wasn't. I was referring to her university course and how she would manage. She said that as the baby was conveniently due at the end of her first year in June, and she'd had no unpleasant side effects so far, she was sure she would manage. She seemed quite determined.'

'She didn't volunteer any comments at all about the father,

132

how he might be involved in her future plans?'

Dr Tremeadow hesitated. 'I rather gathered that it might be a bit complicated – which leads one to infer that the man was probably married. But I may be quite wrong about that.'

'Perhaps,' he said cautiously.

'I'm sorry. This has been a bit of a waste of time for you, I'm afraid,' Dr Tremeadow said, leaning back and stretching her arms above her head.

Simon took it for a polite dismissal. He unwound from his semi-supine posture in the comfortable chair and leaned over her desk again to shake her hand in farewell. 'If you do think of anything else, give me a call.'

There was quite a crowd in the reception area by the time he emerged. The receptionist had obviously given up any attempt at civility or good humour and merely rolled her eyes at him as he waved goodbye.

Dr Tremeadow was right: it had been a waste of time. He was getting rather bored with brick walls and was feeling a dangerous desire to do a little stirring-up. Since he was at the university anyway, he thought it a good time to go and talk to Phillip Beardsley, crony and sidekick of Peter Dawson.

As he entered the main corridor of the psychology department, Hermione Roe was emerging from one of the rooms on his left near Jessie's and spotted him immediately.

She hailed him with all her usual enthusiasm, calling out, 'Chris! Just the man I was hoping to see. Synchronicity – a meaningful coincidence, as Jung would have it.' As he reached her, an uncertain smile fixed on his face, she opened the door again and asked him to step in for a moment.

His face must have been expressive because she laughed and said again, 'Oh, it's only for a moment. I won't devour you, even if I'd like to. Go on, have a seat,' she said, urging him physically through the door.

He sat, looking up at her with bemusement. 'Well? I am a bit busy, Hermione.'

She sat near him on one of the seats in front of her desk and leaned towards him, appearing to hesitate. 'Look, I had to speak to you, Chris.'

He wondered suddenly and horribly whether she was going to start questioning him about his relationship with Jessie or,

133

worse, whether he was available again. His expression again made her laugh and she relaxed.

'It's nothing to worry about, so you don't have to look so alarmed.' She crossed her legs and became more businesslike in manner, if not in posture. 'Did I tell you what my specialism is here, in psychology?'

'No, you didn't,' he said, still wary.

'The paranormal,' she said, watching him closely.

'Oh?' he said blankly.

'I research, investigate, claims of all kinds of extrasensory perception, clairvoyance, prediction, you know the kind of thing.'

'I suppose so.'

'Has your department ever used a psychic? I know that some police forces do and with some success, apparently.'

'Yes, I've heard of it, but I haven't any first-hand experience.' He was feeling more relaxed, even curious. 'It's not exactly foolproof, is it?'

'Oh, no,' she said agreeing with the obvious. 'But it can provide some useful leads, get the police thinking along new lines. There was a psychic – in fact, there were several – involved in the Son of Sam murders in the States. One of them was very close to the mark, and if her insights had been given the credence they deserved, it might have saved some lives.'

'But when you've got several psychics involved, which one do you believe?' Simon had read a little on the subject, but wasn't going to admit to it.

'Most of them had something to contribute,' Hermione said.

'And some no doubt get it completely wrong.'

She shrugged. 'The important thing is to get a reliable psychic in the first place. And I know such a one.'

'Really?' he said without enthusiasm.

'I've asked her to see what she can get on Emily Sanderson's disappearance.'

'Up to you. I can't stop you.'

'No, you can't,' she said, impatient. 'But will you listen to what she has to say?'

'I told you – I'm busy, Hermione.'

'What's the problem? Afraid your mates will laugh at you?

134

I expected that you might be a bit more open-minded, Chris.'

'Sorry to disappoint you.'

'What have you got to lose? You're not frightened, are you? It's not black magic.'

'I thought that was what it's considered to be in some quarters.'

She shook her head impatiently. 'Somthing quite different! And how can it be considered black magic when it's aimed at helping people? Surely the poor girl's sister would be glad of any help to find the body for example?'

He had an alarming vision of Hermione intruding on Charlotte with some colourful old crone in tow.

'All right – you can tell me what she has to say. But don't expect me to go consulting her in some darkened room, because I won't.'

'You really are behind the times, aren't you? She doesn't work in a darkened room. Nor does she dress like the Wicked Witch of the West. She's an attractive woman in her thirties who used to work in the Civil Service.'

He smiled at her annoyance, conscious that she was, after all, only trying to help. 'The stipulation still stands. You can tell me what she said.'

Hermione leaned back, showing an attractive length of thigh. 'You believe that you'll find Emily's body in the river, don't you?'

'Since that was published in this morning's papers, I'm not so far impressed.'

'She told me yesterday it was what you believed.'

Simon shrugged.

'There is no doubt that Emily is dead, Sybil says.'

'*Sybil*? Really?'

Hermione sighed. 'I really don't know why I'm bothering with you. I wouldn't if it was just for your sake, I can tell you.'

'I'm sorry. Is there more?'

'Sybil says that you won't find her body in the river. Emily is buried somewhere.'

'Did she by any chance mention where?'

Hermione shook her head. 'She gave me some notes on the place ...' She reached for her shoulder bag. 'I've got them here.' She produced a sheet of paper torn from a small ring binder and covered with small precisely formed writing.

'I promise to read them,' Simon said, holding out his hand.

Hermione held them away from him. 'She wants to visit the room – Emily's room, in that house.'

'I'll think about it. Did she not have any information on the killer? I was expecting the colour of his eyes, at least.'

She ignored his teasing. 'That's why she wants to visit the room. She says it'll be easier to pick up things.' Hermione watched his face for a moment. 'Don't be sceptical. There's a lot we don't understand about these things. At least have the courtesy to respect the fact that having researched them at some length, I am in a better position to judge than you. Sybil has impressed me over and over again. I assure you, in general I'm a confirmed sceptic.'

'I'm sorry. Like most people, I'm wary of what I don't understand.

Mollified, she handed him the notes. 'I don't know what use they'll be,' she admitted. 'None at all, I imagine, if you don't take them seriously.'

'I promise I'll have a look at them,' he said again.

'And think about letting Sybil visit that room?'

He nodded. 'When the police have finished with it.' He stood up. 'I, um, appreciate your efforts, Hermione. I'll be in touch.'

'Go on with you!' She nudged him with the toe of her shoe. 'You can't wait to get away from this mad woman. Are you going to see Jessie?'

'I'm looking for Phillip Beardsley, actually. Can you point me to his room?'

She unwound her lovely limbs and pulled down her tight skirt with a little wriggle. He couldn't remember any tutors like her in his day.

'Fourth door along on the left,' she said, looking at her watch. 'He should be free about now.'

He pushed the notes into an overcoat pocket and walked the short distance to Beardsley's door, conscious of Hermione's eyes at his back.

Chapter Fifteen

Simon tapped at the door. There was a slight delay before he heard 'Come!' In the small book-lined room, he saw that there were two men present, one of them Peter Dawson. The other man, presumably Beardsley, raised enquiring eyebrows at him but Simon was forestalled from introducing himself by Dawson.

'I do declare it's Detective Chief Inspector Simon!'

'Phillip Beardsley?' Simon asked of the other man, ignoring Dawson.

The man ducked his head in a nod. He was stockily built with light-brown, curly hair, a broad face and deep-set, dark eyes. His clothes, a worn green corduroy jacket over a loose shirt, didn't disguise an incipient paunch as he half rose at Simon's approach.

'Are you cross-examining *all* the blameless members of this department, Chief Inspector?' Dawson asked. He wore his usual bland smile, but his eyes were watchful.

'Just a selected few,' Simon replied civilly. 'It's Mr Beardsley I've come to see.'

'Makes a change.' Dawson turned his back on Simon to face his friend. 'I'll see you later then, Phillip. Don't let this man intimidate you. He seems to have got it into his head that one of us civilised members of society, rather than a roaming psychopath, is responsible for Emily's death.' He faced Simon, a mocking smile still on his face, as he went to the door. 'By the way, it's *Dr* Beardsley. Not *Mr*, Inspector.'

Simon waited for the door to close before turning to Beardsley again.

'Have a seat,' Beardsley said, gesturing.

'Thank you.' Simon sank into a low, comfortable chair as Beardsley perched on the edge of his own, his elbows on his desk.

'I'm not sure how I can help you. I didn't teach Emily – I assume it is about Emily Sanderson that you've come?' He lacked Dawson's urbanity; Simon sensed that he was ill at ease.

'We're talking to people who knew Emily, to try to get some background on her life,' Simon said, in an effort to put the man more at ease. 'You've known Emily since before she came to the university, and I thought you'd be a good person to consult.'

'I see.' Beardsley fiddled nervously with a pen. 'I don't know that I can be of much use. You probably know already that she was a bright, lovely girl – and we're all terribly distressed to hear what's happened to her.' He paused uncertainly.

'You knew her from her job in London. Did you remain friends after she came here?'

'She dropped in to see me occasionally. I wasn't one of her tutors.'

'Did she ever confide in you?'

Beardsley rearranged some papers on his desk. 'I'm not sure what you mean. What would she confide?'

'That she was pregnant, perhaps?' Simon said casually.

There was a definite hesitation before Beardsley said, 'Was she?'

'You didn't *know*?' Simon asked with deliberate disbelief. 'I was given to understand that you were almost her father confessor.' He watched to see whether his guess fell far short.

Beardsley cleared his throat. 'Were you? I'd say that was a bit of an exaggeration. I wouldn't deny our friendship, but I can't say she confided in me.'

'But could you hazard a guess as to who the father of Emily's child might be?' Simon asked.

'Is it important, Chief Inspector?'

He was overdoing the naivety, Simon thought. 'I should have thought that was fairly obvious.'

'A motive for murder? A bit unlikely in this day and age, wouldn't you say?'

Beardsley was definitely uncomfortable with this line of questioning. He continued to fiddle with his pencil, his eyes lowered.

'Not where it concerns people who are in a position of responsibility. Witness our philandering politicians and the trouble they bring on themselves.'

'Not quite the same, is it?' Beardsley said.

'The same as what?' Simon asked quickly.

Beardsley dropped the pencil, bent awkwardly in his chair to retrieve it, returning to an upright posture with a flushed face.

'As *what*?' Simon repeated.

'Well, I imagine you're suggesting that someone in a position of responsibility at the university was involved with – with Miss Sanderson.' Still his eyes would not meet Simon's.

'It seems possible. And as you've been speaking to Dawson, you can hardly expect me to believe that you weren't already aware of the possibility of our likely interest in that possibility.'

'It's ridiculous!' Beardsley said fiercely. 'As if a man like Peter would kill someone like Emily! Over something like that!'

'I admit you know him rather better than I do, but I hardly think that he would see a threat to his status as a "small matter". Do you?'

'Why should it be a threat to his status?'

'Oh, come on, Dr Beardsley. You know as well as I do that it would destroy him. A man in his position, getting a vulnerable student pregnant?' Simon paused. 'I see that it's the validity of motive that troubles you, rather than the likelihood of my premise being true.'

'I didn't say any such thing.'

'No. I can see that you would be reluctant to say anything that might prejudice your friendship with Dawson.'

'Nothing to do with it,' Beardsley said, thrusting out his jaw.

'When did you last see Emily?' Simon asked.

Beardsley frowned. 'I really can't remember.'

'So she didn't come to see you on the day she disappeared? We know she went out that day, but we haven't yet been able to trace where she went.'

'Well, she didn't come here. I haven't seen her since last term.'

'Or heard from her?'

Again there was the slightest hesitation as he took a breath. 'No.'

'Did you know that Emily had moved from her former address in Westwich?'

He frowned again. 'No.'

'Dr Beardsley, you left the departmental party rather early a few nights ago. Where did you go?'

'Who told you that?'

'You are not the only person I've interviewed. My team are making discreet inquiries throughout the department.'

'Was it Dr Thurrow?' Beardsley asked, sarcastically.

'You'll have to acquit her from any accusation that she helps the police with their inquiries, I'm afraid. She is, if anything, overly scrupulous.' Simon was interested to discover that, when Jessie was accused of doing what he had been prompting her to do without success, he leaped to her defence.

Beardsley gave a brief smile. 'I'm sure she is.'

'You still haven't answered my question.'

'Is it any of your business?'

'I'm afraid so. Of course you needn't answer if you have any reason to think it might implicate you in something.'

'Hardly, Chief Inspector.' Beardsley raised his head and looked him in the eye. 'I dislike parties of any form or description. I went home.'

'What time?'

'Soon after half past seven. I was home by ten to eight. It was a slow drive in the fog, it took longer than it normally would have.'

'Can anyone confirm that time?'

'Only my wife.'

What an uxorious lot you are, to be sure, Simon thought.

'You've no news, I suppose, of—'

'Emily? Not yet.' Simon let the pause lengthen, staring out of the window at the low grey cloud being whipped along by a brisk wind.

'We're all terribly distressed,' Beardsley repeated. 'I can't understand—'

'What can't you understand?'

Beardsley scratched an eyebrow, 'How such a thing could have happened.'

Simon was sure he had had something else in his mind. 'How long had her relationship with Dawson been going on?' he asked.

'You should address any question of that nature to Peter, not me.'

'He also left the party early,' Simon said.

'Yes. He went home as well, to help put his child to bed. He came back to the department later.'

'He told you that, did he?'

Beardsley didn't answer.

'What sort of a girl was Emily, Dr Beardsley?'

Beardsley examined his desk in silence for a moment. Then he said, 'I'd say she was rather a sad young woman. You probably know she'd experienced some family tragedy: just her and her sister left. I don't know how much the death of her parents had affected her – I didn't meet her until after they'd died – but she seemed insecure. No stability.'

'Oh?' What Beardsley had said didn't conflict with what Jessie and Dr Tremeadow had thought. 'What do you mean, exactly?'

'Perhaps I mean that she was a bit unpredictable,' Beardsley said slowly. 'I really didn't know her that well.'

'But you know someone who did,' Simon said, getting up. 'Thank you for your time, Dr Beardsley. If you do think of anything that might be of help, I hope you'll let me know.'

Beardsley's expression as Simon left was not happy.

Out in the brick-lined corridor once more, Simon walked in the direction of Jessie's room. Maybe they could have lunch together.

He found her in the act of slinging her bag over her shoulder.

'Oh. Hello,' she said. 'I'm just off. Didn't know you were here.'

'I've been talking to a couple of people.' He felt awkward, afraid he was unwelcome. She was looking particularly bright and beautiful that morning, the reluctant sun, filtering through the branches, lighting up her abundant hair.

141

'It's turned out nice after all,' he said.

She smiled ruefully, 'Look, I'm sorry, I really have got to go. I'm meeting Professor Lamb for lunch.'

'Any chance I can see you tonight?' he asked.

She flashed him another smile. 'Sure you won't be too busy?' she said.

'I can't guarantee the time,' he said anxiously.

'Of course not.' She moved towards the door. 'You're not going to bore on any more about you-know-who, are you? Because—'

'No. Actually, it's Hermione I need to talk about. Urgently,' he said, teasing.

'Hermione?' She turned back, her eyes questioning. 'What's Hermione got to do with anything?'

When he merely smiled she said, 'Come on, Chris, I'm sure you can handle Hermione's advances without my help.'

'I'm not so sure,' he said seriously. 'But I mustn't keep you.' He ushered her through the door and she went off down the corridor casting a puzzled look back at him before she turned the corner.

He stood for a few moments, cautiously cheered by the encounter, then looked at his watch: plenty of time to get to London and see Oliver Harwood.

He had tried to get information on Oliver's exact whereabouts from Mark Whittaker, without success. In the end, Simon had been obliged to ask Charlotte for the information.

'I don't understand why,' she had said. 'What's he got to do with anything?'

He gave the usual explanation: filling in the victim's background, talking to those who knew her.

'But what could *he* tell you that I can't?' she challenged.

She obviously wasn't aware that Whittaker had told him about the way her marriage had broken up. It was understandable that she wanted the police to have as positive a picture of her sister as possible. Perhaps, like many people, she believed they would work harder to uncover his sister's murderer if Emily was portrayed as a pure, innocent victim.

'I don't know,' he said. 'Try trusting me, Charlotte.'

The uncharacteristic appeal had slipped out; remembering it now, he felt uncomfortable. It had, however, recalled her to her usual manner with him. 'I'm sorry, Chris,' she said. 'You understand, don't you?'

He wasn't quite sure what she meant. But, 'Of course,' he had said.

She had given him Oliver's work address, claiming she had no idea where he was now living. 'Give him my regards,' she said, before ringing off.

The watery January sun shone off the wet surface of the road, dazzling him intermittently as the road veered right and to the south. The motorway was not particularly busy but it occurred to him that it was Friday and that his return journey would be caught up in the weekly exodus from the metropolis. Such was his dislike of traffic jams that he considered turning tail at the next junction. He glanced at the dashboard clock; if he was really expeditious, and skipped lunch as well, he might just avoid the worst of the traffic. But he wasn't hopeful.

The road brought him within sight of a river lying like molten lead amid brown, furrowed fields. It reminded him of Hermione and her psychic, a memory that he had been thrusting to the back of his mind. She had said that the body would not be found in the river, but buried ... It wasn't so unlikely after all. The police had already decided that the reason for the removal of the body would most probably have been because of any forensic evidence it might yield. And, although any prolonged immersion in water would probably achieve that object, there could be no guarantee that the body wouldn't be fished up sooner. And it could still provide evidence of the father of the child ...

Throwing the rug in the river had diverted the attention of police, dissuaded them from searching in ever-widening circles, considering other possibilities. Which all went to show, he admitted to himself, that however inclined he might be to dismiss psychics as cranks it didn't do to make assumptions. He shook his head. Longman would love it; the sergeant had a taste for the esoteric. Perhaps he'd hand him over to Hermione's psychic, and make them both free of Emily's room, he thought, amused. Or, then again, perhaps he wouldn't; he imagined Bradley's response to such capers. Still, it might be interesting to ask Jessie what she thought of it all. He'd value her opinion against Bradley's any day.

Chapter Sixteen

The clinic was in one of the narrow backstreets off Tottenham Court Road. After some difficulty in finding a parking space, Simon found he had some searching and walking still to do. London was looking at its bleakest and his moroseness was not relieved by the icy rain falling out of the grey sky. He prayed that the inclement weather would undermine the determination of some of the city's population to head west at the appointed hour.

He was uncomfortably soggy by the time he found the narrow doorway and staircase leading him to Oliver Harwood. A wan and emaciated young woman pushed past him on the stairs, clearly unaware of the existence of another human being in the same space. The small reception area was as drab as the entranceway had led him to expect; paint patches had peeled from walls where posters had been torn down and the floor was pockmarked with cigarette burns. A woman in her thirties was sitting beside a table which had been pushed against the wall. She had short, bleached blonde hair, the dark roots clearly visible. Her unhealthy pallor and look of exhausted defeat made Simon hesitate, unsure whether she worked there or whether she was a client waiting for help. After a moment she answered his unspoken question by raising a questioning eyebrow at him. Simon explained whom he was looking for.

'He's in the rest room,' she said, lighting a cigarette. 'Were you referred?'

Simon felt uncharacteristically aware of the appearance he must present. He took out his identification and showed it to her.

She grinned up at him, obviously reading his thoughts. 'Sorry, love. Not all addicts necessarily look as if they are.' She pushed herself wearily to her feet and opened a door to a dimly lit corridor. 'Oliver!' she called.

Simon heard a voice replying and she returned to her seat, taking another drag from her cigarette. There was an unpleasant mixture of odours in the small room, dominated by cigarette smoke but with an underlying smell of sweat, shot through with the distinctive sweet scent of hash.

'Depressing place, isn't it?' she said, drawing the back of one hand across her brow. 'Can't get the funds, you see. It gets harder all the time.

'I thought the drug problem was being given priority here in London,' Simon said.

She gave a cynical snort. 'If only that were true! Not at this end, it isn't. It's prevention that's the thing, get the suppliers, the dealers, never mind about the poor sods who are daft enough to actually take the stuff. After all, they've only got themselves to blame,' she said sarcastically. 'But I'm talking to a policeman. You wouldn't agree with me.'

'Oh, wouldn't I?' Simon said. He was used to the public's assumption that a police officer must be a right wing bigot.

She looked apologetic. 'I'm sorry,' she said. 'I suppose you're not all the same.

'What can I say? I hate getting into disputes with experts.'

She laughed. 'I've never been called that before. I've been called a lot of other things, mind, but never that. She got up and made a half-hearted effort to rearrange some leaflets on the table. 'This place never closes, you know. It'll start getting busier soon. We're a team, doing shifts. Oliver's just finished one, so he shouldn't be long.'

'You're quite near the university. I suppose quite a lot of students come in?'

'Yep,' she agreed. 'Just because they're better educated than most doesn't make them any cleverer.'

The phone rang and Simon half listened as the woman gave advice to what sounded like a distraught parent. She was still talking when the door to the corridor pushed open and a young man longed against the frame, a jacket slung over one shoulder. 'Did someone want me?' he said.

The Sanderson women certainly had a taste for beautiful young men, Simon thought as he looked at Oliver Harwood. A blond Greek god (thought that expression always puzzled Simon, who had never met a blond Greek) with perfectly carved facial features and a touch of superciliousness around the nostrils and lips. Like Mark Whittaker, he looked as if he too worked out, Simon thought, suddenly conscious of self-neglect.

He stood up and showed his identification once again.

'It's about Emily, I suppose,' Oliver Harwood said, expressionless.

'Can we talk somewhere private?' Simon asked.

Oliver glanced across at Zoe, still talking on the telephone. 'Let's go.' He walked past Simon to the head of the stairs. Simon followed glumly, anticipating another visit to a crowded smoky bar.

Harwood strode ahead purposefully once they reached street level, until they came to a main thoroughfare where he hailed a taxi and leaped in before Simon had had the chance to say a word. Simon followed.

'Regent's Park,' Harwood called to the driver.

'Whereabouts?'

'Anywhere.' The driver shrugged and sped on.

Harwood spent the journey gazing out of the window. Simon assumed the man was either blessed with an extraordinary degree of self-assurance or so concerned about Emily that he was disinclined to make polite conversation. Simon folded his arms and leaned back, contented to gaze out at the ever-frenetic world of central London, more glad than ever that he'd made the decision to leave it several years before for the more human scale of Westwich, where people had begun to take on recognisable faces.

The driver, resisting the lucrative opportunity to drop them at the most distant point of the park, pulled up near Park Crescent. It was only when they had walked more than fifty yards along one of the pathways that Harwood turned to Simon and finally spoke.

'Charlotte wouldn't have me around, you know. I contacted her as soon as I heard, but she seems to be withdrawing into herself.'

146

'I thought so too,' Simon said. He was at a bit of a loss as to how to proceed with Harwood. It was not unusual for Simon to have the outlines of an interview planned and then find, when face to face with the person, that his ideas were in some subtle way inappropriate. He waited for Harwood to speak again, wondering how far he intended to walk in this miserably icy drizzle. There were few people about, just a couple of brave souls huddled into dripping rainwear, dragging unwilling dogs on leads. Yet Harwood seemed oblivious to the weather, his short leather jacket blowing open in the gusting wind. Simon pulled his overcoat collar up and followed in his wake aware that it was time he took charge of this situation.

Harwood turned to him. 'Any news of Emily?' he asked – rather late in the day, Simon felt.

'Nothing more than you've probably read in the papers.'

'So she was dumped in the river?' Harwood asked matter-of-factly.

'It's a possibility.'

The wind was whipping their words away, making it impossible to talk in anything other than staccato shouts. Simon hunched his shoulders up an inch more and started to say that he'd like to be taken to any drinking hole of Harwood's choice when the man painted to a shelter at the edge of the path ahead. Simon followed obediently.

'Sorry about this,' Harwood said, unexpectedly conscious of Simon's misery, looking him over with a wry grin as he sat down. 'After a session at work I have a craving for the freshest air I can get. And this feels fresh, even if it is composed of petrol and diesel fumes.'

Simon shook his overcoat and sat down beside him.

'Is there any particular reason you've come to see me?' Harwood asked.

'There might be,' Simon said. 'I've yet to find out. So – have you seen much of Emily since you left Charlotte?'

'Since she kicked me out, you mean.' Harwood gave another of his wry smiles.

'Because of Emily.'

'Yes. Because of Emily,' Harwood agreed. 'You've obviously done your research.'

'Like to tell me about it?'

'No, but I guess I'll have to anyway.' He rubbed his arms, as if the cold had finally penetrated. 'She saw me kissing Emily,' he said.

'Is that all?'

'It was enough.' Harwood gave a humourless laugh.

'Charlotte overreacted, or did the kiss simply give her confirmation of what she already suspected?' Simon stared out at the rain-washed trees and grass, the dismal flower beds, trying to imagine the scene, to see Charlottle's face.

Harwood shifted uneasily. 'Both, I suppose.'

'How come?' Simon glanced quickly at Harwood's face, pale in the dim light. He seemed reluctant to answer. 'Well?'

'Charlotte was right in her interpretation of what she saw. Even though Emily cried and said that it had never happened before – which it hadn't. But I couldn't stop myself. I found I couldn't keep my hands off her – Emily, I mean. It would have happened again. So that was that.'

'And Charlotte didn't believe Emily?'

Harwood shook his head. 'No. But it wasn't her sister that she blamed.'

Simon regarded him thoughtfully for a moment. 'Do you feel she should have done?'

'Not really. You don't know Charlotte. She's terribly protective of Emily, I suppose because of what happened to the family. And now there's only Anne.'

'*Anne*?'

'Didn't you know about Anne? Well, I suppose you could call her a nonperson. Persistent vegetative state is what they call it. She'll never leave hospital – never do anything again.'

'I assume she's the youngest sister?'

Harwood nodded grimly at the dripping landscape. 'The Brontë syndrome.'

'She was in the same accident as her parents?'

Harwood nodded again, his face expressionless. 'They all were. Charlotte and Emily too.'

'What happened exactly?'

'She hasn't told you? No, I guess she wouldn't. It's not her favourite topic of conversation. Charlotte was driving the car, you see. They were coming back from one of their precious family holidays in Pembrokeshire. It was raining hard – like it is now. She swerved to avoid another car, skidded and hit a tree. Her mother and father were killed outright – they were in the back with Anne. No seat belts. Charlotte and Emily, amazingly, got off relatively lightly – concussion, cracked ribs.' He was silent for a moment. 'And if I'd gone with them, it wouldn't have happened. There'd have been two cars and Charlotte would have been a passenger in mine. Driving's never been her strong point.'

'Where did it happen?' Simon asked.

'Not far from Westwich. The Severn Bridge was closed because of the weather, strong winds with the rain so she was planning to cross the river further north.'

'You were married to Charlotte at the time?'

Harwood nodded. 'We'd been married a year. I was in advertising, had a big contract on and didn't want to tear myself away for some rural family get-together. So they all went in my car because it was the biggest, and Charlotte drove,' he said bleakly.

'When was this?'

'Four years ago now.' Harwood got up and leaned against the shelter wall, staring out at the rain.

Simon felt reluctant to press for more details. The accident had obviously left a lot of guilt and misery behind – for Charlotte and Harwood, anyway. He wondered if that was why Harwood was now working in a drug-rehabilitation unit – as an atonement for imagined sins.

Harwood turned to look at Simon. 'So after that, Charlotte felt responsible for Emily. She became very protective. They were always protective of each other anyway, as a family. They were very close, did things together. Emily never had a wild, rebellious youth. Perhaps that was why she succumbed to me for a while.' His mouth twisted and he paused. 'Charlotte can't do anything to help Anne. It's too late for that. Which made her even more intense about Emily. That's why she reacted as she did when she found us together.' He gave a brief laugh. 'I thought at the time she was just jealous. But it wasn't that. She wanted Emily to be happy more than anything. I actually think that if Charlotte felt I would have been good for Emily, she would have given us her blessing.

But I was part of the guilt, you see. After the accident our days were numbered as a married couple.'

'How did Emily feel about it all?' Simon asked.

There was silence for a while, apart from the patter of rain on the roof and sudden loud spatters as the wind hurled down droplets from the overhanging branches. Harwood cleared his throat. 'She was very upset when Charlotte and I split. She thought she was to blame. Oh, she had feelings for me, too – at the time I thought she wanted me as much as I wanted her. But I think now it was just a craving for affection, for reassurance, after all that had happened. It was as if she wanted to share in our closeness – Charlotte's and mine.' He paused. 'She was lonely, I suppose.'

'Did you see much of Emily after you left?'

Harwood nodded. 'She came looking for me.'

'And what happened?'

'You mean, did I have my wicked way with her?' He smiled sadly. 'Maybe it was she who had her way with me.' He sat down again beside Simon, shoving his hands in his pockets. The damp had released that strong smell peculiar to wet leather from his jacket; Simon had always felt that leather jackets carried the aura of death.

'Look, Chief Inspector, this may be all very interesting, but it's hardly to the point, I'd have thought. Baring my soul won't help you find Emily. Why don't you tell me exactly what it is that you're after?'

'When did you last see Emily?'

Harwood wrinkled his perfect brow. 'I can't remember exactly. Some time before Christmas.'

'Where did you see her?'

'She came to the clinic.'

'How did she seem?'

'All right, I think.'

Simon waited expectantly and Harwood shrugged his shoulders impatiently. 'So what do you want me to say? That I ravished her on one of the couches?'

It was a possibility, of course. Simon was making an effort to unravel the complicated byways of Emily's relationships with the men in her life.

'Did you?'

'No. That was all over. We were just friends.'

'And that was why she came to see you?'

'Is that so unbelievable?'

'What did you talk about?'

A glimmer of irritation passed over Harwood's features. 'I don't know! Work. My work and hers – her psychology course. The psychology of the addict – obviously I've got some experience of that and Emily had been reading about it.'

'Did she mention the fact that she was pregnant?'

Simon was watching closely for Harwood's reaction. He found it hard to interpret. It looked near to anger, but the expression passed very swiftly, leaving Harwood's face perfectly composed.

'She didn't, no,' he said a bit tightly. 'Who was the father?'

'I wish I knew,' Simon said.

'Silly cow,' Harwood said softly. 'But you surely don't think that that's got anything to do with Emily's death?'

'I don't know, Mr Harwood.'

'Oliver. No one calls me Mr Harwood, not even my tailor.' He grinned, the first genuinely light-hearted expression Simon had yet seen on his face. 'So you think Emily was murdered by someone she knew?' His face was serious once more.

'We think it's likely.'

'Now we get to the main point, do we? I suppose you want to know where I was that night?'

Simon nodded.

'I was with my girlfriend. I'm sort of living with her.'

The precarious sound of this predicament reminded Simon of his own position. Did women ever move in with men, or was it always the other way around? 'You'd better give me the name and address.'

'Arabella Loxton. *Lady* Arabella Loxton, 15 Vanbrugh Mansions, W2.'

Simon made a note of it. He wondered whether Lady Arabella was a former client, a rich girl with a drugs problem. It reminded him anxiously of Rose; he must try and make contact again when he got back to Westwich.

'Will that be all?' Harwood asked, standing up. 'Because I'm bloody frozen.'

It was your idea to hold a meeting in a rainstorm, Simon

thought acidly. He joined Harwood on the step outside, stamping numb feet and rubbing his hands together. The rain had eased to a mizzle and the park was shrouded in a dense mist of half-darkness. Had it not been for the traffic's endless roar, he could have imagined himself far away from the city.

Harwood set off abruptly, as he had done before, with Simon following briskly in his wake.

In the taxi heading back towards Tottenham Court Road, Harwood again withdrew into silence. Simon realised that the man had expressed no sorrow or regret at Emily's death; he had seemed far more saddened by the loss of Charlotte, the destruction of his marriage. Did he hold Emily responsible for that? Had he, for that matter, really ceased his sexual relationship with her? The child could have been his; it had been conceived before Emily moved away from London to Westwich. What if her visit before Christmas had been to tell him of her pregnancy and she had expected him to marry her? He was now involved with what was presumably a woman of wealth as well as title; he wouldn't want to throw away a second chance of domestic bliss.

'Do you still see Charlotte?' he asked Harwood's stony profile.

'Occasionally. We're friends. At least, we aren't enemies.'

'How long have you been involved in your present relationship?'

Harwood gave a faint smile, perhaps in recognition of Simon's thought processes, of where this line of questioning was leading. 'Over a year now.'

'And you stopped seeing Emily before that?'

'Good God! What kind of a Lothario do you take me for? Of course. And what must you think of *her*? Emily wasn't man-mad. Besides, she's got a boyfriend, hasn't she? Has had for some time.'

His indignation sounded genuine. But Harwood was a hard man to judge.

As Harwood got out of the cab, Simon gave him his card. 'Just in case you think of anything else.'

'I hope you find whoever did it. I was very fond of Emily.'

That remark gave Simon a more charitable impression of him, until he realised that Harwood had left him to pay the cab fare.

152

Chapter Seventeen

Longman ment Simon on his arrival back at HQ. 'Guess what? Someone wants to talk to you.'

Simon pulled a face. 'Bradley I suppose.'

'Him too.'

It was only to be expected that Bradley should heave into view demanding an update on progress, or the lack of it. Simon hadn't been too surprised at his absence at the meeting that morning; Bradley seemed to shift from headquarters as little as possible, venturing out only on the occasion of an official dinner or similar event. One quick look at the scene of the crime, then keep pulling the strings to make others dance, seemed to be his method lately. Simon, trying to be charitable, wondered again if he was unwell.

Longman was still gazing at him expectantly.

'Who else? Simon asked irritably. The journey back had been as tedious as he had feared; congestion on the roads seeping into his brain.

'Dr Dawson!' Longman said triumphantly.

'Is he *here*?'

'I said he could come in at seven. I assumed you'd be back by then.'

'Well, well. Dr Dawson Helps the Police with Their Inquiries. I wonder what's brought this on?' Simon cast his mind back, wondering what he had done to provoke Dawson into making a move. Nothing, surely, since he'd seen him that morning out at the university. If he'd had an axe to grind, he could have done it then. Having Beardsley present wouldn't have inhibited Dawson from tearing Simon off a strip. Simon wondered if it had been his talk with Beardsley himself that had prompted the call. Perhaps he was worried about what his friend might have said and was coming to sound Simon out.

He suggested this to Longman.

The sergeant puffed out his cheeks. 'Could be. I thought those two were supposed to be pretty thick together, though – if you can use that term about a pair of dons.'

'That's only an assumption on our part. Dawson seems to be the dominant one of the two. Perhaps he's afraid his little friend may kick over the traces.'

'Did he?' Longman asked doubtfully.

'Far from it.' Simon filled him in on the day's interviews since he'd left Longman with Edwards.

'Poor Charlotte,' was Longman's comment, after Simon had recounted his conversation with Harwood. 'It must be worse than if Anne'd died, her sister being in that state.'

'What did you get from Edwards? Anything useful?'

Longman brandished a page covered with his own clear handwriting.

'I got the statement down and signed. Nothing to add, except he was a bit clearer about the times. He says he went out at eight in his car, gave some of the lads a lift, left his car at Jack Singleton's in Redworth.' This was an area of the town about a mile southeast of Acacia Road. 'He got back home about twenty past nine.'

'Did he take his car from the garage, or was it parked on the road before he went out?'

'I didn't ask. Does it matter?'

'Only in so far as we are interested in what cars may have been parked near the house that night. For obvious reasons.'

'I'll ask him,' Longman said glumly.

'Odd, isn't it?' Simon said.

'What?'

'He's certainly not an up-with-the-lark type, and I bet they're not either. So why did they break up the evening's entertainment at such an early hour?'

'Maybe they were doing away with Emily Sanderson,' Longman said.

'It's within the realms of possibility. I bet Edwards has never been able to keep his eyes – or hands, for that matter –

154

off any decent-looking girl who's moved in there. There are no other women in the house – I doubt they'd stand it for long. We're going to have to look at Edwards a bit more closely. Him *and* his friends. I want them all checked out.'

'Always a pain with types like that. They're always as slippery as hell.' Longman was looking depressed.

To cheer him up. Simon gave him an account of his talk with Hermione.

'Why not give it a go, sir? There's a lot in that sort of thing. The local force need shaking up a bit.'

'I thought you'd say that,' Simon said. 'After all, the only thing I've got to lose is my credibility. Can you imagine Bradley's reaction?'

'But he doesn't have to know, does he? We could sneak her into Emily's room and no one would be any the wiser.'

'Isn't she likely to be a bit conspicious?' Simon was half-serious. 'All those scarves, Gipsy earrings, tasselled shawls and so forth.'

'You're out of date, sir,' Longman said earnestly. 'They look quite normal these days.'

'And she used to be a civil servant. Apparently.'

'Well, there you are then! You can't get more normal than that. I'll take her to the house if you like,' Longman ventured, clearly taken with the idea of a genuine psychic.

'I'll think about it,' Simon said, hoping Jessie might have something helpful to say that evening. 'So what did you find out about the lad who got beaten up the night of Emily's disappearance?'

Longman had not only located the young man but had visited him at the city hospital. He had regained consciousness only shortly before Longman's arrival and the uniformed branch had decided, not unreasonably, that they took precedence over Longman as far as interviews went.

'So I haven't managed to speak to him personally yet,' Longman admitted. 'But I know a man who has – or rather, a woman.' He glanced at his notebook. 'PC Collings was there. She said the lad, Gary Wyman, told her he was beaten up by a gang. But he didn't see who they were.'

'Why?'

Longman looked at Simon blankly.

155

'Why was he beaten up? Did he have any idea?'

'Said they just set on him.'

'Well, we weren't really expecting to discover he was attacked by an axe murderer, who'd already got our own victim tucked up cosily in the boot of his car—'

'He was found at eight,' Longman interrupted. 'Could have been the same attacker.'

Simon looked disparaging. 'The time he was attacked is more to the point.'

'Said he couldn't remember. He was hit on the head.'

Simon's expression changed to one of scepticism. 'So he says ... He was found just inside someone's garden – was the house empty at the time?'

'Must have been. I read the report and there was no mention of anyone from that address having been interviewed.'

'The lad was probably trying a bit of breaking and entering,' Simon said. 'That's why he's being evasive. He'll have been set on by some local lads who think of it as their patch.'

'That's what Inspector Perfect thinks,' Longman said. 'Still, the neighbour who found him might have seen something.'

'Or not – as seems generally to be the case. Have we had any reports at all of a car being seen near number 25 around the relevant time?'

'Not so far.'

There was a knock on the door. Simon looked up, expecting Bradley to lumber into the room, but it was Rhiannon Jones.

'Sir?' She opened the door only a short way and eased through, closing it partially behind her. 'I've got Dr Dawson waiting in the corridor for you. The one that's on television.' She was evidently impressed; and Simon's good opinion of her plummeted.

She appeared even more pleased with Dawson's appreciative look-over and thanks as she showed him through the door. Simon was cynically aware that Dawson's behaviour was deliberate and conscious and that this was a kind of male territorial attack.

Despite his efforts at behaving true to form, Dawson looked less at ease than in his own surroundings of university and home. Unusually, he did not take the initiative and speak first, but stood waiting on Simon.

156

'Have a seat, Dr Dawson,' Simon said, taking his own behind his desk. 'You stay, Sergeant. You can take notes.'

They both quietly assumed their accustomed interview positions, Longman seating himself out of sight of Dawson, on a chair by the wall.

'Dr Dawson. What was it you wanted to see me about?'

'It's not a confession to murder, Chief Inspector, in case that's what you're hoping for.' Dawson's habitual sardonic smile was back on his face.

'I asked you what it was, not what it wasn't.' Simon was annoyed at himself for rising, as always, to Dawson's bait.

His obvious irritation broadened Dawson's smile. 'Let's say I've decided to – level with you. Isn't that the correct police terminology?'

Simon looked at him expressionlessly and waited.

Dawson shifted in his chair. 'I did receive a telephone call at the departmental meeting. From Emily, I mean, not from my wife. I lied to you.'

Simon remained impassive.

'She asked to see me.' Dawson paused.

'At her bedsitter?'

'No!'

Simon's surprised expression seemed to gratify Dawson. He leaned back, more relaxed now, and produced a packet of cigarettes. 'Do you mind?' he asked, lighting up regardless.

'If you must,' Simon said, jealously watching the curling grey smoke drift upwards.

'My wife won't let me smoke in the house, and the university is getting as bad. Bloody PC nonsense.'

'Don't let the purity of our lungs put you off, Dr Dawson. Where and when did she ask you to meet her?'

'Lovers' Bridge. At eight o'clock that evening.'

Lovers' Bridge, on the river, was just over a mile from Acacia Road, to the west of the city, not far from the city centre.

'I do hope you are not going to trot out the usual phrases about wasting police time. I would prefer not to be involved. I have enough demands on my time as it is.'

Simon silently ground his teeth. 'Oh, we understand, Dr Dawson. All this must be very inconvenient for you. But then murder has a habit of putting people out. So, did Emily say why she wanted to see you so urgently?'

'She didn't,' Dawson said coldly. 'But she sounded upset and I didn't like to refuse.

'Considerate of you.' Uncharacteristically so, Simon thought. 'So you went to the bridge at eight?'

'I did. Proceeding in my motorcar, as I believe the police put it, and arriving promptly at eight o'clock.'

'And?'

'Emily wasn't there. I waited in the car. It was not a very pleasant night for standing around in the open.'

'Where were you parked?'

'St Mary's Street. I could see the bridge clearly from there. And, to cut an overlong and very simple story short, Emily did not put in an appearance.

'How long did you wait?'

'Until twenty minutes past eight.'

It was a long enough time to show that Dawson had not wanted Emily to think he had failed to turn up, Simon thought. 'Weren't you worried when she didn't arrive?' he asked.

'Not particularly. You know what women are like.'

'I'm sure you're more of an expert on that Dr Dawson. Didn't you go to look for her in Acacia Road?'

'I didn't know she was living there,' Dawson said smoothly.

'How about Sinclair Road? Her previous address?'

Dawson raised his eyebrows and didn't answer.

'Is there anyone who might confirm what you've just told me?' Simon asked.

Dawson shrugged. 'Shouldn't think so. There weren't many people around, not on a cold, foggy night like that.'

'And you then drove back to the psychology department?'

'I did.'

'What's your car registration number?' Dawson gave it and Longman noted it down.

'Well, if that's all—' Dawson stubbed out his cigarette and began to rise from his chair.

'No, that's not all. We'll need a statement from you, for a start,' Simon said sharply.

Dawson sank back. He looked at his watch. 'Could we do it

some other time? Perhaps your sergeant could visit me? Only we have been rather long about this and I am a busy man.'

Simon smiled. 'Sorry, but it's better done immediately. So, why did you find it so difficult to tell me this in the first place?'

Dawson was not used to being in a position in which his authority counted for nothing. He stood up, his colour heightened, his lips compressed.

'I should have thought that was bloody obvious,' he said loudly. 'You barge into my house without so much as a by-your-leave, at a time when my wife is expected home—'

'Any problem, Chief Inspector?' Bradley's bulk appeared in the doorway.

Simon was unsure in that moment which of the pair – Bradley or Dawson – he would happily have tossed from his third-floor window. 'Dr Dawson seems reluctant to supply us with a statement, sir. Apparently it's not convenient right now.'

Bradley ignored him, coming round to park his sagging frame on the edge of Simon's desk. 'You're Peter Dawson, aren't you? I've seen you on television.' Simon doubted it; rugby and quiz shows were more in Bradley's line. The superintendent extended his hand and Dawson leaned forward to shake it, managing a tight smile.

'Well, now.' Bradley turned a cold gaze on Simon. 'I understand that Dr Dawson volunteered to come to talk to you this evening. No doubt he's given you some useful information. I'm sure we can accommodate him just this once.'

'I haven't finished interviewing him yet,' Simon said through his teeth. 'Sir.'

Bradley shifted from the desk and Simon hoped for a moment that he was planning to leave. Instead, the superintendent transferred his considerable weight to a chair midway between Simon and Dawson forming a physical as well as a metaphorical barrier. 'Carry on, lad. I'm sure you've no wish to cause unnecessary hassle to someone as public-spirited as Dr Dawson's clearly been.' He smiled benignly and leaned back in his chair, clearly there for the duration.

It was unforgivable behaviour in a senior officer, beyond the pale even for Bradley, whose toll of trespasses Simon had not even begun to forgive. Still, Simon had no option but to continue the interview in front of his unwanted audience.

'So why exactly didn't you want your wife to hear the truth about that evening? Was it that you didn't want her to know you'd been having a relationship with Emily Dawson?'

'That's very astute of you, Chief Inspector.' Dawson was at his most patronising. 'Imagine she might have assumed just what you are assuming, if she heard that I had gone to meet a young woman that evening.'

'But your wife originally corroborated your story: that you went home to help put your child to bed. If you persuaded your wife to lie to us on your behalf, what did you tell her?'

'That I'd just gone for a drive and didn't have an alibi.'

'In that fog? Hardly plausible. And why should you think that you needed an alibi?'

'That was afterwards,' Dawson said patiently, 'after you'd been to see me. At the time she just went along with me. She's a loyal wife and she wouldn't contradict me in front of the police.'

'So after we had left, you told her that you had left the department "to go for a drive"?'

'Yes.'

'And she believed you?'

'Yes. She had no reason not to.'

'Would you describe to me, now your wife isn't here to listen, the nature of your relationship with Emily Sanderson?'

Bradley shifted warningly on his seat.

'We were *friends*. I'd known her from her days working for Hyde Books. If she was in trouble over something, I suppose it was quite natural she should call me.'

He was a blatant bloody liar, Simon thought.

'So exactly what did Emily say in that telephone call?'

Dawson leaned to one side and extracted his cigarette packet and lighter; Bradley solicitously passed him an ashtray.

'All she said was, would I please meet her at Lovers' Bridge at eight, and that it was important. She didn't go into details of why she wanted to see me but she wasn't a melodramatic girl, so I assumed it must be a matter of some urgency.'

'What about the letter she sent you, asking you to meet her at her new address? Did she tell you why she had changed the venue?'

Dawson blew smoke insolently in Simon's direction.

'I have already explained to the chief inspector.' Dawson addressed Bradley, 'that I did not receive any letter from Miss Sanderson.'

Bradley gazed reproachfully at Simon. This was hopeless, Simon thought; he wouldn't get anywhere while Bradley was in the room. 'Very well,' he said. 'If Superintendent Bradley is happy about it, you can make your written statement at another time.' He stood up. 'I'll leave you both to make the arrangements.'

He left the room, followed hastily by Longman.

'D'you think they're both Freemasons?' Longman asked as they turned the corner of the corridor.

'I think they're both bastards,' Simon said.

Chapter Eighteen

Simon arrived outside Jessie's cottage in one of the back lanes of the village of Oxton just after nine. Usually she would come to the door when she heard his car and stand in the porch waiting for him; not tonight though.

The sky had cleared to reveal a low moon. It was bitterly cold. He stood for a moment preparing himself, determined that tonight he would not put a foot wrong, say a wrong thing, disturb the universe of his relationship with Jessie any further.

He called out to her as he turned his key in the lock.

'In the sitting room,' she said.

She was seated on the floor in front of a blazing log fire, a glass of red wine in her hand and a book in her lap. She smiled up at him. 'How's it going?'

The first evasion beckoned. 'Fine.' He smiled, and kissed the top of her head.

'Wine?'

He nodded. 'I'll get it. In the kitchen?'

'Right here, on the hearth. You'll need to get a glass.'

So she hadn't been expecting him; either that, or she was being unusually sparing with the welcome mat. He came back with a glass and sat down opposite her on the old sofa.

'Have you eaten?' she asked.

He cast his mind back. Had he? If he had, he couldn't remember when. But he didn't want to be distracted by messing about in the kitchen. 'I'm not hungry. Perhaps I could have something later?' As he said so, he realised that he was, in fact, ravenous. He held up his glass. 'Wine's nutritious, or so I'm told.'

She didn't, as she normally did when he came in late after a long shift, insist on giving him something, if only a sandwich, to sustain him. Instead she observed him through lowered eyelashes. 'You look tired,' she said.

'*You* don't'

'Don't let the dim lighting deceive you. I look haggard. Usual beginning-of-term trauma.'

He didn't rush to deny her claim. But, tired or not, she looked thoroughly desirable to him at that moment. They sipped their wine quietly. It was enough for him to be there; he had no need to talk. The words of a poem came into his mind: 'I wish I knew a woman ...' Something about drawing near her in the red stillness of the dusk, taking delight in her without having to take a chill talking to her. D.H. Lawrence. Jessie was equivocal about Lawrence and would probably be even more so about the sentiment of that particular poem. Another time he might have quoted it to her, but not tonight. He couldn't risk equivocation.

'What are you smiling at?'

'Sorry.' He pulled an exaggerated frown. 'Better?'

'An improvement. So what was that question about Hermione?' Jessie leaned sideways and sloshed a little more wine into her glass. 'Is it personal or professional?'

'Oh, professional. Absolutely.' The wine was quickly going to his head.

'*Not* psychic support?'

Simon nodded dreamily.

'She's been longing for the opportunity to try out her stuff with the police for ages! You've obviously provided her with it.' Jessie looked amused.

'I was wondering what you thought. I didn't know if what she was saying had any academic credence, or whether she was cranky. I suppose it's a legitimate interest, or the department wouldn't make space for it.'

'It probably wouldn't, not if Dawson takes over.'

'D'you have any views on it?' he asked cautiously, watching her through half-closed eyelids.

She gestured with her wine glass. 'It's a wide field. I don't think there's any doubt that some of the phenomena exist. Why not? The problem lies with scientific method – repeating experiments in a way that will ensure reliable results. But since scientists have recognised that the experimenter influences the experiment, there's been a more open-minded attitude in some quarters.'

'That's a reasoned answer, but what do you think personally?'

'Something along the usual lines of "There are more things in heaven and earth than are dreamt of in your philosophy." '

'So you think it's worth considering?'

'I think it's always worth being open-minded. The fact that there are plenty of weirdos out there jostling for their fifteen minutes of fame doesn't mean there isn't some truth at the root of it.' She sipped wine thoughtfully, staring into the fire. 'I'm not the expert, anyway, Hermione is. Don't let her dizzy exterior mislead you. She's no fool.'

'But what do you *really* think?' he said.

'You mean, what do I really *feel*.' She prodded him with her foot. 'God, Chris, you look half-cut ... I really feel you should suit yourself. You've got nothing to lose, and you might learn something.' She shifted to put another log on the fire. 'More wine?' He handed out his glass.

'So how's the case going? *Really* going, I mean?'

He undulated a hand. 'So-so.'

'You don't want to talk about it?'

His anxiety to avoid sticky subjects had dissolved to some extent; maybe it was the mellowing effect of the wine. At the moment he could view Dawson with quiet dispassion. 'Sure,' he said. 'It might help me get my thoughts in order.'

'Chris, I'm sorry I gave you a hard time.' She was looking at him squarely. 'I overreacted. You were on my territory, I didn't know how to handle it.'

'No. I was being boorish. It was a difficult situation and—'

'Dawson made it even worse,' she finished.

'He didn't make it easy,' he agreed.

'At his house, when you came in ... He was using me to get at you. He's the one with the real territorial obsession.'

Simon remembered Dawson's lingering looks at Rhiannon. 'I know what you mean,' he said.

'So.' She reached out a hand to touch his. 'If there's anything else you want to talk about ... But,' she warned,

'I'm not happy discussing colleagues' private lives.'

He decided he could afford to push it just a little. 'Not even when someone's been murdered?'

'You know,' she said, leaning back against the arm of the chair, 'that question encapsulates all sorts of moral dilemmas.'

'What?'

'You know what I'm talking about. How far can we make inroads into the civil liberties of the individual in the name of protecting the masses?'

He understood exactly what she was saying. And he agreed with what she was getting at. But he said, 'Isn't that extrapolating a bit?'

She threw a cushion.

'OK, OK. You're right,' he protested. 'So would you still like me to tell you how the case is going?'

She nodded. So he told her, beginning at the beginning and ending with his ignominious exit from his own office.

'I can't imagine that Peter, of all people, would have put himself to the inconvenience of going to meet Emily that night unless she did have some sort of hold over him,' Jessie mused when he'd finished.

He looked at her in surprise.

'I'm allowed to speculate,' she said defensively. 'But not to sneak.'

'If he did indeed go to that bridge and not to her room,' Simon suggested.

'Why tell you at all then?'

'I don't know. He could have pre-empted her and got to her room before she left – just. And he's bust his own alibi, which was dutifully backed up by his wife. He could have stuck to his original story – there was no one to disprove it.'

'Perhaps someone saw him,' Jessie suggested.

'Where? At the bridge, or at Acacia Road?'

She shifted to a more comfortable position. 'I still think you're focusing too closely on one person,' she said.

'They're all being checked out,' he said 'All we can do is interpret the facts we have. Jess, what sort of relationship do Beardsley and Dawson have? Are they very friendly?'

'Pretty friendly, yes.'

He imagined she had said as much as she was prepared to,

but she added, 'Peter's the dominant one. Phillip follows where Peter leads.'

'So Beardsley would be loyal to Dawson? Whatever happened?'

'Within reason. Phillip hasn't got Peter's bravura, he's rather a timid sort. But Peter's useful to him. Reflected glory, maybe.'

'I imagine that Beardsley does most of the donkey work on the books they've done together, and Dawson gets all the credit.'

Jessie smiled wryly. 'I get that impression too.'

Simon said no more for the moment, aware that Jessie had probably said as much on the subject as she was going to.

'What's the sister like, Charlotte?' Jessie asked.

Simon gave Jessie an account of some of her history. 'She's understandably distressed about Emily, in view of all that.'

Jessie eyed him thoughtfully. 'That's not quite answering the question,' she said, adding a smile.

'Perhaps because whatever she is like is hidden behind all the grief and anxiety,' he said.

'Does she give that impression then, of being hidden?' Jessie's tone was one of cool interest.

'No. That's not what I meant. But people aren't really themselves at such times.'

She got up to throw another log on the dying embers. 'Have something to eat now.'

'I'm not really hungry.' The wine had taken the edge from his appetite.

'You know, I think you need to stay closer to the kind of person Emily was to get at the truth of all this.' She kicked at the log with her toe.

'There speaks the psychologist. What are you thinking?'

'Just that. The fact that she was pregnant isn't the only fact of her life. She had other attributes.'

'Like attracting a lot of men. And not being the most stable of characters.'

'That too.'

'Which reminds me. I forgot to ring Rose.' He told her about his last conversation with his mother.

'Ring her from here,' she offered. 'It must be daylight over there.'

'She'll probably be in bed.'

'So you'll maybe catch her in.'

He looked out the number and sat on the sofa to punch it out. Once again, the call went unanswered.

'No answerphone?' Jessie asked, returning with the remains of a casserole for him. 'I thought all Americans had them.'

'Perhaps they switch them off.'

He had already finished his meal by the time she returned with coffee.

'I've missed you,' he said, pulling her down on to the sofa beside him.

'You and your stomach,' she said.

Chapter Nineteen

Next morning in the bedsit in Acacia Road Simon finally had a look at the slip of paper that Hermione had given him: the notes from her psychic protégé. The woman had recorded a series of impressions, none of which made any immediate sense to him. 'Long blonde hair' (nothing new there); an 'important letter' (probably true, and that fact had not been reported in the newspapers); 'a woman involved' (vague enough to escape contradiction); 'a sense of anguish' (unsurprising); 'things being confused' (when are they not?); 'feelings of desperation' (being murdered would have that effect); 'not the river. It is not where she is.' And that last was written – as were the others, according to Hermione – before the rug had been found.

He scrunched up the sheet and shoved it back into his pocket, sitting back in the chair and allowing his mind to wander into a directionless thoroughfare, letting thoughts arise and depart as they would.

'Having a rest? No time for that, son. You're ballsing it up good and proper, aren't you?' Bradley thundered into the room and plumped himself down on the bed, waving a newspaper at Simon.

'Sir?'

'You haven't seen it?' Bradley raised puffy eyes ceilingwards, then threw the rolled-up newspaper at Simon. 'It's part of your job to know what the media are saying. But not you, oh no, you think you can swan along with your head in the bloody clouds. A cut above ordinary coppers.'

Simon opened the newspaper. Peter Dawson's face stared

168

back at him, the familiar smile fixed on the handsome face, an expression entirely inappropriate to the headline: 'MEDIA DON AND MISSING STUDENT: Peter Dawson, the well-known media don, was giving his assistance to the police late last night at Westwich Police Headquarters.'

There was little of any substance in the article. As in most tabloids, the photograph and headline took up most of the front page. The facts, such as they were, were accurate; the press had obviously been doing some digging and had caught on to the fact that Emily had known Dawson before she came to the university at Westwich, that the two had met previously, on a number of occasions, in London. Nothing libellous, nothing even scandalous, but damaging nonetheless. They had carefully avoided the prejudicial phrase 'helping police with their inquiries', Simon noted, but they were still sailing pretty close to the wind.

Simon's reaction as a policeman struggled briefly with a sneaking delight at the thought of Dawson's face at being singled out, though he was careful not to let Bradley see it. He steeled himself for the aftershocks of the initial explosion.

'Well? What have you got to say for yourself? And you can give that back here. I'm going to have it framed on my wall, as a reminder to others of the cock-ups your sort are capable of when you take your eyes off the ball.'

Simon smiled inwardly at the quality of the metaphor, but handed the paper back to Bradley in silence. He knew that any attempt to exonerate himself would simply fuel Bradley's rage.

Bradley swiped at the bedhead in lieu of Simon. 'Well? I asked you what you've got to say for yourself?'

'You're in charge of media relations, sir. How could I have stopped this? You know what they're like.'

'You *knew* the press had been hanging around at HQ!' Bradley fumed. 'You should have warned Dawson, taken some steps to prevent this!'

'I didn't see any reporters. And I left him in your safe care, sir, if you remember,' Simon said quietly.

'Yes. After you ponced out of the room in a huff. Most unprofessional.'

Simon stared back at him. What about Bradley's own

behaviour while Dawson was being interviewed? Hardly the height of professionalism.

'There'll be hell to pay at the university,' Bradley said bitterly, sinking back with a heavy thud on to the bed.

Simon could understand why Bradley was so concerned. He had devoted the better part of his career to keeping on the right side of the right people.

'You'll be meeting the press to give them an update soon, sir,' he said. 'That'll give you the chance to set the record straight, lead them in the right direction.'

'Oh, yes?' Bradley sneered. 'And what direction exactly might that be?'

Simon was still so convinced of Dawson's guilt he found it hard to frame a reply.

'Well, obviously we're considering all the options. We can't rule anyone out, but at this stage we haven't definitely ruled anyone in.' Simon decided to take the bull by the horns. 'The thing is, sir, we may be on the right track with Dawson. If you started declaring his innocence, it could make the situation even worse.'

Bradley was almost purple. 'How could it possibly be *worse*?'

'If I were you, sir – I'd just say that we're speaking to everyone who knew Emily, which includes a number of staff at the university. And ask them to make another appeal for information from anyone who saw a long-haired blonde in the vicinity of Acacia Road or Lovers' Bridge last Tuesday evening.'

'Hmm. And warn them about prejudicing prosecutions with their wild speculations!' Bradley looked purposeful. He rose ponderously to his feet, with much accompaniment from protesting bedsprings.

'Sir?' Watkins tapped at the door and came into the room. 'There's a call for you.'

Simon glanced at Bradley, who was wrapping his scarf firmly around his neck. The superintendent nodded a dismissal and preceded Simon from the room.

'Who is it?' Simon asked Watkins.

'Somebody Roe.'

Simon picked up the phone. 'Hermione?'

'Have you seen the papers this morning?' she said.

'I have,' Simon said warily.

'I bet Peter's steaming!' She didn't attempt to hide her amusement.

'We're not too happy about it, either,' Simon said. 'But that wasn't why you phoned.'

'No.' She paused. 'And this isn't really why I phoned, either, but you might be interested.'

Simon had the feeling that some kind of quid pro quo was in the air. 'Well?'

'I was in the Theatre Bar last night. Dawson came in and joined Beardsley.'

'Is that it?'

'Of course not! They had a row. I was watching; things seemed to get a bit heated, then suddenly Phillip got up, growled something at Peter, and walked out of the bar. Peter followed him. Makes a change; it's usually Phillip following Peter.'

'Did you hear what they were talking about?'

'No,' Hermione said regretfully. 'It gets pretty noisy in there.'

'What time was this?'

'About ten. The film had just finished, *Night and Fog*, it was.'

How apt, Simon thought. 'Did you see them meet up?'

'They were already in the bar when I came out.'

'Well, thanks for telling me,' Simon said, about to put down the phone.

'Chris?' she said quickly.

The payoff, he thought. 'Yes?'

'Have you had any more thoughts about Sybil?'

He felt cornered. But Hermione was the only person in the department who seemed to have no inhibitions about passing on what was probably to her mere gossip. 'If she can be here at Acacia Road to meet Sergeant Longman at two o'clock today, I'll indulge you. In the interests of research, of course,' he said.

'Wonderful!' Hermione sounded triumphant. 'Did you make anything of her notes?'

'Not much.'

171

'Oh, well. We'll see what happens today, eh?'

He rang off with a gut feeling that he'd just done something really silly and a hope that he wouldn't be found out. He should have asked Hermione for some discretion on the subject. Discreet, it appeared, Hermione was not.

Most of the team on the case had begun assembling in the incident room to share their latest reports and to delegate new inquiries. There was a general buzz of conversation about the prominence of Dawson in the news that morning; Simon made no comment but told them about the interview with the don the night before, pointing out the reduced time available to the killer if Emily had indeed planned to leave the house to meet Dawson at a quarter to eight or even earlier.

'*If* he's telling the truth,' Rhiannon Jones commented.

'Yes,' Simon agreed. 'Checking whether anyone saw his car or himself near Lovers' Bridge is one more thing to be working on.'

'*Two* more,' Monkton murmured.

Simon ignored him.

The inspector spoke again, more loudly this time. 'It may be this other chap, Beardsley. Why aren't we looking at him?'

Simon waited, eyebrows raised.

'His wife says that he didn't come home after the office party,' Monkton said, pleased with the general stir that the information created.

'Was it you who spoke to her?' Simon asked.

Monkton nodded, smiling, an expression that oddly emphasised his sinister looks.

'So tell us about it, Bob.'

The inspector leaned back in his seat still smiling. 'Not much to tell, really. She just said that as far as she recalled, he hadn't been home that night. I got the impression that was nothing unusual.'

'What was her manner?' Simon asked.

Monkton considered for a moment, then looked to DC Rodgers for confirmation. 'Indifferent rather than embittered, wouldn't you say?'

Rodgers nodded agreement. 'Wasn't keen to talk. Just answered our questions, very businesslike. She couldn't give us much time – said she was busy.'

'What's she like?' Simon asked.

'Nice-looking woman. Smart. She's head at one of the city comprehensives.'

'And I bet she hasn't got an alibi, either,' Rhiannon piped up.

'You got a down on your sex, or what?' Monkton asked aggressively.

Rhiannon ignored him.

'Did you ask Mrs Beardsley where she was that night?' Simon asked Monkton.

'No.'

'Did you ask her if she knew Emily Sanderson?'

'*No.* As Rodgers said, she was busy.'

'Well, it's Saturday today, so maybe she'll be a bit less busy. Go and see her again. Perhaps this time you'll make sure you ask the right questions,' Simon said. 'And I want Beardsley brought in for questioning.'

Simon told them about the row that Hermione had observed between Dawson and Beardsley.

'Looks like one of them knows something incriminating about the other,' Rhiannon said.

Monkton scoffed. 'More likely they were arguing about who was going to win the big match. Anyway, what about the boyfriend, Whittaker? If the girl was pregnant and he wasn't the father, he's surely got a motive? We've only got his word for it that he didn't know about the pregnancy. If he went to Westwich to see her, confront her, he could have lost his temper and lashed out at her. Maybe he didn't mean to kill her, but he could easily have worked out where to dump her body.'

'I've had a call about Whittaker,' Simon said. 'He was seen by a neighbour putting out his rubbish at soon after nine o'clock on Tuesday night.'

'He's in the clear, then,' Monkton said grudgingly. 'The fastest I've ever made it to London and that was in a marked car, was two hours. Where exactly does he live?' Monkton asked.

'Shepherd's Bush.'

'No way, then. She was definitely alive at seven thirty. And then he'd need time to attack her, get her out of the window, put her and the rug in the river. At least another fifteen, probably twenty, minutes, that'd take. The neighbour was sure of the time?'

'Absolutely. He was watching the BBC evening news. Besides, only half an hour later Charlotte Sanderson called him to ask him to drive her to Westwich.'

Simon went on to report his meeting with Oliver Harwood and the man's story of the accident that had decimated the Sanderson family. He noticed Watkins and Rodgers exchanging glances.

'You two know something we don't?'

'We were just going to say, sir,' Watkins began. 'We followed up some of the reported sightings of Emily that last Tuesday. The one from the city library, at about eleven am fits. She was looking up local newspaper files from four years ago. Could be she was reading up on the accident.'

'The librarian couldn't be more exact about what she was reading?' Simon asked.

'No, sir. She just remembered the date the girl asked for – April, four years ago.'

'You'd better go back and find out whether there's anything of particular relevance in the report,' Simon said. 'Any other follow-ups?'

'We showed Emily's photograph to the woman in Copperfields Café in the centre. She was positive it was the same girl. Said she was sitting at a table with a ginger-haired woman at half past one or thereabouts. We got the local radio station to put a police request out for the woman she was talking to. The papers'll do the same.'

'Well done,' Simon said. 'Any other reports of sightings?'

'The usual ones from Scarborough, Edinburgh and Brighton. Not to mention the south of France,' Monkton said. 'I'll follow those up if you like!

'Any we've already followed up,' Simon emphasised. Monkton was beginning to jar, 'So, we've still got the time between her presence in the café at half past one, and the time she returned home at twenty past six, unaccounted for.'

'Is it really that important where she was that day?' Monkton interrupted. 'I mean, it's where she was that night I'm more interested in.'

'Fine! As you're so keen, you get on to it. Find out what you can from the people living at the Lovers' Bridge end of Mary Street – whether anyone saw Dawson, or noticed his car. Or saw Emily anywhere in the vicinity.'

Monkton went on, 'We finished talking to the Dawsons' neighbours. For what it's worth, nobody noticed the wife drive her car out that evening. One of them saw Dawson coming in at ten thirty.'

That left the inquiries into the landlord's activities; Edwards's cronies had confirmed his timings for the night in question. 'Seems OK as far as it goes, sir,' Watkins said. 'Except that they're not a crowd whose word I'd trust easily.

'You thought they were lying?' Simon asked.

'I doubt they're in the habit of doing anything else. But whether that's so in this case—' Watkins shrugged.

A draught of icy air heralded Longman's entry into the room. 'Just been talking to young Gary, the lad who was mugged,' the sergeant said, by way of apology, as he took a seat.

'And?'

'I think you're right that he was planning to break into one of these houses – not that he's actually admitted it,' Longman said, rubbing his hands together. 'All he says is that he was waiting for a mate and this gang jumped him.'

'Did he see anything useful while he was so-say waiting for this mate?' Simon asked.

'He says he arrived about half past seven and was waiting about for "a bit" before he got knocked about. He wasn't more specific than that. When I asked if he'd seen anyone beforehand, anyone arriving or leaving at number 25, he said no. It was foggy and there wasn't much traffic around, so he would have noticed. A car drove down from the North Road end but passed him, going on down Acacia Avenue.'

'And he was sure about this?'

Longman pursed his lips. 'Seems to have his brain back in gear.'

'Any idea at all what time he got knocked on the head?'

Longman grinned. '*He* didn't have. But, believe it or not, we have a bit of classic evidence. He fell into the rockery inside the garden and his watch got damaged. It stopped at seven fifty-two precisely.'

'But it was a foggy night,' Monkton said drily. 'Which means that even if he wasn't knocked unconscious till seven fifty-two, he was probably only able to see cars, not people. And if someone took Emily Sanderson away in a car it might have been later than that anyway.'

'Have you spoken to the man who found Gary Wyman?' Simon asked.

'Yes. He wasn't much use. He came from the opposite end of the road – he was giving his dog a quick breather – and didn't go any further after he found Wyman, so he didn't pass number 25. He doesn't remember any cars. But then, he was a bit preoccupied with Wyman.'

'And it was about ten minutes before an ambulance and the police arrived,' Simon said. 'And they'd no reason to look for a car, or a pedestrian, come to that. They'd have known Gary's attacker would be long gone. So whoever left the house with Emily wasn't likely to be noticed.'

They moved on to other reports: still nothing useful from the questioning of students and other university staff, apart from the fact that a few fellow students had seen Emily in the company of both Dawson and Beardsley. 'But they weren't giving much away, sir,' Rhiannon said wryly. 'You know students – they always think we're the enemy.'

'Is that so? I thought they were a more conservative lot these days. With a big C as well as a small one. Ah, well, never mind. If Emily was having a serious relationship with Dawson or Beardsley, none of them would have advertised the fact more than they could help. But keep trying. Right, that's about it.' Simon shuffled his papers together. 'I'll let you have the report from forensics as soon as it's ready.'

The phone rang; it was Oliver Harwood, wanting to talk to Simon.

'When we met, you asked me to call you if I had any new information. About Emily, I mean.' He sounded oddly hesitant, almost reluctant.

'Yes?'

'I should have said something at the time, but it seemed unfair to Emily just to come out with it. It seemed almost like betraying her confidence. Besides, it was only a vague impression, but I've been thinking about it, and I felt I should come to you.'

176

'Right.' Simon was getting impatient, straining to hear the man's next words as the room emptied noisily.

'Well,' Harwood said, 'I could be wrong, but I got the impression that Emily might have been experimenting with drugs.'

'Drugs? What made you think that?'

'Well, there were all those questions about addiction. Oh, she said it was for her studies, but it did seem a bit suspicious. Even so, I wouldn't have put two and two together, but her manner was strange. Defensive. Put it this way, she wasn't herself. I've been working around drug users long enough to know the signs.'

'But students try drugs almost as a matter of course, don't they? Perhaps she was just curious.'

'It was more than that. Most students share the odd spliff at a party, sure, but they don't act like Emily did that day. I don't have a clue what she was using, but whatever it was she can't have been doing it for long – she looked too healthy for that. But she was jittery, unsettled somehow. Nothing I could put my finger on, but in my line of work you do develop certain instincts. And my instincts told me Emily was using.'

'Any ideas who might have been supplying her with drugs?'

'None at all, I'm afraid. I'd really lost touch with Emily – I didn't know any of her Westwich friends. One thing's for sure, it wouldn't have been her boyfriend. Whittaker feels guilty as hell that he smokes now and then. He's not the type to get involved with drugs – works out, you know.'

Simon was sceptical. In his experience, anyone was capable of doing almost anything, despite appearances to the contrary. But he agreed that Whittaker wasn't a particularly likely type.

'You've been very helpful, Mr Harwood. I appreciate it.' A thought occurred to him. 'By the way – which hospital is Charlotte's sister a patient in?' Simon had suddenly realised that Anne might in fact hold the key to Emily's whereabouts on the afternoon of her disappearance.

'The Cotswold Memorial. Just outside Cirencester, on the Westwich side. But I'm afraid she won't be able to help you with your inquiries.'

And on that somewhat bitter note, Harwood rang off.

Chapter Twenty

The drive to the hospital was a pleasant one along high Cotswold roads with fine views to the west and east. Dark rain clouds filled the sky to the west, but up here the day was bright and sunny with just a few clouds scudding low in the pale sky. Simon took the journey slowly, enjoying the absence of company and regretting, as he frequently did, having the phone connecting him by a never-ending thread to the centre of operations. He felt its presence like a constraining lead, confining him, restricting the thinking time which driving, with its element of hypnotic automatism, provided for him.

He tried nevertheless to let his mind drift over the elements of the case, allowing ideas to surface subconsciously and at random. The more he pondered, the more he realised that he had been going down what was, for a policeman, an inexcusable path: searching single-mindedly for evidence that would confirm his belief that Dawson was guilty. Now he resolutely made the effort to lift himself out of that mire; to speculate, as Jessie had suggested, on the character and motivations of Emily, and see where that led him.

Emily's chief characteristic seemed to have been her insecurity and poor sense of self. And, perhaps as a result, her relationships were primarily with those who would most freely give her the affection and reassurance she so obviously craved: men. Apart from Charlotte, Emily didn't appear to have been close to any woman. And even Charlotte hadn't been told of Emily's pregnancy until a month after it had been confirmed.

That mysterious pregnancy ... Where had Emily been and

whom had she been with during September, the month her baby was conceived? It took only moments to conceive a child; it could have happened anywhere, any time. But no one had suggested that Emily slept around. Unless she had indulged in an unaccustomed one-night stand, the choice of possible fathers was limited.

Then there were the drugs. But he couldn't visualise the beautiful, elegant Emily doing furtive deals on seedy street corners. It seemed far more likely that her supplier was someone she knew and trusted. His mind turned to Peter Rudley and his pathetic, squalid death. Students were so vulnerable; bereft of parental guidance, they were determined to assert their independence, kick over the traces. And evidently drugs were widely available on the Westwich campus.

Despite his efforts he kept coming back to another Peter: Dawson. Dawson loved power, loved to manipulate; Dawson, whose close friend Beardsley had apparently lied about where he was the night Emily died. So were they both involved in what had happened to Emily? Were they, for that matter, involved with drugs? Through his London media connections Dawson would almost certainly have known where to get drugs. If Dawson had been dealing, and Emily had known, he would have had a strong motive for wanting her dead if she threatened to expose him. Not to mention the baby, the potential for sexual scandal.

And Dawson must know the area around Westwich. He'd have known exactly where to dispose of a body, where to leave it so it would never be found. Maybe Hermione's psychic would solve that particular puzzle. He smiled to himself at the recollection that Longman, at this minute, would be trailing around Acacia Road in her wake.

This trip to the Cotswold Memorial Hospital was to some extent self-indulgence on Simon's part, a chance to get away for a few hours rather than a strictly necessary inquiry. Even if Emily had visited her sister that day, it did no more than fill in a doubtless unimportant gap in the file that was getting fatter every day with what was mostly irrelevant detail. He wondered how often she or Charlotte had made the journey to sit with their unconscious sister. Probably Charlotte would have done so most often, to assuage the guilt that Harwood had said she felt, guilt arising from an anguished sense of responsibility.

This train of thought reminded him of Emily's apparent interest in the newspaper reports of the accident. He was still puzzling over what she could have been trying to find out when the sign for the hospital appeared.

The driveway wound through woodland for almost a mile before ending at a gravelled parking area in front of what looked more like a country house than a hospital. The building was Victorian, covered with the tendrils of a leafless creeper, with a large porticoed entrance. Instead of turning off into the less convenient visitor's car park, he placed the car at the end of a row in front of the house, no doubt, he thought, usurping some important medic's right of place.

As soon as he entered the double doors, the familiar hospital smell vanquished any country-house illusion. The place did not otherwise resemble a large, centralised general hospital. It seemed almost unnaturally calm.

'Can I help you?'

A dark-haired woman with a formidable bosom had emerged from the office behind the reception desk. Simon explained that he was there to visit Anne Sanderson, as part of a police inquiry.

The woman nodded curtly. 'Her sister Emily – the missing student. We did hear. Though I can assure you that Anne is in no state to help you.'

'I didn't suppose she would be,' Simon said. 'But *you* might be able to.'

'In what way?'

'I wondered whether Emily came here to visit her sister last Tuesday.'

She gave a dismissive shrug. 'I didn't see her. She may have done.'

'Is this a specialist hospital?' Simon asked. It was not one that had featured in any of the cases he'd worked on since he had been in Westwich.

'That's right. Used to be for TB and contagious diseases years ago but now it's a regional neurological unit.'

The TB history explained the isolation of the place, Simon

thought. 'I see. So is there anyone else who might have seen Emily – if she came here?'

She shrugged again, straining her vast bosom against her white coat. 'You could ask some of the staff. Anne's room's at the end of that corridor,' she said, made suddenly helpful by the prospect of getting rid of him. She pointed to some doors to the left.

Simon thanked her and set off down a highly polished corridor which seemed to traverse half the length of the building. Some doors opened off the corridor, revealing two-bedded and one-bedded rooms containing still, silent patients hooked up to a variety of blinking and bleeping machines. There were trolleys laden with various items of medical equipment but he saw no sign of any nurses, doctors, physiotherapists or any other kind of staff. The rather eerie atmosphere was troubling him by the time he reached the last pair of closed doors. As he debated which one to try, a voice by his shoulder spoke. 'Can I help you, love?'

A young black nurse was gazing up at him with clear, untroubled eyes and a generous smile.

He explained again why he was there, showing her his identification.

'Anne's in here,' the nurse said, indicating her room. 'But she's not capable of talking. As far as we can tell, she's not aware of anything.'

'I understand that. But did you, or someone else, perhaps, happen to see her sister Emily last Tuesday, visiting Anne?'

The young woman's expression lit up. 'Oh, yes! I saw her.' The light went out of her face as she remembered. 'All that lovely, long blonde hair ... What a terrible thing to happen!' Her eyes widened and she looked worried. 'It was that night that she went missing, wasn't it? It never occurred to me ...' She put her hand to her mouth. 'I'm so sorry. I should have told you before. I didn't think it could be relevant.'

'The newspapers.' Simon said, 'asked the public to come forward with any information, no matter how trivial it might appear.'

'I don't get much time for reading newspapers. Full-time job here, two children at home. I'm so sorry.' She looked contrite.

181

'What time was Emily here?'

The nurse thought for a moment. 'It was around four o'clock. I was just going off for a quick cup of tea and I popped my head around the door to see that everything was all right. And Emily was sitting by the bed.'

'Did you speak to her?'

'I said hello, that's all. She smiled, and then I went off.'

'So you don't know exactly what time she arrived or left?'

The nurse shook her head sadly. Then she added, as if in compensation, 'Do you want to see Anne while you're here?' She gestured to the door again.

Simon nodded and followed her into the room.

The silent figure was tucked neatly beneath the sheets, her arms, with blue veins tracing the white skin, placed tidily at her sides. She looked as if she was simply asleep. There were no tubes and machines hooked up to her, as there had been to some of the other patients in the rooms Simon had passed, no indication on her perfect features of the car crash that had destroyed her life. He didn't know what he had expected; after all, it was several years ago now, plenty of time for injuries to heal. She looked very young, hardly more than a teenager, her hair, blonde like her sisters', cut to an easily manageable length. He could see a clear family resemblance to Charlotte, but Anne's lightly veined eyelids hid from him whether her eyes were the same dazzling shade of blue.

'Is there any hope that she might come out of this?' he asked.

'It happens.' The nurse cast a sad look at the figure in the bed. 'That's why she's here, because we haven't given up hope. But it doesn't look good. Her sister Charlotte wants us to keep trying. She often comes in to talk to her. Head-injured patients need a lot of stimulation if they're to stand a chance. Sometimes she came with Emily. I suppose now Anne's all Charlotte's got left.'

'So Emily didn't often come on her own?'

'That Tuesday afternoon was the first time I saw her here without Charlotte. Of course, she'd moved to Westwich, so that was a bit nearer for her.

'Did anyone else see Emily that day?'

She shook her head slowly. 'No, I don't think so. I'm sure

182

they would have said, after what's happened. But you can come and ask, if you like. I'm just off for some lunch. Would you like a cup of tea?'

Simon declined, attractive though the prospect was. He had confirmed what he had come here to confirm, that this was where Emily had been; there seemed no point in proving it over again.

'Well,' the nurse said, hesitating to leave him for her no doubt well-earned break.

'You go and have your cup of tea,' Simon said. 'I'll just sit down here for a few moments, if I may. And thank you, Nurse—?'

'Sister Akande. And you sit wherever you want.' She beamed at him and made her soft-footed exit.

Simon lowered himself into the chair Emily must have used that Tuesday, facing the french windows which looked out on lawns and evergreen shrubbery. Poignantly, an effort had been made to make the room homely, cosy even, with pictures on the wall and a teddy bear sitting on the locker beside Anne's bed. But the presence of the hospital equipment – monitors, a trolley of syringes and bowls pushed against the wall, the institutional bed – vanquished the attempt.

He found that he was avoiding looking at Anne, feeling that to do so was in some way voyeurish, intruding without the consent of the girl who could not give it anyway; that he had no such rights, familial or even professional.

He stood up again and went over to the windows. The view was very English, green and restful, designed to aid the recuperation of those who originally had been kept in these rooms, those with some hope of recovery. There was a stone terrace outside where they would have sat on warm summer days when the trees were in green leaf. He tried the door handle and found it locked by a lever action on the inside and turned back for a final look at the girl Anne. She appeared terribly vulnerable lying there alone. The number of single rooms were a hangover from the days the hospital had been for contagious disease cases, he assumed. Hospital security seemed non-existent, because, he supposed, there were no babies to steal. But there were other forms of attack on patients in understaffed hospitals. Her isolation made him feel

183

acutely uneasy suddenly. Because of what's happened to her sister, he told himself as he closed the room door firmly behind him. Again he saw no-one as he made his way along the corridor and out to his car.

Soon after Simon left the hospital, Monkton came on the line. 'They've got a floater turned up on the north Somerset coast.'

'You mean, a drowned person?' Simon was known for his preference for the English, rather than American language.

'Yes, sir.' Monkton made no attempt to hide his impatience. 'A young woman, blonde hair, stab wounds. Only been in the water a few days.'

Regional as well as national police forces had all been officially notified of Emily Sanderson's disappearance. This could be she – the timing fitted and north Somerset was a possible area in which her body might emerge if it had been dumped in the river at Westwich.

'Have they started a postmortem?'

'No. They'll wait. But they're able to say she was dead before she went into the water. She didn't drown. They've taken her to the main mortuary at Taunton. I assumed you'd want to see her. I've already contacted Miss Sanderson and she says she'll meet you there.'

Simon felt annoyed at Monkton's peremptoriness. 'I presume you've arranged for a car to take her there?'

'She said she preferred to drive herself.'

Monkton had probably not even thought to suggest the kinder alternative. 'Did she seem all right?' he asked. It was obviously an extremely distressing prospect, having to identify the body of someone close, especially when the body was in effect that of your only living relative.

'Didn't notice,' Monkton said.

Chapter Twenty-One

Charlotte arrived soon after Simon, at three o'clock. The body had been placed in a separate room, as far as possible from other bodies and the unpleasant odours of the dissecting area. It made some difference, but not much; the distinctive smell of decay and mortality was everywhere; the atmosphere of the place, it seemed to Simon, could only serve to heighten the despair of the thousands who came to see loved ones for the last time in this alien and unforgiving place.

Charlotte looked frightened, paler than ever, her eyes large and dark. She put her hand on his arm. 'What do I have to do? You'll come with me, won't you?' she whispered.

He assured her he'd be at her side. Shortly afterwards the pathologist led them into a small room where the covered body lay on a trolley.

'Are you ready?' the woman pathologist asked.

Charlotte nodded, her grip on Simon's arm intensifying. Simon not much less tense himself, steeled himself for what he guessed would be something fairly shocking. He had seen a number of dead bodies, some of them from the river, in the course of his work, but the experience never got any easier.

The pathologist, concerned eyes on Charlotte's face, slowly folded back the sheet. Simon felt rather than heard Charlotte draw in her breath. He bitterly regretted he had not prepared her more before she had been allowed in.

The skin, wrinkled and loose through prolonged immersion, distorted the features, giving only a vague impression of what the young woman had looked like in life. The skin hung slack on the neck and shoulders too, like a grotesque body mask that had stretched too far. The hair was a dull blonde, the eyes closed. The pathologist had revealed only the head and shoulders, waiting for an indication that she should do so before she moved the sheet any further.

The soundless gasp that had come from Charlotte as the woman threw back the covering had changed into a cry, high-pitched and on the verge of hysteria. She turned away from the body and bent almost double, between the trolley and Simon, as if she had been punched in the stomach.

Simon, at a loss, glanced at the pathologist, whose eyes were sympathetic above the mask. He put his arm tentatively around Charlotte's rigid shoulders. She tried to pull away, and as she did so, she came close to that other, dead woman and turned quickly away, moaning under her breath, hyperventilating.

'Charlotte!' he called sharply, and leaned forward awkwardly to see her face. Her eyes were turned upwards, showing mostly only the whites. 'Charlotte!' He shook her, her eyelids flickered and the terrible moans turned into recognisable sobs as her body slackened.

The pathologist was offering a glass of water, indicating a chair against the wall. Simon manoeuvred Charlotte backwards to the seat and pressed the glass to her lips. She was suddenly silent, eyes closed, with tears seeping through her eyelashes and falling on her hands, which lay clutched in her lap. He lifted one of her hands and clasped it around the glass, holding it for a moment until he was sure she had a proper grip. He was angry that she had been allowed to come like this, with no friend to support her, to keep her company.

'I'm sorry,' she murmured at last, wiping at her eyes with some tissues the pathologist had supplied.

Simon glanced at the dead body, the grotesque simulacrum of the lovely, vivid girl in the photograph. 'It's Emily?' he asked gently, still feeling shaken.

She turned her head from side to side. In a low voice she said 'I don't know. How can I tell? She doesn't look like a human being.'

The pathologist gestured silently towards the body. But there was no point in Charlotte seeing more. Emily had no particular distinguishing marks. He shook his head and the woman

186

covered the head and shoulders and pushed the body out of the room, returning immediately to stand inside the door.

Charlotte opened her eyes, lashes wet and spiky, and looked at Simon. She took a deep breath. 'Clothes?' she said indistinctly. 'Can I see them?'

'Are you sure you're up to it?' Her skin was as white as the tiled walls.

She stood shakily, leaning on his arm. 'I don't think it was her.'

The pathologist indicated a room across the corridor. The young woman's clothes had been placed in plastic bags and tagged ready for forensic examination. Simon knew, from Richard Lee's account, what Emily had been wearing on the evening of her disappearance, though it was of course possible that she had changed before her anticipated meeting with Dawson.

Charlotte was shaking her head as she touched a bag containing a pair of blue denim jeans. 'No,' she said, 'Emily never wore jeans. She didn't own a pair.'

'You're absolutely sure?'

'Absolutely.' She fingered another bag containing a red sequinned knitted top. 'No, it's not her. Poor girl! I wonder who she is.'

It was a sad coincidence for Charlotte, he reflected, that such a body had turned up at such a time. On the other hand, if the time came for another identification, at least she would know what to expect.

As they stepped outside the building, it was clear that Charlotte was far from recovered from her distress. It seemed obvious to Simon that this had been the first time that Emily's probable death had become a reality for her. He should have realised that it would be so and done something about it. Except that he'd had no chance. Bloody Monkton had pre-empted him.

She agreed to a cup of coffee, so he took her to one of the town's older hotels and seated her in a quiet lounge bar. He ordered a brandy for her to go with it and gradually some colour and calm began to return to her face.

'That was awful,' she said. 'I still pray that she'll turn up somehow.' He realised uneasily that, at the same time as

187

bringing the possibility of Emily's death into her conscious imagination, and shocking her as it had, this most recent experience might in some ways encourage her belief in the opposite possibility.

As she relaxed she began to ask him questions about how he investigations were going. As he had thought she would, she referred to the newspaper reports that morning about his questioning of Peter Dawson.

He explained that Dawson had come to see the police of his own accord.

'He's admitted now that he did get a telephone call from Emily that evening. He says she asked him to meet her by Lovers' Bridge, at the river.'

'And you believe him?' She was watching him intently over the rim of her brandy glass.

'I don't know. We're checking his story of course.'

'Do you think you're getting anywhere?' she asked.

'Hard to tell, yet.' He wished he could be more positive.

'Why did you go to see Oliver?' she asked. 'Surely you don't suspect him? He's always been so fond of Emily.'

A slight distortion of the truth, Simon felt, but there was no irony in her voice. Harwood had obviously contacted Charlotte after Simon's visit. He gave the usual explanation about talking to as many people as possible who knew the victim and mentioned his visit to the hospital that afternoon.

'Why didn't you tell me that you have another sister? Why didn't you tell me about Anne?'

She gulped some coffee. 'I don't have another sister.' Her face hardened slightly. 'That's not my sister Anne, lying in that bed ... Did Oliver tell you all the sad story?'

'He told me about the car crash, how it all happened.'

'Well, forgive me if I don't indulge your curiosity any further.' She put down her cup in a gesture of finality.

'That was where Emily went to on Tuesday afternoon. She went to see Anne,' Simon said.

'Did she?' Charlotte blinked a few times, as if hearing this had moved her.

'I went there today. One of the nurses said she was there in the afternoon.'

'You went there?' she echoed. 'So you saw Anne?'

'Yes.'

'She didn't see you, though, did she?' Her voice hardened to bitterness again.

'No,' he said quietly, wondering just how long Anne would be expected to live in such a condition.

'I don't think we should let her stay alive much longer,' Charlotte said, as if reading his thoughts. 'Pumping drugs in to keep her alive when she gets infections. It seems hopeless.'

He had wanted to ask her if she knew anything about Emily's interest in the reports of the accident but decided to leave it for now. It was obviously all still a raw subject and Charlotte had had enough to deal with today.

'You're not still in that house on your own, are you? You ask too much of yourself,' he said.

She drained her brandy glass. 'I'm fine,' she said. 'It'll be afterwards, when I know what's happened, when you've arrested someone, that I'll really have to face it.'

Only after she had assured him emphatically that she had truly recovered did Simon agree to her leaving. When he had dropped her at her car, he headed back to Westwich.

Chapter Twenty-Two

Early next morning – Sunday – Longman joined Simon in his room at headquarters. They had both had time off the night before; Longman had managed to visit Stratford to see *Twelfth Night* with his wife and Simon had spent a mixed time with Jessie.

Everything had been going well until, lulled by their relaxed companionship, Simon had rashly started questioning Jessie about Dawson and Beardsley. He had been trying to broach some discussion of the drugs scene at the university, but never got that far. She had exploded, reminding him that she would not and could not discuss colleagues with him. He had been tempted to ask why Hermione could and she couldn't, but thought better of it. The night had been spent with Jessie pointedly keeping to her own side of the bed and Flossie, purring heavily, on the pillow between them. Simon had left early after a quick shower and no breakfast.

Longman semed to have had a more enjoyable time, dropping several quotations and extolling the virtues of one of the leading actresses in the play before Simon woke up and recalled him to business.

No one had yet been able to locate Beardsley. Monkton and Rodgers had visited Kathleen Beardsley again and had little to add to what she had told them the day before. She had been home doing some administrative work for school last Tuesday night and she had never, to her knowledge, met Emily Sanderson. More importantly, her husband had not been home the night before. In fact, she hadn't seen him since breakfast on Friday.

'We'd better speak to Dawson,' Longman said. 'Since he was seen having a row with Beardsley on Friday night.'

'I should talk to Beardsley's wife too. Did she seem concerned about her husband?'

'I gather they lead fairly separate lives. Not much love lost between them, I'd guess.'

Simon described his trip to the Cotswold Memorial Hospital.

'One more detail in place,' said Longman. 'Doesn't help much, though. I gather the trip to Somerset was a waste of time.'

Simon told him briefly what had happened at the police mortuary.

'Nasty experience for her. Something I never get used to, and when it might be a relation—' Longman sighed in commiseration.

Simon had no desire to dwell on the memory. He was acutely aware of his inadequacy when confronted with a distraught Charlotte. 'To get back to Emily visiting the hospital – I was wondering how she got out there,' he said. 'It doesn't look as if it's on any bus route.'

'Taxi?' Longman suggested.

'Either way I'd like it checked out. Someone may have given her a lift.'

Longman made another note in his notebook.

'I thought you'd be bursting to tell me how you got on with the Sybil,' Simon said. 'I hope you were discreet?'

Longman chuckled. 'She looked business-like enough. There was no-one else much around anyway.'

'So has she solved the crime?' Simon stretched back in his chair, arms folded behind his head.

Longman sat down, an earnest expression on his genial features. 'She's definitely got a gift. Told me things about myself and my family—'

'Which you knew anyway.' Simon gave a mocking smile.

Longman was miffed. 'It still doesn't alter—'

'Get back to the issue, Geoff. I'm not interested in whether your granny is having a whale of a time in the Elysian Fields.'

Longman, offended, got up with a sigh and went over to the window, staring out at the city. 'She had a few things to say about the crime. If you're interested.'

Simon waited and, as he knew he would, the sergeant came and sat down again. He riffled through his notebook and cleared his throat. 'I jotted a few things down as she was talking. She goes into a sort of different state of consciousness—'

Simon tried to smile encouragingly.

Longman coughed. 'It's mostly just impressions.'

'Go on.'

'I'll just read them out as I jotted them down.' Longman frowned in concentration at his notebook. 'Buried near a bridge – near water – fields around. Far from here. Sees a needle, syringe. There were drugs involved, she was taking drugs. Emily was afraid. Perhaps of her situation, perhaps of a person. There's a man, an older man, with power. A lot of fear and sadness. A lot of anger, too.' Longman stopped. 'She got a bit upset. The vibes got to her, or something. She said she'd try again at home.' He closed his notebook and looked at Simon a touch defiantly.

'Hmm,' was all Simon said at first. Longman waited, restless.

Relenting, Simon mentioned the call he had received from Oliver Harwood. 'Drugs again!'

'It's a problem everywhere. It's not just kids on council estates. We know that well enough,' Longman said.

Simon was again reminded of his sister Rose. He must try again to get hold of her.

'The older man could have been supplying them. Dawson, perhaps?'

'Or Beardsley.'

'Not without Dawson,' Longman said firmly. 'Suppose that was the motive for attacking Emily – suppose she was going to report the fact that they supplied drugs.'

'I've wondered whether that might have been it. It's all a bit speculative, though. I mean, we've got no evidence that either Dawson or Beardsley were using or supplying.'

'What about Edwards?'

'She'd only just met him. I'm sure of that.' Simon shook his head. 'No, I think I know what Edwards was up to that night – and it had nothing to do with Emily.'

192

'Oh?' Longman said. 'What?'

'It's pretty obvious.'

'Not to me,' Longman said grumpily.

'Forget Emily for a moment. Remember the stuff in his room. He's a type, is Edwards.'

'The videos?'

Simon didn't answer.

'The magazines. Pornography mostly. So – ah. Military.' Longman paused.

'The other event in Acacia Road that night?' Simon prompted.

Enlightenment dawned. 'He and his little gang are self-appointed vigilantes! Is that what you think?'

'Makes sense, doesn't it? Gives them the chance to practise what they think of as a little justified violence. They wander about looking for anything vaguely suspicious and have a lot of fun putting the boot in.'

'Because, even if the police catch them, British justice won't give 'em what they've got coming to them.' Longman nodded. 'It figures.' He looked more cheerful. 'The timing fits, doesn't it? He admits he took his mates home about eight o'clock.'

'Yes, they all scarpered just before the police arrived.'

'Are we going to see him?' Longman asked.

'We've got enough to do. I think we'll pass it straight on to Perfect.'

'Inspector Perfect's got a thing about vigilantes,' Longman said, smiling.

'I don't like them much myself.' Another lot who projected their own innate violence on to others and called it justified, Simon thought.

'So what do you think?' Longman held up his notebook.

'About the Sybil? Doesn't really tell us anything new, does it? And the burial place could be anywhere. There are hundreds, thousands of rivers or lakes far from here.'

'But the other stuff,' Longman insisted, 'that's pretty close. The least it does is confirm what we're already thinking.'

'Perhaps she was just reading your mind.'

'But it's still impressive,' Longman said stoutly.

'The point is, there's nothing we can go on there.' Simon

was wishing he had never allowed himself to get into this. But it brought the benefit of Hermione's cooperation, he reminded himself.

Longman had decided, albeit reluctantly, to let his psychic encounter go. 'Charlotte doesn't seem to have suspected Emily was using drugs,' he said.

'If she did, she certainly hasn't mentioned it.' Simon made a mental note to ask her a direct question.

'My, my. Talk about fiddling while Rome burns.' Bradley heaved into the room and flung one of the Sunday tabloids on Simon's desk, toppling the in-tray and scattering papers over the floor.

'Sir?' Longman said, craning his head to make out the newspaper headlines.

Simon busied himself on the floor, gathering papers together.

'More bloody publicity for the university!' Bradley said. 'Get up, Chief Inspector Simon, I want to talk to you. Who's leaking all this stuff?'

'They say any publicity is good publicity, sir.' Simon resumed his seat and unfolded the newspaper.

Longman winced, but the expected outburst didn't come. Bradley, dressed in Sunday-morning casuals and looking most unlike himself, lowered himself into a chair. 'Who's behind all these leaks, Detective Chief Inspector Simon?' he repeated.

The offending article centred on Beardsley's mysterious disappearance and the questionable goings-on among 'the staff of one of our most prestigious universities'. Beardsley's photograph was there, a flattering one, doubtless taken from the jacket of one of his books.

'They're jumping the gun a bit,' Simon said calmly. 'Still, perhaps it will bring him out into the open.'

'You haven't attempted to answer my question.' Bradley snapped.

'I don't know the answer, sir. I'll have a word with the team.'

'Well, make sure you do,' Bradley said, standing up. 'I suppose it's no use asking you if you're getting anywhere?'

'We're narrowing things down, sir. I've got a few people to see today. May have something for you tomorrow.'

194

'The university's not going to like all this talk about drugs one bit,' Bradley said. 'Especially after the death of that student last week.'

Simon had not had the opportunity to read the whole article. 'You mean the press is actually suggesting Beardsley is involved with drugs?'

'Not in so many words.' Bradley slapped the rolled-up newspaper against his broad thigh. 'They ever so subtly remind the reader that a colleague of Beardsley's has already been interviewed by the police – they don't name him, but it can only be Dawson – and go on straight after that to say that since arriving at the university, Miss Sanderson had allegedly been introduced to the delights of various illegal substances. Then there's a whole paragraph on Peter Rudley and the usual hypocritical crap abut the lethal effects of drugs and the apparent failure of the police to do anything about what they call "the drug epidemic".' Bradley snorted. 'So where the hell are they getting it all from? If I were you, I'd get on to them straight away, and see if they're prepared to reveal their sources. The reporter's name is Nicola Dennis. Get on with it!'

Bradley pushed his way through the door and the change in atmosphere was immediate.

'Go out and take a look at the Sundays, Geoff. See if that's the only one carrying the story. Bring back any others that are.'

Simon located the number and called the newapaper; Nicola Dennis wasn't there. After some argument, they rang Simon back and gave him her home phone number, but she wasn't there either. Simon passed it on to Rhiannon Jones and told her to keep trying.

Longman came back with most of the Sunday newspapers. 'I've only skimmed through them,' he said. 'Most of them have just done a recap of the week's reports and they all picked up on Dawson. But only one's mentioned Beardsley's disappearance.' He unloaded them on Simon's desk. 'You'd better take a proper look.'

The both spent half an hour scanning the variety of articles. The 'quality' papers had focused on violent crime against women, using the Emily Sanderson case as an example; the tabloids, as usual, had dredged up whatever personal details of

195

the victim they had been able to find. These didn't amount to much, although some of them mentioned the tragic accident that had deprived Emily of most of her family and left her younger sister a 'vegetable'. There was indeed only one that mentioned both Beardsley and drugs.

Watkins called in as they were still looking through the newspapers: no more news of the woman seen with Emily in town that Tuesday, but he had managed to get a look at the newspapers reports that Emily had requested in the library. 'Apparently there was another car involved, probably driven by a woman, but she didn't stop,' Watkins said.

'Yes. Harwood did mention something of the sort,' Simon said, his head still buried in a newspaper. 'Thanks, Watkins.'

Longman put his paper down and stood up, stretching as he did so. 'Shall we go and see Kathleen Beardsley now?' he suggested.

Simon was glad of any excuse for action. On the way out, they called in on Perfect to pass on Simon's theory about Edwards. Simon requested that, if Perfect managed to get a confession out of the man, Edwards be questioned again about anything he might have seen that night of relevance to the Emily Sanderson case. Perfect agreed readily.

'Nice fellow,' Longman grunted as they walked away from the inspector's room. 'D'you think he tries to live up to his name?'

'God help him if he does,' Simon said.

'But names are very influential—'

'You said something of the kind before.' Simon interrupted another of Longman's speculations. 'Yours didn't do much for you, though, did it?'

Longman looked up from eight inches' disadvantage. 'Ah, but you forget, sir – I'd have been considered a long man by my ancestors. They were all about five foot tall in those days.'

Chapter Twenty-Three

The streets of Westwich were almost empty of traffic on this dismal Sunday morning. A few people were hurrying home in the drizzle, clutching newspapers under their arms or using them as protection from the weather. As Simon pulled up at some traffic lights, Beardsley's eye glared balefully at him from a distorted front page held to a pedestrian's head. Newspaper hoardings, predictably as this was local news, took the lead from the *Sunday Mirror* and shouted the disappearance of one of the city's dons.

'He's not been gone that long,' Longman commented as they passed another such hoarding. 'Might have just gone off for the weekend somewhere.'

'If he has, this lot should bring him back fairly quickly,' Simon said.

'The bit in the paper about the drugs—' Longman hesitated.

'Well?'

'I wonder if he knew Peter Rudley.'

'Why should he? Even if Beardsley *is* involved with drugs, it's not as if he's going to be the only supplier. Or the only other user. We'll search his house, if Mrs Beardsley will let us. Will that satisfy you?'

Longman shrugged. 'So who d'you think is responsible for all this leaking to the press?'

Simon had been wondering about that. Privately he had been considering Monkton as the offender; the inspector had been stirring things a bit lately and this was an easy way to create embarrassment for a senior officer on a case. He wasn't going to admit his suspicions to Longman, though.

'Someone wanting to make trouble for Dawson and Beardsley, obviously.' Longman answered his own question.

It could be that those two were the target, Simon thought. 'We'll speculate when I get to speak to the reporter.'

'Protect their sources, don't they?' Longman said glumly.

Simon took a roundabout fast on to the inner ring road heading north as the beginning of suburban Westwich approached. Large detached houses sat sedately amid shrubberies; there was none of the usual Sunday-morning activity – people washing cars, pottering in the garden – in this wet weather. The smell of fried bacon was adrift in the mist and Simon became conscious of having missed his breakfast.

'If something's happened to Beardsley, it's going to change the look of the Emily Sanderson case,' Longman said.

'That depends on whether he's committed suicide, been murdered or decided to disappear,' Simon replied. 'So we can't speculate.'

'Any of those possibilities suggests his involvement in what happened to Emily,' Longman persisted.

'I certainly got the feeling he knew more than hc was telling,' Simon said.

'Wonder if he told his wife anything.'

'I wonder if she'll tell us if he did.' Simon turned into a quiet road of large thirties houses. The trees that lined the road had grown mature in the years since the houses were built and their trunks were defaced with yellow posters indicating that this was yet another Neighbourhood Watch area.

The woman who opened the door examined their IDs carefully before inviting them into the sitting room. It was pleasantly, if conventionally, furnished and looked unlived in. There were no personal touches, no comfortable clutter.

Kathleen Beardsley was plump and neatly dressed on a day of the week when she might have felt entitled to relax a little. Her hair was grey, cut in an orderly pageboy style with a rather severe fringe. Her plump face was almost unlined and she wore no make-up.

She stood in the middle of the carpet, hands clasped in front of her, and looked them over with pale eyes while she waited for them to speak. Simon, quickly glancing round the room on

198

the way in, had noticed a copy of the *Sunday Mirror*, together with the *Sunday Times*, lying on the sofa.

'You've seen the papers then, Mrs Beardsley,' he said.

'Evidently,' she said. 'But *I* haven't reported him missing.' Her emphasis on the 'I' sounded like a reprimand.

'Do you know where he is? You were unable to tell the officers yesterday,' Simon said neutrally.

'Why don't you sit down, both of you?' she said, seeming to thaw slightly, gesturing to the two armchairs while she subsided on to the sofa. 'No,' she replied to the question, 'I don't know where he is. But that's not necessarily significant – I often don't know where he is.'

Simon wondered how genuine her indifference was. 'So he often goes off for several days without telling you his whereabouts?'

She said precisely, 'Not for as long as this. Often overnight, though.'

'You aren't concerned?' Simon asked.

She lifted her rounded shoulders slightly. 'I suppose I should be, shouldn't I? I did ring round a couple of acquaintances, including Peter Dawson at the university. He said he saw my husband on Friday night.'

'Forgive me, but are you and your husband estranged in some way?' Simon was unsure how to put the question; perhaps this was normal behaviour in the Beardsley household. Other people's marriages were frequently a mystery to outsiders.

She gave a faint smile. 'Oh, I think you could say that. We live fairly independent lives these days.'

Mildly encouraged, Simon said, 'Does he perhaps have a relationship with someone else?'

'I would think that that is very likely, Chief Inspector.' She repeated that rather prim smile.

Obviously she was prepared to provide answers to questions but not to venture anything without being asked. Simon couldn't blame her. It was always humiliating to admit betrayal and she struck him as a woman who was particularly careful of her dignity. The day's newpaper publicity had probably hurt her more than she would care to acknowledge.

Longman, his sturdy body sunk in the floral armchair, spoke. 'Do you have any idea, Mrs Beardsley, who that relationship might be with?'

'I'm afraid not.'

'So you couldn't make a guess where he might have gone?'

'I've already told your officers, I saw my husband on Friday morning at breakfast. I haven't seen him or heard from him since and I have no idea where he is.' She sounded strained.

'What do you make of the comments in the *Mirror*? About drugs?

'It's probably true,' she said coolly.

Simon was surprised at her frankness. 'Your husband did take drugs?'

'I don't think he was an addict, Chief Inspector. But since the suggestion is made, I'm hardly shocked by the idea that he indulged, as so many do, in recreational use – dangerous and foolish though that is. I see too much of it at school. And if we have the problem in the city schools, I've no doubt it is even more common at the university.'

Her face remained expressionless, but Simon noticed a slight heightening of colour.

Longman leaned forward to ask another question. 'Did you know of Emily Sanderson, Mrs Beardsley? Did your husband ever mention her?'

'The student who's gone missing? No. Not even after she disappeared. He may have known her – she worked for his publisher in London, after all.'

'You didn't ask him after you read about the case?'

'I don't gossip, Sergeant. Even with my husband.'

Especially with your husband, Simon thought. Yet it was an odd response.

'Mrs Beardsley,' he said, 'would you mind if we searched your house? To see if your husband kept any drugs here?' In view of what the papers were saying, she might regard the request as inevitable, one she had already anticipated. Simon wondered if she had herself searched for any evidence of the truth of the story.

He waited while she thought over her answer. There was no real reason why she should agree, except that principle and propriety seemed to have overcome the passions in this woman's life and she might consider a refusal to be standing in the way of justice. A search warrant might be obtainable soon, anyway, if Beardsley failed to appear after the day's publicity.

Perhaps she had thought of that, too, because she finally nodded. 'I'll show you to his room.' She rose from the sofa, holding her skirt modestly over her knees as she did so, and led them back into the hall. The house was silent, immaculate, empty; the stairs, thickly carpeted, muffled the sound of their three pairs of feet ascending. She showed them into a room at the back of the house. It contained a single divan bed with a tweed counterpane and was otherwise furnished as a study. A pair of slippers had been kicked off under the desk, which held a personal computer, and other items of male clothing were draped on chairbacks and on the half-open door of a wardrobe.

Kathleen Beardsley fastidiously picked up a brown Shetland sweater and a pair of cord jeans, folding them neatly. 'This is his territory. I don't generally come in here, except to collect his washing.'

Simon wondered slightly at this untypical wifely concern until she added, 'Can't have the house smelling. He wouldn't think to put it in the washing machine himself.' She sighed, looking critically at untidily placed books and papers. 'He didn't appreciate it when I tried to tidy up, so I haven't attempted it for some time. If he does have supplies of illegal substances, Chief Inspector, your guess is as good as mine where they might be.'

Simon moved over to the window, which looked over a big garden. Having a mother who was a keen gardener, he tended to notice other people's gardens; this one had obviously had a great deal of time, effort and expense put into it, though at this time of year it was hardly looking its best. Kathleen Beardsley came to join him and gazed down at what was presumably her creation.

'I shall feel better when I can get back in the garden again. There's not much to do in January.'

'You do it all yourself?'

She gave a little humourless laugh. 'He doesn't help! Can't tell a weed from a lily. A man comes in to help with the heavy work.' She turned away. 'Well, I'll leave you to it. I hope you don't fine anything that you shouldn't, of course, but I expect you to inform me.'

201

Simon and Longman waited for an interval until she had moved out of earshot.

'Blimey! I should think it goes without saying that he's got some other woman tucked away somewhere. I should think *she* finds lovemaking messes the bed up too much.'

'Never make assumptions, Sergeant. Underneath cool exteriors can lie passionate hearts.'

Longman looked doubtful. 'But where's *her* passion directed? Compost heaps,' he said disgustedly.

'Her husband doesn't seem to be the object of any kind of passion, either positive, or negative,' Simon agreed, beginning a search of the desk. 'Did you notice she never referred to him by name?'

'I did.' Longman opened the wardrobe. 'Do you really think it's likely he's left anything incriminating where she might come across it?'

'She says he prefers her to stay out of here, and perhaps she does.' Simon extracted a sheaf of papers from one of the desk drawers and began shuffling through them. They consisted mostly of student essays which Beardsley or someone had marked; none of the names at the head of the papers meant anything to Simon. Another drawer contained folders of what he took to be research notes for another book.

Longman was going through pockets in coats and trousers. 'I doubt if he'd leave anything in his clothes, not if she's in the habit of cleansing the house of his intrusive body odours.'

Simon started looking through the file drawer. Beardsley seemed reasonably organised when it came to paperwork; there were letters from Hyde Books, university personnel and psychology departments, car documents and a file of personal letters. It was obvious that Beardsley was a bit of a hoarder; mundane communications from friends and colleagues, several from other universities, had been carefully stored in their envelopes. Judging by the dates on them, the man appeared not to get many such letters. Who did, though, in the age of the telephone? Even so, Simon wondered at the loneliness of a man that would bother to keep these lukewarm reminders of human connection.

At the back of the collection, out of date order, Simon found an stiff envelope, too firm to be holding a letter. It bore a Welsh stamp; the postmark read St David's, with a date in January. Simon took it to the window but couldn't make out the exact date. It had been posted to Beardsley at his home address. Inside was a postcard with an artistic view of the sea at evening, the water the colour of rolled metal. The writing on the other side was large and bold, written in ballpoint. *It's been a wet Christmas. Charlotte's being kind. Did you do what I asked? Love, Emily.*

Simon held out the card for Longman to read.

'So what did she ask him to do? Speak to Dawson for her, d'you think?' Longman suggested.

Simon shrugged and continued the search, but there was nothing of any further interest in the desk. He began on the bookcases.

Longman, finishing with the wardrobe, went over to the desk himself. He tipped out and upended the smaller drawers; under the bottom one on the left he found a taped package. He peeled it off by the corner and held it up to Simon. 'Not very original, is it?'

Longman pulled on some gloves while Simon watched. There were separate packets of tablets and white powder. 'Amphetamines and cocaine, by the look of it,' Longman said, examining them. There were only small quantities of each. 'Shall we keep looking?'

'Of course.' Simon went back to the bookcase.

Strains of Berlioz drifted up the stairs, along with the smell of freshly made coffee. Simon's stomach yearned in response and he considered leaving Longman alone while he went in search of sustenance.

An hour later they had searched the room thoroughly but found nothing else of interest.

'She'd obviously already been in touch with him before she wrote that card,' Longman said. 'Perhaps there's another letter.'

'If there is, its not here.'

Downstairs Simon showed Kathleen Beardsley the envelope from St David's and asked if she could recall the arrival of any envelopes bearing similar handwriting.

'I always put his letters in a separate pile. I don't examine them, Chief Inspector.'

'Perhaps he had a telephone call from Emily,' Simon suggested.

'If he did, I'm afraid I'm not aware of it,' she said.

Simon told her what else they had found.

For the first time, emotion showed in her face. 'I'm very sorry. This is going to mean trouble, isn't it?'

She showed them to the door, asking no questions about what would happen next, or what steps they might be taking to find her husband.

'She's a cold fish,' Longman said as they drove through the heavy rain.

'Controlled rather than cold, maybe. For all we know, she's sobbing her heart out right now.'

'I doubt that somehow.' Longman belatedly fastened his seat belt. 'Time to search Dawson's house as well?'

'Not immediately. And we'll need a warrant in his case.' Simon drove on to the inner ring road. There was still very little traffic – they seemed to have the city to themselves. 'I'd like to get hold of that reporter first, and find out if there's any more news of Beardsley.'

'You're not worried the smouldering Kathleen will tip Dawson off? Maybe she's one of his victims too.'

Simon smiled at the image of straitlaced Kathleen in Dawson's impassioned embrace. 'Now that would really surprise me.'

204

Chapter Twenty-Four

Beardsley's whereabouts were clearly now a matter of concern. Simon asked Longman to circulate his car registration number and description to the divisions.

Rhiannon finally tracked down Nicola Dennis and put the call through to Simon's office.

'Detective Chief Inspector Simon? The police officer didn't say, but I assume it's about the *Mirror's* front page this morning?' The accent was mid-Atlantic with a hint of cockney.

'That's right. We want to know where you're getting your information. Can you tell me who has been speaking to you about this case?'

She gave a rasping laugh. 'Come on, Chief Inspector! You know we never reveal our sources.'

This was all much as anticipated. 'No, I know that. But can you just confirm whether it was the same person who tipped you off about the visit Peter Dawson paid to headquarters here the other day?'

'Ye-es,' she said cautiously, 'I suppose I can go that far.'

'Thank you,' Simon said. 'By the way, do you actually check on the accuracy of what's fed to you?'

'We check,' she said shortly.

'You realise, Ms Dennis, that you make our investigations a lot more complicated when you carry on a trial by newspaper like this.'

'Oh, come on! Hardly. The story was getting tired, we spiced it up a bit. Peter Dawson is always news. Just the fact that he knew the victim is enough to sell newspapers.'

'I understand your commercial imperatives, but you might spare a thought for the families of those involved.'

'But I do, Chief Inspector. What harm's been done by keeping the case in the headlines?'

'Ask Peter Dawson that. Or Phillip Beardsley's wife.'

'Dawson can take any amount of publicity. And maybe the front page will flush Beardsley out.'

'In which case you might have been some use. But you prejudice cases before they come to court by carrying on like this.'

'Hey, can I quote you on what that implies?'

The bloody woman was irrepressible. 'I wasn't implying anything – I was stating a general fact.'

'I've heard it before,' she said drily. 'Have you finished the lecture? Because I have a busy day.'

'You don't help your cause by alienating the police,' he said, hoping she'd pick up the hint.

'Yeah, we tread a tricky path. So might you have something for me soon, maybe?'

'Can you tell me whether your informant was a man or a woman?'

'I *could*,' she said slowly. 'What's it worth?'

'Probably not much,' Simon said honestly, 'but you never know.'

'OK. It was a woman. But whether she was nine or ninety, British, Russian or Polynesian, that I won't tell you.'

'Thanks,' Simon said, satisfied that that was as much as he'd get, and hung up.

'Sir?' Rhiannon Jones put her head round the door. 'There's someone come to see you. She wouldn't say what it was about but I think it's something to do with the Sanderson case.'

The girl who came into the room looked very young. Her hair was almost black and cut very short. She wore loose red trousers and laced boots with a bulky multicoloured jacket. Her face was small, dark-eyed and full-lipped, her skin attractively flushed.

She solemnly held out a hand to Simon and then to Longman. 'I'm Laura Stacey. Dr Beardsley's mistress.'

Simon caught Longman's expression; he was sure it reflected his own surprise – though whether they were struck more by the girl's youth, her beauty or her frankness he wasn't sure. She must be older than eighteen, surely, Simon thought. He said, unable to curb his curiosity, 'You're one of his students?'

She gave a small smile. 'Not really. I'm a postgraduate, doing a psychology PhD.'

So she was probably in her early twenties. Simon felt that age was beginning to distort his perceptions. He gestured to a seat. 'You know where Dr Beardsley is?' he asked, perching on the edge of his desk. Longman leaned on the windowsill, clutching his plastic mug, unable to take his eyes off the lovely Laura.

She shook her head. 'No, I don't. I wish I did. I was hoping you might be able to tell me. I haven't seen him since Friday evening. He wanted to see a film but I didn't want to go. I don't like flaunting our relationship around the university, for obvious reasons. Anyway, he didn't come back that night. I don't like to ring him at home, so I had no idea what had happened. And then I saw the newspapers this morning.' She looked up, her expression now anxious, at Simon. 'He should have contacted me by now.'

'Well, if you've come to see me in the hope that we know where he is, I'm afraid—'

'I didn't really think you'd know. It's not that. It's what they were implying in that article.' She gestured with a small white hand at the pile of newspapers still lying on Simon's desk.

'You mean the drugs?'

'Not that either – though that's bad enough. No, I mean the stuff about his involvement in Emily Sanderson's disappearance.'

'Oh?'

'He was with me that night – last Tuesday night. All night. He *couldn't* have had anything to do with it. I didn't know there was any suggestion of it! He didn't tell me, and until I saw the newspapers—'

'He hasn't been accused of anything,' Simon said, 'He was questioned, interviewed as someone who had known Emily for a while, but that was all.'

'I'm worried about him,' she said, a frown on her small face.

Simon thought that in the circumstances she might be justified. 'I suppose he didn't tell us he was with you that night
because he's married. Is that it?'

She nodded. 'I suppose so. We try to be as discreet as
possible. It's all got so ... ' She hesitated. 'Everyone's so
intolerant about staff–student relationships. Even though I'm
not an undergraduate. And scandals don't help careers. He
didn't want to hurt his wife, either,' she added as an after-
thought.

'Mrs Beardsley did tell us that he wasn't home that night,
which made things potentially more difficult for him,' Simon
said. 'Where is it you live, Laura?'

'Elm Avenue. Only there aren't any elms now. In a basement flat, number 39.'

Simon looked across at Longman, trying to remember
where that might be.

'Elm Avenue runs north off Acacia Road, sir,' Longman
said significantly.

'What time did Dr Beardsley get to you last Tuesday night,
Laura?'

'It was about quarter to eight.'

'Are you sure of the exact time?'

'I've thought about it and that's as near as I can get. I didn't
think about it at the time, there was no reason.'

'You can be more precise about the time if you're able to
Laura. We're not trying to trap Dr Beardsley.'

She raised her pointed chin defiantly. 'I'm telling you the
truth!'

'He didn't say anything to you afterwards about what had
happened? Anything about Emily?'

'Well, of course he did, when we heard what had happened.
He'd known her from Hyde Books.'

'Nothing else? He didn't say that he had heard from her
over the Christmas vacation?'

'No.' She sounded less confident.

'The newspaper allegations about drug use,' Simon said,
'do you know anything about that?'

She was dismissive 'He probably used now and again. Most
people do, don't they?'

Simon didn't answer, but kept his eyes on her face.

The lovely flush appeared in her cheeks again. 'I don't, in fact, Chief Inspector. So he didn't take anything in my company.'

'Very wise of you,' Simon said. 'Is there anything else that you can tell me?'

'I don't think so.' She began to zip up her jacket.

Simon thanked her for coming in.

She turned back in the doorway, a look of appeal on her absurdly youthful face. 'You will let me know if you hear anything, won't you? That's one of the worst things about being a mistress, it's always the wife that's kept informed, gets to be by the bedside.'

'We'll let you know if we have anything definite,' Simon assured her. She left, as quietly self-contained as she had arrived.

'Well, well,' Longman said, coming to sit in the chair that the girl had vacated. 'Maybe Beardsley did see something that night. Elm Avenue is at the other end of Acacia Road to North Road. Beardsley would have driven along there to see his girl-friend that night.'

'He could have called into Emily's place en route,' Simon said.

'But why? And he wouldn't have had much time to do anything, if he arrived at Laura's at quarter to eight.'

'*If* he did.'

Longman folded his arms. 'So why has Beardsley disappeared? Is he guilty? Or has he been got at, because of something he knows? Seeing Dawson in Acacia Road that night, on his way to kill Emily, would be one good reason for getting rid of him. Why don't we go and talk to Dawson?'

'I told you – I want a search made at the same time. The warrant's in hand. I don't want to put the wind up him now, give him the chance to clean everything out.'

Since Bradley was huffing and puffing his way around a golf course that day, Simon had spoken to Chief Superintendent Williams about the need to conduct a thorough search of the Dawson household. The discovery of drugs in Beardsley's room had made a considerable difference to his cause, but the powers that be were still nervous of causing unnecessary offence to such a distinguished member of the university. 'Does it follow,

209

Simon, that Dawson's in possession, too?'

Simon had given him several reasons why that might be the case, adding that Dawson had also been the last person, as far as they knew, to have seen the missing Beardsley. Not entirely hopeful, he had left the warrant in Williams's hands. Meanwhile, Simon seemed to have come to an impasse, so he got on with some overdue reports.

Later, as he stood at his window and watched the early-evening gloom settle over the city, the orange streetlights pricking out the arterial roads, Monkton came into the room. They had found Beardsley's car down by the river.

Chapter Twenty-Five

Beardsley's blue Vauxhall Cavalier was in the car park near the old Water Mill restaurant. Between the car park and the mill was the approach to the narrow footbridge which crossed the river just above the weir, half a mile downstream from Lovers' Bridge. It had stopped raining, but there was a heavy mist, aureoles forming around the orange streetlamps. The recent rains had swollen the river and now it swirled blackly before falling in a roar over the weir. In summer, with water lilies just above the bridge, with coots and swans, it was a charming scene and a favourite place for walkers. In midwinter now, and at night, it felt sinister, the blackness of the water a bottomless pit.

The uniformed police officers who had discovered the car were waiting, along with Longman and Rodgers, who had got there just before him, for Simon's arrival.

'It's locked, sir,' Longman volunteered.

'Any clues to how long it's been here?'

Longman glanced towards the restaurant, its striped awning in darkness. 'I thought that would be a good place to ask if anyone had noticed the car. But it seems they don't open on Sundays.'

Simon turned to Monkton, taciturn at his side. 'See if you can locate the owners. We'll have to do some kind of a search along the river, I suppose. But with the darkness and all that flood water swirling around, I think we'd better wait till morning and get a proper search together.'

'But if he's in the river, he may be lodged somewhere near and swept away by morning. Hadn't we better take a quick

211

look now?' Monkton was, as always, impatient.

He had a point. It was better to check and if Monkton was that keen, then he could organise it.

'All right. You get a team together and I'll try and track down the restaurant owner.' Simon looked round at the larger group of police officers. 'Anyone know the name of the people at the restaurant?'

Rodgers said, 'They live above it, sir, so you shouldn't have far to look. Can't remember their names, though. It's a man and wife – at least it was, last time I ate there.'

As the car was being taken away for examination, Simon set off the short distance to the mill, reflecting that he would look – in Monkton's terminology – a right prat if Beardsley came strolling back from an evening walk along the riverbank. Highly unlikely, though, in mid-January and in this weather.

He had to wait some time after ringing the doorbell before there was any response. He could see no lights anywhere in the building and had begun to turn away when a light showed through the inner hallway door and a rattling of keys indicated that the door was being unlocked.

'Yes? You do realise we're closed tonight?' The man didn't bother to disguise his annoyance at being disturbed.

Simon held up his identification and introduced himself. 'You're Brian Godwin?' The proprietor's nameplate hung over the door.

Godwin nodded. He was dressed only in a towelling robe, its belt tied insecurely beneath a straining gut, and his feet were bare. He shivered and looked out at the night. 'You'd better come in. I'm not hanging about here.'

Simon followed him inside and up the stairs, reflecting, not for the first time, on the misanthropic manners peculiar to many of the restaurateurs and publicans of his acquaintance.

They went up a further carpeted flight of stairs and Godwin led him into a comfortably furnished and softly lit room. The windows were uncurtained and wide, showing the lights of the city ringroad to the southwest and, in daytime, probably an impressive view of the river and the distant Welsh hills.

There was a blonde woman, in comparable deshabille, lounging on a large sofa. Godwin perfunctorily introduced her as his wife and mumbled something to her about police before

212

going over to a drinks table and topping up a whisky glass. The woman swung a pair of plump, naked legs to the floor and gazed with interest at Simon.

'So what's it about?' Godwin asked, sitting beside his wife and putting an arm round her satin shoulders.

Simon explained about the car in the nearby car park and asked if either of them might have noticed it there earlier, or the previous day. 'The car park your customers use,' he added.

Godwin grunted. 'You're asking a bit. As you can see, we don't look in that direction from where we live up here.'

'I can see that, but perhaps when you were seeing your customers out last night?'

'What d'you think, Judy?' The man glanced at his wife. 'Can't remember anything much about last night meself. Had some mates in, so I wasn't entirely *compos mentis*, if you know what I mean.'

Judy appeared to be considering the matter. 'Yeah, I think there was a car when Mike and Steve left. I waved them off and there was only one car left there. I remember wondering if we'd still got a customer on the premises.'

Simon, who hadn't been invited to sit down, wandered over to the window and looked down towards the river. He could see torchlights waving on both banks, their beams directed mainly at the river's edge. They hadn't wasted any time getting started.

'Could you describe the car, Mrs Godwin?'

She giggled nervously. 'Well, it was shiny and dark. I couldn't tell you much else.'

'Whereabouts in the car park was it?'

'Oh, over near the riverside. Near the footpath exit.'

Where Beardsley's car now was. Simon supposed that customers from the previous night might also remember seeing it, but it hardly seemed worth the trouble trying to trace them.

'What size car?' he asked.

She looked at him blankly. 'Not as big as ours. Not a small car, though. Family-saloon type, I suppose. Don't know much about cars.'

'This got something to do with the murder case in the city?' Godwin asked. 'Only you don't usually get detective chief

213

inspectors out looking for stolen cars on a Sunday night.'

Simon didn't answer. 'Nice view you've got here, Mr Godwin. So did either of you notice any visitors to the car park earlier on yesterday? Perhaps people taking a walk along the riverbank?'

'In that weather? You've got to be joking,' Godwin said. 'No. We're busy on a Saturday.'

Given confirmation that the car had been there overnight, Simon wanted to know just how long altogether it had been there.

'Would perhaps any of your Saturday-lunchtime customers have noticed the car earlier in the day? Do you know any of them personally?'

'Sal came in,' Judy said to her husband. 'She was on her own. I sat down with her for a bit. She might remember. We weren't actually that busy, it being such a nasty day. I can give you her number if you like,' she said to Simon.

She unwound her legs and went over to a mahogany desk at the far side of the room. After rooting around in a capacious handbag, she scribbled something down and handed it to Simon.

He thanked them both and Godwin saw him back to the door, locking up again after him with much jangling of keys.

Longman was in the car park watching preparations being made to tow away the blue Cavalier. The mist had turned to drizzle and it was miserably cold after the cosy warmth of the Godwins' sitting room.

'I doubt they'll find anything in this darkness,' Simon said to Longman. 'And they'll probably trample to nothing any useful evidence, even if they do.'

Longman nodded towards the nearby footbridge. It was badly lit, slippery and precarious in the dark. 'That's the most likely place he'd go in.'

'Depending on whether he jumped or was pushed.'

'Either way.'

'I've got a phone call to make. And I'm doing it from my office,' Simon said. 'Monkton can take care of things here.' He was still wondering how to approach the question of the leaks to the press with the inspector.

Longman crossed the bridge to speak to Monkton on the

214

other side of the bridge and Simon watched the flat-footed caution with which the sergeant stepped, careful to grasp the chain hand support, before being swallowed by the gloom on the far side. It was a very easy place to lose one's footing, Simon thought.

Back at headquarters he found a handwritten note from Inspector Perfect on his desk. Edwards had confessed to being responsible for the attack on Gary Wyman. 'Seems to think he'll get the sympathy of the court,' Perfect had added. The sympathy of the tabloid press and the public, anyway, Simon thought. None of the group had apparently seen anything suspicious, apart from Gary Wyman, that Tuesday evening. They had begun their patrol at around half past six that night and knocked off as soon as they had scored a hit.

Simon passed the note to Longman.

'Oh, well, at least you've solved one case, sir,' he said cheerfully. 'Maybe you're on a roll.'

'I wish I felt that optimistic.' Simon picked up the phone to ring Sal.

'Yes, that's right,' she said. 'I went there about one yesterday, I suppose, for a bit of lunch.'

No, the car park had been quite empty when she arrived and there was no blue Cavalier there when she came out, either, maybe a couple of hours later.

If it had been a coin-meter car park, Simon thought, she might have remembered exactly when she had gone back to her car. He thanked her and rang off.

'So Beardsley didn't arrive until Saturday lateish afternoon at the earliest,' Longman said.

'So where was he meanwhile? Where did he go on Friday night, after quarrelling with Dawson? And was he still there on Saturday, when his car arrived in the riverside car park?'

'Are you suggesting that someone else may have driven the car there?'

'It's possible.' Simon tapped a pencil nervously on the edge of his desk.

'To make us think he's in the river, and perhaps waste time looking in the wrong place? Maybe he met someone there.'

Simon pushed back his chair and went over to the window.

215

'There are too many unanswered questions altogether,' he said irritably.

'Like who's leaking stuff to the press?'

'Has Monkton got a woman friend?' Simon glanced over his shoulder at the sergeant.

'I don't know. He's a bit bitter about women since his divorce. You don't think he's making trouble, do you?'

'It's possible. But don't let the speculation go any further.'

Longman nodded thoughtfully at Simon's back.

'I have wondered if it might be Hermione Roe. It's more likely, I suppose.' Simon was speaking almost to himself, Longman straining to hear.

'Why should she do that?'

Simon felt he was being humoured. He turned around, leaning on the windowsill. 'A mixture of things, really. I just get the feeling that I'm being manipulated in some way. The psychic, for a start – some of the things she said pointed so obviously to Dawson, and the reference to drugs ... Then the two leaks to the papers, both of them damaging to Dawson and to Beardsley, and again the hint about drugs being involved.'

'You don't think Dr Roe's got anything to do with Emily's death, do you?'

Simon paused. 'I don't know. I can't think of any reason she would have to want to hurt Emily. It was just something Jessie said about Hermione's job being on the line if Dawson becomes professor of the department. He's not supportive of the work she's doing, apparently.'

'So you think she may be helping the case along by encouraging you to go for Dawson as the main suspect?'

Simon shrugged.

Longman looked sceptical. 'A bit extreme, isn't it?'

'Not if she felt there was some justification anyway.'

'You mean she believes one or the other of them is guilty, and is just helping the police in a roundabout way?'

Simon sighed. 'Something like that. I don't know.'

'Why not just tell you directly?'

'If it's only suspicion, it could backfire.'

'And you think she primed the psychic?'

'I think it's possible,' Simon said.

216

'Does this affect your ideas about Dawson being the one who attacked Emily?'

Simon went to his desk and sat down again. 'Not really. I'm just not feeling comfortable about things. And there are so many other questions in the case that are still open,' he said irritably.

Longman settled back in his chair. 'Such as?'

'That letter, for a start. The letter that Emily sent to Dawson, that Dawson says he never received.'

'Well, he would, wouldn't he?'

'But he admitted she phoned him. And why did Emily change the meeting place? Why go out on a dark night to meet him in a lonely place, when she could have met him in her bedsitter?'

'You've only Dawson's word for it that she did change the meeting place.'

'So why admit it at all? He didn't have to tell me he'd gone to meet her. And why did she move to that awful little bedsitter? There are other places to rent, less grim than that.'

'Just a temporary measure, probably.'

Simon pulled at his chin and made no comment. 'Then there's this business of Emily reading up on the accident. Have we got things all wrong? Maybe she was trying to track down the other woman in the accident, the one who made Charlotte swerve the car.'

'The ginger-haired woman she was talking to in the café, perhaps?' Longman's head jerked up. 'Didn't Sybil say something about a woman being involved?'

Now it was Simon who looked sceptical. He shook his head.

'Anything else, then?' the sergeant asked.

'They're all little things, nothing in themselves. Just a feeling of things being out of key, somehow. Like, why didn't Harwood mention the fact that he suspected Emily was on drugs when I went to talk to him in London? It's his job, for God's sake, so why not say at the time?'

'He forgot. People do.'

'Perfectly possible,' Simon said sourly. 'And how did Emily get out to the hospital? They've checked there are no buses from Westwich that would take her there, and they haven't found any taxi service or hire car that took her. So who gave her a lift?'

Longman compressed his lips.

Simon threw the pencil across his desk. 'I know. They're not terribly important questions in themselves. They're just making me uneasy.'

'So when are we going to talk to Dawson?' Longman said.

Simon looked at him blankly for a moment, then said, 'Tomorrow morning early, if everything's in order. We'll do the search and bring him in for questioning.'

'If we find drugs.'

Simon nodded, his thoughts still elsewhere.

Chapter Twenty-Six

The search for Beardsley would resume again at first light, but it was still dark when they left headquarters next morning for Dawson's house. The early hour was not designed to intimidate, only to ensure that the household's inhabitants were all present. Simon, his thoughts on the child, wanted their entrance to be as low-key as possible in the circumstances. The satisfaction he might have anticipated in treating Dawson to search and questioning was muted. Simon no longer felt sure that Dawson had caused Emily Sanderson's death, though he was still convinced that the don was involved in it somehow.

For now, he focused on the drugs issue, serious enough to warrant this degree of investigation, particularly with someone in Dawson's position with influence over young and impressionable minds. His main anxiety was that the publicity linking Beardsley's name to drugs would have prompted Dawson to dispose of any incriminating evidence.

Simon's concern about drugs had deepened since the day before. He had at last heard from his sister Rose, who had phoned him from the States the previous night. She was coming home, she said. She had to get out of it.

'Of what, Rose?' he had encouraged her.

'Drugs, Chris. It's too easy, too much a way of life where I'm at.'

He tried to get her to talk about her experiences, but she obviously wasn't going to do so on the phone, anyway. All she said was 'Some people cope with it. They have the ability to sustain an outward kind of life. Not me, I've learned that now. Gus can do it. He paints like mad and then flakes out. Not me,' she said again. She asked if he could have her to stay for a while. 'Don't tell Mum yet. I need to recover somehow.'

With a greater willingness than he felt, he had agreed to that. How could he refuse? But quite what he would have to deal with when she arrived, and how he would cope with it, he had no idea, only an anxious foreboding that he might not fulfil whatever her needs were.

He thought of Jessie, who would probably know what was needed. When this case was over, he promised himself, he would take his leave no matter what, and he would go and stay with Jessie, if she would have him, and Rose could have his flat to herself, if she was well enough to be alone. And if Jessie really did not want to marry him, he would accept whatever she did offer.

The streets were shiny and black with the fine rain that was falling. He had been driving on automatic pilot, Longman untypically silent beside him, and Rhiannon and Watkins, equally morose at the early start, in the back seat. The drug team was following behind.

He pulled into the Dawson's drive behind their two cars. There was a faint light showing in one of the upstairs rooms, a night light, he thought, for the child sleeping there. Considering that presence, he told Monkton and the others to wait in the car and went with Rhiannon at his side to rouse Dawson.

The man answered the door without much delay. There was a twitch of curtains above and then the muffled sound of moving feet on the stairs. Dawson appeared, tousled from sleep, with glasses on the end of his aquiline nose. Simon had never seen him wearing them before. He showed Dawson the search warrant. Surprisingly, there was no protest. Dawson silently stood back to let them enter.

'We'll do this with as little fuss as possible, if you'll cooperate, Dr Dawson,' Simon said.

'I don't want my son disturbed,' Dawson emphasised. 'You lot will terrify the life out of him.'

'Perhaps you should wake your wife,' Simon suggested, and indicated to Rhiannon to follow Dawson back up the stairs. Dawson paused there as he realised he was being followed, and cast Simon a look of contempt. Simon went

220

outside to call in the others.

While they searched the house, Dawson sat in the kitchen drinking endless cups of coffee and smoking cigarettes. His wife stayed in their son's bedroom. She had not spoken to Simon, had merely, like her husband, given him a look of scorn as she carried bedclothes to her son's room.

The search was thorough and included the kitchen and its contents, so that Dawson was forced to remove himself. Simon had searched Dawson's desk and study, hopeful of finding, if not drugs, at least some communication from Emily Sanderson.

The grey light of the day was probably as bright as it was going to be that day when they gathered in the study to admit they had none of them found anything incriminating.

'We'll check outside, sir,' one of the team said. Dawson handed over keys to the two sheds with a supercilious smile. He had taken a shower and dressed as soon as that was allowed, and then sat reading a book with a bland look of unconcern.

Simon, who had been expecting a barrage of verbal attack, preferred this mode of protest and steered clear of him. But when it became clear they had drawn a blank, he went to speak to Dawson.

'You might care to remove your wife and son to your bedroom, Dr Dawson, so that we can complete our search in his room.'

For the first time Dawson's poise faltered. Simon noticed with interest, even some sympathy, that the skin over his cheekbones whitened. 'You're not serious? If you are, I protest. Most strongly.'

Simon shrugged. 'You'll probably need your solicitor anyway when we've finished here.'

'Right.' Dawson reached for the phone.

'After you've spoken to your wife, if you wouldn't mind.'

Dawson hesitated, then made for the stairs, appearing for once resigned rather than resistant. He was too intelligent not to know when the time for protest was over.

Simon again sent Rhiannon to follow Dawson and heard the high, querulous notes of a child, accompanied by low, soothing voices. There was hardly ever a time when Simon could not find it in him to regret human frailties – including his own – and the damage they inflicted on all around them.

They found drugs, some the same as they had found at Beardsley's house, and larger quantities of other substances, stuffed into the pillow on his son's bed. The act of concealing them there had a taint about it that made Simon's task easier when it came to arresting Dawson and taking him in.

Simon was on his way out to his car when the call came that Beardsley had been found, his body caught on the branch of a willow tree nearly a mile downstream from the footbridge and the mill. He was already on the way to Havers for examination.

Simon rang to pathologist after he got back to headquarters.

'All I can make any comment on,' Havers said, 'without looking into him properly, is that he has marks on his face which may have been made when he went into the water and before he drowned. So if you're wondering, as I'm sure you are, whether it was suicide or murder, I'm afraid I can't help you. I'll let you know when I'm ready to look at him properly.'

'Can you give me any estimate of time of death?'

'A day or so ago. Not long. But you know I can't—'

'Two days?'

Havers sighed loudly into the phone. 'Probably not that much, but at least twenty-four hours.'

This suggested that Beardsley had driven the car to the river himself.

'What's he wearing?'

'So you haven't seen him yet? I thought you were in charge of the case?'

Simon forbore rising to the implication that he had been lolling in bed until now. Havers liked to bait people. It livened up an otherwise deadly occupation. 'His clothes?'

'Jacket, shirt, trousers and the usual undergarments. Had you some suspicion he was a transvestite, perhaps?'

'Just wondered if he was wearing an overcoat.' On such a cold night, if he had intended being out of his car for more than a few moments, he would have worn something more substantial than a jacket.

'Why didn't you say so? No, just a lightweight cord jacket.'

Simon arranged for Kathleen Beardsley to be notified and remembered to send someone to see Laura Stacey as well.

Dawson's solicitor had turned up and was waiting with his client and with Longman in attendance in the stark little interview room.

After some preliminaries, Simon switched on the tape recorder and spoke the date, time and names of those present.

'You have been arrested for possession of listed drugs and on suspicion of supplying the same, Dr Dawson. Will you tell me to whom you have supplied drugs?'

Dawson looked haggard. 'I haven't supplied drugs,' he said.

'We found a similar supply in Dr Beardsley's house. Was it he who supplied you, then?' Simon's voice was injected with disbelief.

'No comment,' Dawson said, glancing at his solicitor, who had shifted suddenly in his seat.

The solicitor was elderly and had gravitas. He was from one of the older-established firms in the city. While it was a pleasant change not to be faced with one of the more abrasive types from the younger school of legal representatives, Simon was aware that Charles Seedman would not miss any advantage for his client. The two had had a short time alone together and either Seedman or Dawson had decided that the silence to which Dawson had right was not going to be the most advisable course.

'Who supplied you?'

'I don't know his name. Just a man I meet. In Kings Cross.' Dawson seemed to realise that he might have implicitly answered the former question. 'The same person that Beardsley gets them from.'

'Of course,' Simon nodded. 'We realise that you would both have to travel a considerable distance, there being such a shortage of sources in Westwich.'

Dawson made no response to the sarcasm.

Simon felt a surge of anger. 'Did you know the student Peter Rudley, who died of an overdose in Westwich last week, Dr Dawson?' Even Simon thought it was unlikely, but he aimed to gain a moral point by linking Dawson's name to one of the victims of drug abuse.

'I'd never heard of him until his death was reported,' Dawson said. 'And never met him as far as I'm aware.'

There was little hope that Simon would get any admission from Dawson on the extent of his own use and the supply of harmful substances to those with whom he came into contact, whether or not they had included Peter Rudley. Such evidence would have to be obtained by other means. Even with what the police had now, there was irreparable damage done to Dawson's career, especially with the added likelihood that he had supplied to students in his care. Simon was determined to pass on all relevant information to Detective Inspector Odell in the drug squad. He would go and have a talk with him when all this was over.

'What were you arguing about with Dr Beardsley on Friday night?'

Dawson didn't answer, glancing again at his solicitor.

'Dr Beardsley was found dead this morning.' Simon watched for any discernible reaction.

Dawson stared at Simon and swallowed.

'You are the last person to have been seen with him. You followed him from the university theatre bar after he left you and after the argument.'

'Spies everywhere.' Dawson made an attempt at a sneer.

'You don't seem surprised at his death.'

'Of course I'm surprised. Who can behave normally in these circumstances? But I've got nothing to do with it. How did he die, anyway?'

'Where were you from the time you left the bar following Dr Beardsley on Friday night until Saturday evening?'

'I went home to my wife.We spent the whole of Saturday together with our son. We went shopping, otherwise we were at home together.'

'Did you supply drugs to Emily Sanderson as well as Dr Beardsley?'

'No comment,' Dawson said again.

'The argument with Phillip Beardsley, Dr Dawson. You are inevitably under investigation with regard to his death. If you have nothing to do with it, it would be wiser for you to be open with me.'

Now that they were face to face in these official conditions,

Simon felt detached from his earlier animosity towards Dawson. The man had shrunk to the proportions of any other suspect in a case. Simon simply wanted to get at the truth, whatever it was.

'May I have a word with my client alone, do you think?' Seedman asked politely. 'This particular investigation and the reference to the girl were not on the agenda when I was called in by my client.'

Simon nodded, spoke into the tape recorder and switched off. He and Longman went outside for a few minutes.

'Jumping around from one thing to another doesn't seem to be throwing him off much,' Longman commented.

So much was obvious. 'When he's had chance to think a bit, he may decide to cooperate more.'

'Or otherwise.' Longman looked pessimistic.

When they began the interview again, it appeared that the solicitor had advised Dawson to help the police with their inquiries.

'I suppose there's no reason not to tell you what the argument was about,' Dawson said. 'He thought I should admit to the police what my relationship with Emily really was.'

'Why did he think that?'

Dawson looked contemptuous. 'He was afraid that you'd keep on digging and he'd be drawn into it. The more you asked questions, the more likely it was that you'd find out about the drugs.'

Simon frowned. 'What made Beardsley so concerned?'

Dawson sighed. Doing as his solicitor suggested obviously went against his own inclinations. 'He had a letter from Emily when she was in Wales.'

'More than one, I think,' Simon said.

'Yes. She was pestering him to get me to contact her. I didn't, and she wrote another letter, a last one, in which –' Dawson paused. 'Phillip, the idiot, seemed to think he ought to show you the letters but I told him he was stupid. He should have forgotten about it.'

'The letters mentioned drugs?'

Dawson nodded and felt in his pockets for his cigarettes. 'The last one did.'

'What else did it say, the letter?'

'I don't know exactly.' He paused again while he lit up. 'He wouldn't show it to me. I think he thought I'd take it from him or something.'

'Do you know what bothered Beardsley about it?'

'She threatened something about making use of the drugs, or the fact that we had—' Dawson stopped speaking as if realising he was making yet another admission.

'Had supplied them?'

Dawson examined the end of his cigarette.

'In fact, he thought it gave you a motive for her murder. Which is why he hesitated to hand the letter over.'

'No, it was the mention of drugs. They implicated him as much as me.'

'I don't think so, Dr Dawson. You were the one who was involved with Emily Sanderson. You were the one who got her hooked.'

Dawson again didn't answer.

'The letter mentioned you specifically, did it not? Emily had been trying for some time to contact you to tell you that she was pregnant with your child. And if you try to deny that fact now, you must surely be aware that it will be confirmed as soon as we find her body. Or do you think that we won't find her?'

Dawson took a drag on his cigarette. 'I admit that if Emily was pregnant, it's possible I was the father. I deny absolutely, however, that I have harmed her in any way. I haven't seen her since last term, for God's sake!'

'Encouraging her to use drugs might be construed as harmful, don't you think?'

'You have no proof that she used drugs only after meeting me,' Dawson said, 'but I suppose it's hopeless to point that out. Anyway, for God's sake, it wasn't as if it was anything heavy.'

Was Dawson as naive about drug use as he was pretending? Simon wondered. He doubted it and that increased his contempt. He decided to make a stab in the dark. 'How did you and she use the heroin? Injecting?'

'No,' Dawson said, sounding outraged. 'That's squalid. We smoked it.'

'I suppose without needles it's much easier to get people to

226

share with you. People like Emily who hadn't used before. And you think that's not squalid?'

Dawson looked away.

'So, on Friday night, when you were having this argument with Phillip Beardsley, it was all about his worry that we'd find out about the drugs. Tell me more of what happened that night.'

'There's nothing much to tell.'

'Why should he expect us to find out? Presumably the threat had passed after what happened to Emily?'

'He was right, though, wasn't he? Because you did find out,' Dawson said, as to one of lower intelligence.

'He thought it was you who had attacked her, didn't he? That's why he was in such a hurry to get away from you. Did he see you in Acacia Road that night?'

'No. Because I wasn't there. And it wasn't like that. He didn't go off in some dramatic horror at what he thought I'd done. It was after the argument about whether I should admit to you that I was involved with Emily. We'd been talking about the letter and he suddenly got up and walked off.'

'And you followed him out.'

'Only as far as the car park. He drove off and I went home.'

Simon leaned back in his seat for a moment. 'What about that scarf of yours that we found in her room?'

'I haven't seen that since last term, either,' Dawson said. 'She probably brought it to give back to me.'

There was no way they could prove otherwise, of course. It was merely suggestive. Simon said, 'Would she be likely to be worrying about returning your scarf after the way you'd treated her? When she was pregnant and on drugs?'

Dawson looked bored.

'And you still insist that when she telephoned you she changed the venue of your meeting from her place to the bridge across the river?'

'She didn't *change* it. There was no previous arrangement. I went to meet her by the bridge but she didn't turn up.'

'And unfortunately no one saw you to confirm you were there rather than at her bedsitter.'

Dawson stubbed out his cigarette. 'Not surprisingly. It was a cold, foggy night.'

227

Simon got no further with his questioning of Dawson. The man stuck to his story through an ever-thickening haze of cigarette smoke. At lunchtime Simon arranged for sandwiches to be brought in and went off with Longman for his first food of the day in the canteen.

'So what do you think?' Longman asked as he munched through a plate of ham and eggs.

'I wish I knew who was telling the truth in all this.' Simon swallowed hard on some food 'I mean, just suppose that Dawson is. Now that we've found drugs in his possession he's not likely to be lying about everything. Suppose he didn't hurt Emily and he wasn't responsible for Beardsley's death. What then?'

'You've presumably been thinking about it,' Longman said noncommittally.

Simon paused in his chewing and looked at Longman without seeing him. 'Yes,' he said slowly. 'There was something he said.' He swallowed again. 'What was it? Something that could be taken another way, have a different meaning.'

Longman finished his meal while Simon continued to think, chewing his food ever more slowly.

'What I want to know is, where was Beardsley before his car arrived at the river?' Longman said. 'From what Havers says, he must have driven it there himself. So where was he after he left Dawson, if Dawson really didn't get rid of him? And if Dawson did get rid of him, I'd have thought Beardsley would have been in the river since Friday night rather than twenty-four hours later.'

Simon stared at him. 'Yes,' he said. 'Exactly.' He took a gulp of tea and stood up. 'Charge him,' he said. 'Just with the drugs offence for now. I'll be back later.'

Longman's burgeoning eyebrows shot up as he watched Simon almost run from the canteen.

Chapter Twenty-Seven

Simon stood on a windswept hillside, a railway bridge behind him and the grey ocean below, the small seaside village of Porthgwar huddled under the hill. At his feet was turned brown earth, a bunch of faded flowers and a simply made wooden cross, blown already at an angle by the fierce prevailing wind. The cross was decorated with painted flowers, which would take longer to fade than those others, entwining a simply printed name: 'Emily Harwood'. In smaller print was written, 'She was the last and best. Care for her.'

He stayed there for some time, imbued with the melancholy of the place, until the bitter wind chilled him to a different awareness and he returned to his car. His phone was bleeping, he could hear it from some yards away, an alien sound in this bleak graveyard high above the sea.

'Yes,' he said, 'I'm on my way, tell him. And make arrangements, will you, to bring in Miss Sanderson for questioning.'

He switched off Longman's exclamations and questions. Bradley could wait until he returned.

It had not taken him long after he had arrived in this part of Wales to locate the local newspaper offices and find the report on the death of a young woman staying here in a holiday cottage for the Christmas period with her sister for company. It was tragic, sudden, unexpected, but there were few details.

'Yes,' the young man in the office had said when Simon was having the report photocopied, 'someone else was in enquiring on Saturday morning.' He had not asked for a photocopy, though.

A call on the coroner had been more fruitful. Simon took notes of the information supplied by the sister. Details had been sent on to the young woman's GP in London. Everything was in order, the inquest carried out quite soon after the death. What was the problem? Why were the police now making inquiries?

Now, after leaving the graveyard, Simon paid a courtesy call to the local police station. He would keep them informed.

The drive back to Westwich, motorway most of the way, passed quickly, his thoughts all centred on what had happened and how. There was relief that it was all almost over but there was no satisfaction to be found in any of it. When was there ever, really, in a murder case? And who could say whether the punishment could ever fairly fit the crime? Who could ultimately pass judgement other than a higher authority than mere mankind?

Chapter Twenty-Eight

She was brought into headquarters not long after Simon had returned. He wanted the chance to speak to her alone before they began the official interview. He wanted the whole story and believed that she would more willingly tell it to just him alone. The delay before the taped interview would give her a chance to consider her official story, too, though he was still uncertain that it was right to give her that opportunity. Bradley, subdued by the fact that Simon seemed to have solved the case, made no objections, even going so far as to say that all that fuss over the newspapers causing trouble hadn't really been necessary, not now they knew what had been going on. It was a fairly typical backhanded apology coming from that source.

Longman was still smarting from having been left out of the trip to Wales. 'You might have told me,' he protested.

'I wasn't that sure,' Simon said. 'Really I wasn't,' he added at Longman's disbelieving expression. 'It just felt as if the fog might be clearing. It was only when I was actually on my way that I could see how it had all happened.'

He offended Longman further by his insistence on speaking to Charlotte alone.

Simon had her brought into his office, where he had talked to her before under such different circumstances. When she had seated herself, watchful and still, and looked back at him with that same luminous blue stare, he could not find it in himself to condemn her. It was her rage that had transformed love into a dark force. He thought he understood, but he still needed her to tell him the how and why of it, to confirm that understanding.

'You know why we've brought you in?' he began.

'Why don't you tell me?' she said quietly.

'We found Beardsley's body this morning.' It seemed much longer ago.

'I'm sorry,' she said conventionally.

'I know, Charlotte. I know what you've done. Why didn't you just tell me? Leave it to the law to pass judgement?'

She made a scornful exclamation. 'What would the police have done? Busted him for possession, if that. That man killed my sister, as surely as if he had stabbed her to death. And not just with the drugs he foisted on her. With the use he made of her, and the way he threw her away after he made her pregnant.'

'Not Beardsley, though.'

'No? He was involved. It was his own fault that he died. If he had left it all to me, he might still be alive now.'

'What happened?' From the chill in her voice Simon could tell that the warmth she had shown towards him was a pretence like all the rest. Yet he still found himself being gentle with her, as with any wounded creature.

'Beardsley? He went to where we stayed in Wales and found out what had happened, as you no doubt already know, if you've worked it all out. He telephoned me from there, told me he knew what I'd done, said he was going to the police.'

She got out her cigarettes and took her time over lighting one. 'I begged him to speak to me first, to let me explain. In the end he said that he'd meet me in Westwich when he got back from Wales, by the mill footbridge at six o'clock.'

She blew a stream of cigarette smoke. 'Then I got the call from your inspector about identifying a body. It was a bit of a shock. But I realised that if I went in my own car I'd just make it to Westwich in time to meet him.'

'You followed me back up the motorway,' Simon said. He found the thought disturbing.

She nodded.

'You obviously did get there in time.'

'Yes. But when I met him, he wouldn't listen. It wasn't enough that he'd found me out, that he could mock me and my efforts at some kind of justice. He attacked Emily, said she was just another feckless girl who couldn't look after herself

... ' Her voice was tight with renewed anger at the memory.

'I tried to tell him that it was Dawson I wanted to see pay for what had happened, but he kept on about the drugs. I asked him to just leave it to me, I just wanted Dawson punished for her death and there needn't be any mention of drugs, and that Beardsley didn't have to be dragged into it.' She drew deeply on her cigarette and her hand trembled slightly.

'But he wouldn't go along with it?'

Charlotte shook her head. She must have been totally obsessed not to have realised that he never could have done so. He was bound to be dragged in, whatever happened. But perhaps she had just said whatever served her, and been glad to send him to his death as a proxy for Dawson. Simon's ready sympathy wavered and he felt himself withdraw to a more cautious and objective distance.

Charlotte glanced at him. 'Then he started going on again about Emily. He said a lot of things that I won't repeat.'

'How did you get him on the bridge? You did push him from the bridge?'

She nodded, her mouth tight. 'It wasn't difficult. I decided, once I could see he wouldn't listen, to just let him talk, pretending that I was in the wrong. I let him lecture me, and I kept walking slowly. He was so absorbed in justifying his dear friend Dawson and himself, he didn't notice where we were. When we were in the centre of the bridge, I turned on him. I told him just what I thought about him and his friend Dawson. It took him by surprise. I hit him in the face and the bridge was slippery. He went over backwards, fell on the stone slope of the weir and disappeared. It wasn't very likely he'd survive. There was a lot of water.' Her eyes were blank and cold. There was no emotion, just the memory of something done that had to be done.

She could not disclaim the guilt for Beardsley's death, for it was a kind of victory for her, a last, satisfactory part of her campaign. But, Simon thought, he must make sure she had a legal representative to talk to before she came to her official interview.

'You didn't plan to kill Beardsley that night, then?'

Her eyes focused on him again. 'I thought it would probably

233

come to that. I didn't think it was really possible that he would just keep quiet. When it came to it, I was glad to kill him because I thought that if you decided it must have been Dawson who killed Emily, you would get him for Beardsley too. Especially for Beardsley, since you didn't have Emily's body.'

It could so very easily have turned out that way, as Simon was acutely aware.

'What happened to the letter he had from Emily? The one that he didn't understand at first.'

'In which she was threatening to kill herself, using the drugs Dawson had given her,' Charlotte finished for him. 'He told me all about it. I didn't know she'd written it. That's what he was going on about, how weak she was, that it was her own responsibility. He had it in his hand when he went over.' She seemed to retreat into the memory again.

'But really it was Dawson that you wanted, wasn't it?' Simon said.

'I wish it had been him that night, not his little pal,' she said coldly. 'Perhaps not, though.' She looked into Simon's eyes, but wasn't seeing him. 'No, what I wanted for Dawson was what would hurt the most – the loss of status, the humiliation and, if it was possible, finally the conviction for her murder. It might have happened, mightn't it?' she asked Simon. 'You might have got him convicted?'

'It was a possibility,' he agreed. He wondered if she was aware just how close she had come to manipulating him into thinking so. She could have no idea, though, how his own jealous prejudices against Dawson had so readily partnered her own darker vengeance. 'So tell me. Tell me what happened to your sister.'

'You know already, don't you?' she said coldly.

'I only know some of the facts. I don't know what it was like.'

'No. How could you know?' She stubbed out her cigarette and lit another. 'All right, I'll tell you. She was in a terrible state, very depressed, desperately trying to get hold of Dawson. One minute trying to convince herself that it would all work out and the next in a state of hopeless despair. The night it happened she was OK, I thought. She seemed to have decided that she could sort it all out with him when she got back at the beginning of this term. She'd calmed down. We went to bed.'

Her voice caught and she swallowed. 'I didn't know. I didn't know she'd got that stuff with her. I should have known.' She stopped, blinking back tears.

'Did you know, then, that she had been taking drugs?'

Charlotte produced a handkerchief, nodding. 'Yes, she told me. Only because she became so fearful about the baby, that the baby would be damaged. That's why it didn't occur to me that she had any with her, or that she would do what she did.' She wiped her eyes and blew her nose, her face blotchy and tired.

Simon's wariness was overtaken by a desire to put his arms around her. Her aloneness was tangible.

'It's how she got pregnant. She didn't know what she was doing a lot of the time. She forgot to take the pill.'

'She was living with you still, at the time, in London,' Simon said. It was not an accusation, just a realisation.

'It didn't occur to me that she was taking drugs. There wasn't really anything in her behaviour. Not really different,' she added uncertainly.

Her watchful companions at Seymour Road hadn't had any suspicions either, or they would have been sure to say so. Emily had been, in some ways, a very controlled person. It was one of the things that had made her life so hard to interpret.

'And you knew earlier on that she was pregnant, didn't you?'

She nodded. 'I couldn't tell you all these things.'

At the moment he felt too confused to remember quite what was true and what wasn't, she had rewritten the tale so thoroughly.

'Go on,' he said.

'I got the whole story out of her, of how she began using with Dawson when they were first together in London.' Charlotte rubbed her nose with the screwed-up handkerchief. 'It wasn't that she was an addict,' she appealed to Simon. 'She didn't inject or anything.'

Was this a wisdom received from Dawson? Simon

235

wondered. It occurred to him that, if she had come off heroin during the Christmas vacation, it would have made her more susceptible to overdosing.

Charlotte's voice hardened again. 'It was his rejection of her that drove her to suicide. He was the cause and he handed her the instrument.' She took a deep breath and got up, going over to the window to look out on the darkness.

Simon watched her reflection for some moments. 'You found her in the morning, then?'

She spoke in a dull tone, without turning round. 'She was cold. She'd made sure. The doctor said she must have done it soon after she went to her room the night before. A deliberate overdose of heroin along with whisky to make sure. It was my drink, whisky.' Her voice broke. 'She hated it. She must have got up and gone into the sitting room after I'd gone to bed, and taken the bottle.'

She paused and Simon watched her reflection compose her features.

'I was in a state of shock when I found her, blaming myself terribly for not having looked after her properly. I just sat there in her room for a long, long time – I don't know how long – looking at her, knowing I'd never talk with her, be with her, comfort her again.' She turned to face Simon, the tears shining on her face. 'And then, as I sat there, I decided that I would make him pay for it somehow.'

'You planned it all then?'

'Not really. Not in detail. When I sent for the doctor, I gave him my married name and he assumed it was Emily's surname too. That gave me the idea of trying to keep it secret somehow.' She looked down at her left hand and rubbed the ringless third finger absently, speaking slowly, as if trying to recall just what had happened while she was still in that state of shock. 'There was another doctor.' She looked at Simon, concentrating. 'There had to be two to sign the death certificate. It was afterwards, after they'd taken her body away, that I thought of what I could do, how I could get Dawson for what had happened.'

'Weren't you afraid it would all come out with the official documentation?'

'Not really,' she said simply. 'These things can take ages to

236

go through the system. I remember how it was after the accident. The only real connection that can be made is through the information being passed to the dead person's GP. I gave a false name for her doctor and gave his address as Oliver's clinic. I asked his receptionist to pass it on to me when it arrived, told her a friend just wanted a postal address temporarily. It still hasn't come through. They'd never have found out. They'd got their inquest and the body buried. It was all over as far as they were concerned. They'd never connect it with a missing student in Westwich.'

Simon remembered that, among the reports of sightings of Emily, there had been at least one from that area of Wales – disregarded, since they had been trying to track her movements in Westwich itself a week later. And, after all, they had known she had been in Wales. It had not occurred to him that the caller might have had anything different to add. One, maybe two, among many calls from around the country.

'You didn't think anyone would recognise Emily's photograph, anyone who had been involved in the inquest in Wales?' Simon asked.

Charlotte shrugged. 'Not many saw her after her death. And people look different when they're dead. She looked peaceful. I was glad about that.' She swallowed, her mouth pulled tightly, resisting the image. She cleared her throat. 'Nobody knew us, really.' She managed a taut smile at Simon. 'But I did give you a not too clear picture of her, just in case. And you, of course, got a better one from the university. I didn't think of that.'

'I might have asked you for a clearer one,' Simon said.

'But you were so careful, so gentle, weren't you? Did all you could to disturb me as little as possible.' She said it softly, robbing the words of any mockery.

There was a moment's silence while Simon avoided her gaze. Then he said, 'The inquest was held quite quickly. What if it had been delayed?'

She shrugged. 'It wouldn't have made any difference. As I said, there was nothing to connect her with the missing student.'

'And you carried it all out yourself and told no one?' He still found it hard to believe that she could have sustained such a fiction alone.

237

'It was easier that way. Mark had lost her anyway. His distress was no different from what he would have felt if he had known what really happened. Maybe not even so bad in some ways. Perhaps I would have told him one day.'

'So when people tried to contact her, when you got back from Wales, you just said she was out?'

Charlotte sat down again. 'I was afraid, I admit, that you would realise that no one who knew her had seen her since before Christmas, except me.'

'And one of the girls she shared the house with. She thought she'd seen Emily, driving off. By the way, you forgot to take Emily's patchwork bedspread with you.'

'It seemed safer to leave it. I wasn't sure whether it was hers. That was a close thing ... I went there well before the beginning of term, thinking there wasn't any chance I'd run into them. It was lucky I'd had to park further down the road. The little dumpy girl was standing by the door, staring at the car as I drove past. She'd probably only seen the back of me getting into the car, and you can't see into cars as clearly as you can see out. She didn't doubt I was Emily, did she? It's the hair, you see. When someone has long blonde hair, that's all they really see. It's easy to buy a convincing wig nowadays. Besides, when I wore it with some make-up to give me more of Emily's colouring, I looked very much like her.'

Conscious of the time, Simon kept the questions coming. 'I suppose you asked the man across the hall for change just to establish that you were there and making a phone call at that time.'

She nodded. 'That's right.'

'You must have left the house in Acacia Road straight after phoning Dawson.'

'Straight away. I kept my car nearby, in a car park. I needed to get back home as quickly as possible. I used a mobile phone on the journey back to make my first phone call at nine o'clock. Then I called from home at half past nine. I got the landlord to call me back, just in case any doubt might arise that I was where I said I was.'

'Why did you change the arrangement and ask Dawson to meet you at the bridge?'

'There was no change. I wrote the letter, knowing you'd

238

find it on the computer, to point you in Dawson's direction and make you think he was at Emily's that night. I didn't print it or send it. I couldn't have him actually coming there. Someone at the house was likely to see him trying to get to see Emily. It was more likely to prove an alibi than the opposite.'

She leaned back in her chair, folding her arms. 'And I phoned him to get him to a place where he wouldn't have an alibi. And, of course, to establish that Emily had phoned him that night.'

'The scarf,' he said. 'That was an added detail.'

'Emily used to take it to bed with her,' she said, anger in her eyes again. 'She said it smelled of him.'

'And the blood in the room?' Though he thought he knew it all now, it seemed important to let her tell her story. If in this way the cathartic process would free her to take greater care for her defence, it was the best that he could do for her now.

'I wasn't so happy about that.' Her eyes seemed to look inwards again, rather than at him. Then she smiled another mirthless smile and glanced at him. 'I didn't want you to find out about Anne. I thought you'd be more likely to guess where the blood had come from when you learned I'd got another sister alive. Alive,' she repeated, her eyes in some distant place again.

After a moment she resumed her story. 'But it was one thing that Anne could do for Emily. I'm sure she wouldn't grudge it. Oh, I didn't hurt her, I'm sure. It's not difficult to draw blood. I've had plenty taken from me. I was ill not long after the accident – some virus.

'There were always syringes lying around at the hospital. No one would be likely to comment on a plaster inside Anne's elbow. People forget to write things up.'

Simon raised his eyebrows. 'You must have used a lot of syringes.'

'Quite a few,' she said matter-of-factly. 'But it doesn't take that much blood to make a very suggestive mess. Blood's thinner than I thought. I made a zigzag on the wall to suggest that an artery might have been cut, and poured some over the edge of the rug to make it seem that most of it was on the rug that the attacker took with him.' She glanced at Simon. 'I had to leave it as late as possible to keep the blood fresh.'

239

It was true that a little blood went a long way, Simon thought. A bad cut while shaving could make it look as though murder had been done. In common with most men, he had a horror of needles, but he felt that his own justifiably stemmed from an experience with a ham-fisted doctor in his youth, who had pierced an artery while attempting to extract a tube of blood. Instead, the stuff had hit the opposite wall and splattered all over it. The doctor had coldly assured him that he had lost only an ounce or two and not to worry. Yet it didn't take a lot of blood to make the police suspicious. They were bound to investigate what looked like an attack.

'Weren't you afraid you'd be disturbed while you were taking the blood from her?' Simon tried to avoid picturing the scene.

Charlotte shrugged. 'I know the hospital's routine. And the layout of the place makes for privacy. Anyway, it didn't take long.'

Simon examined the ceiling, unable to rid himself of the image of Charlotte coolly bleeding her comatose sister. 'We still haven't had the result of the DNA test,' he said.

'But I knew you'd do one. It's standard. You would have wanted a match with a near relative. Otherwise I would have left my own blood there.'

'You've read about procedures in such cases, then?' he said.

'Oh, yes. There are quite a few books now, aren't there, on police procedure and murder methods.'

Simon stretched his cramped legs. He had to believe that she must have suppressed a lot of anguish to do all these things apparently so cold-bloodedly. He said, 'And by disposing of the rug in the river, you could make it seem that much more blood had been spilled.'

'And make you think the body was there. I did that when I got back from the hospital, so that I could go straight back to London as soon as I'd set the scene at Acacia Road. I was a bit worried, I admit, because you wouldn't have a body. But people have been convicted without, haven't they?'

Not many. But it had happened, in not so dissimilar circumstances. 'Forensic reports take a while,' he said. 'We still haven't had the results from the rug, either. When we received

240

them they would have shown insufficient blood, despite the immersion in water.'

'Not necessarily,' she said. 'You still had to investigate. For all you could know, she died after she was removed from the room. Drowned or something. Anyway –' she smiled – 'you got him. He's been fixed, one way or another. He's finished, is Dr Peter Dawson.'

Simon watched her for a moment, the distant smile still on her face, and wondered how much all that had happened had unhinged her. And whether these machinations and deceits might have pushed her further over the edge. There was a kind of awful sanity in her actions, though, in the planning to bring about Dawson's punishment – one way or the other. He shook his wonderings away. Her actions were for the psychologists to interpret, not for him. He was too conscious of the way in which he personally felt betrayed by her.

'Why didn't you identify the body we went to see as Emily?' he asked. 'It would have answered your need for a body.' The fact that she hadn't had been one thing that had made him doubt his ideas when he was on his way to Wales.

Charlotte raised her brows. 'I wasn't that stupid. You might have asked for her dental records or something. Besides, that poor girl probably wasn't pregnant.'

She had been so very wary, despite her apparent shock and distress at the time. 'Why did you avoid telling me what you knew about Dawson and your sister – even the drugs?'

Charlotte had been pacing around the room, pausing sometimes while she spoke. She sat down again now and examined him with a faint smile. 'I was afraid that if I had told you what I knew, that I had plenty of reason to hate Peter Dawson, you'd be more likely to suspect me.' She thought for a moment. 'I did get Oliver to tell you about the drug taking. He didn't know, you see. I just asked him, would he pretend to know, because I didn't feel able to discuss it with the police. It seemed best if it appeared that I was in ignorance about as much as possible, and you found out everything for yourself.'

'Of course,' he agreed, still stunned by the thoroughness of her deceit. 'The newspaper publicity on Dawson and Beardsley must have helped.'

'I got impatient,' she said.

So it had not been Hermione or Monkton. The whole orchestration had been in Charlotte's hands.

'The news about Beardsley I can understand,' he said, bemused. 'I mean, who knew better than you that he'd disappeared? But how did you know I was questioning Dawson that night?'

'I didn't,' she said simply. 'But I knew that you would question him at some point soon. So when I decided to speak to the woman at the *Mirror*, I suggested she put a stringer on to watching him.'

Simon, bemused by all that she was telling him, was struggling to remember all the things he wanted to ask in the time he had left.

'The library,' he said. 'Why were you there, looking up the newspaper reports of the accident?'

She compressed her lips. 'I had to go somewhere. I couldn't stay in that awful little room. I think I had some idea of putting everything behind me after all this was over. I was trying to make myself face it, the accident. I've tried to suppress the memory for so long. Reading about it, I hoped it would seem like just another car accident among the thousands that happen every year.' She gave another twisted smile, as if she recognised that it would all be rehashed in detail when it came to her defence.

'And the woman you were talking to in Copperfield's café?'

Charlotte frowned and looked up at him, puzzled. 'What woman?'

'A ginger-haired woman. She was talking to you, the assistant said.'

'No, I wasn't there. I didn't want to hang around in Westwich. I might have run into someone who thought I was Emily. But you see what I mean? It's the hair that people see. It must have been some other woman with long blonde hair.

'Well?' Charlotte leaned forward in her chair impatiently, as if she had waited for his questions to be over before she asked her own. 'You have got him on a drugs charge at least? You did do a search? Or has all this been for nothing at all?' She was tense, waiting for his answer.

She had achieved most of her objective. Dawson had fallen heavily and would find it hard to recover his former status, especially after Charlotte had her say in court. 'Yes, we found drugs at Dawson's and at Beardsley's. I'd say you'd succeeded in part,' he said drily.

Had all that grief really made her mad? he wondered. A grief that had begun four years ago and might never end. And what would she do now, now that her mission was finished, if not fully accomplished? He wondered if, now that she'd been given the chance to tell him her story, she might reconsider her official statement. Was she capable of relinquishing her role of avenging angel in order to try to save herself?

He rose and put a hand on her shoulder as he passed her. 'I'll bring your solicitor to you. He should have arrived by now.'

Chapter Twenty-Nine

After paying a courtesy call on Hugh Smith next day, Simon went in search of Jessie. He was wondering what her reaction would be to Dawson's temporary incarceration, and whether she would think Simon in some measure responsible for the fact that Beardsley was dead. If he had listened to her cautions about both Charlotte and Emily, things might not have gone as far as they had. Even without Jessie's comments, there had been enough that didn't feel right to have justified his looking more closely at Emily's recent past, those lost days in Wales over Christmas and the New Year.

His meeting with the university administrator had had no such background, and the man had expressed no criticism over the way the case had been conducted. Smith had been disturbed by what Simon had to tell him, his patrician countenance taut and his manner showing none of the urbane ease with which he had greeted the inspector on their first meeting.

'There will have to be an investigation – among the students, I mean. The fact that two lecturers apparently involved students in these practices is very serious indeed,' Smith had mourned.

It was. The police had managed to obtain information from some students at the fringe of the group that Dawson had gathered around him, enough to make clear that he had been at the centre of drug experimentation with a significant number of his students. The drug squad would intensify investigations and searches in Westwich but, after all this publicity, users and suppliers would be more cautious for a while.

Smith's reaction to the story of Charlotte's machinations

244

was of more interest to Simon. After an initial expression of shock, he had raised his hands expressively, saying, 'Poor girl! How much she has suffered! Who can judge her?' Then he had sighed and added, 'If it were not for what she did to Beardsley. That is harder to accept. After all, it wasn't really he who drove her sister to what she did, was it? So what will happen to her now?'

When Simon remained silent, impressed with the quickness of the man's wits, but unable to confirm his suppositions about Beardsley's death, Smith added, 'I'm assuming that she was responsible for what happened to him?'

'I can't comment,' Simon said. 'I have no idea whether the police will decide that there is enough evidence to bring a prosecution in that connection.' He rather doubted it himself. After her conversation with Simon, she had requested a little time before seeing her solicitor. It had been enough for her to decide to save herself as far as she could, and deny that she had anything to do with Beardsley's death. Simon supposed that she was still hoping Dawson would be found responsible for his death.

'There will be a prosecution brought against her, of course, for what she does freely admit to,' he added.

'Wasting police time?' Smith raised a sardonic eyebrow.

'Oh, a little more than that.'

'But unless she is charged with murder, she's going to gain a lot of sympathy when her story is told.'

She would make certain her story did get told, too, one way or another. She had said quietly to Simon as they led her off to the cells, 'It's all written down, all of it.' She would make use of the press as she had already, if she felt she needed to. He nodded his agreement with Smith. 'Yes, I think she'll manage to get plenty of sympathy.'

And now, as he drove slowly around the university's perimeter once again, he wondered what Jessie would have to say. She could no longer feel that his pursuit of Dawson had been unjustified when all was known.

In the utilitatian corridor he met Hermione. On the whole he would have preferred not to have done.

'Chris!' She came close. 'You sorted it all out. Terribly clever of you. It's all over, then?' She made big eyes at him.

'Well, not quite,' he said, backing away.

'And Sybil must have been some help, surely?' Her eagerness widened her eyes even more.

He had sort of forgotten Sybil. Now he could not avoid remembering, and there was a question he just had to ask. 'Um, Hermione? Just how much did you feed her, you know, when you sent her to my sergeant?'

The flash of guilt was unmistakeable.

'I imagine she told you afterwards what she told us?' he prompted.

'Yes,' she said slowly.

'Well?'

'Only a bit, truly, I promise.'

'The bit that mentioned drugs, and an older man in authority?'

'She didn't do it deliberately,' Hermione said very firmly. She looked into the distance over his shoulder and murmured, 'I talked to her a little a day or so before, that's all.'

'Not terribly professional of you.'

Hermione's eyes sought his again and looked down submissively. 'No. But she was right about some other things, things I didn't know, wasn't she?'

'None of it terribly helpful. Hermione, if you knew all that stuff, why the hell didn't you just come to me and tell me?'

She shrugged expressively. 'Just not done. You know, reporting on colleagues.' It was a concept not unfamiliar to him, but she had told him some things.

'Even when you know they're pushing drugs to students?'

'Ah, but I didn't know, you see. I just thought that they were. Peter, anyway, and Phillip always followed where Peter led. But I was pretty sure about Peter's involvement with the girl. I saw them together on more than one occasion.' She put the palm of one red-nailed hand against his chest. 'Chris, I couldn't tell you that either, you must see that. I mean, you don't suspect colleagues of murder when one of their girlfriends disappears.'

'But you told me about the row they had.'

'That was afterwards,' she said calmly. If there was a logic she adhered to, he couldn't follow it.

'It was just the drugs you wanted me to know about, then?'

She nodded.

'I suppose your job is likely to be secure now that Dawson's in the pan?'

Her creamy skin flushed at that, and she said, more with resignation than resentment, 'Not much seems to get past you.'

'You're going to, I hope,' he said, making a move to get by her. 'I'm trying to find Jessie.'

'Oh, Chris,' she said as she stood aside, 'you won't mention any of this to her, will you?'

She had a wonderful repertoire of facial expressions, Simon thought, looking down at her. 'Why ever not?'

The anxious frown looked genuine. 'It wouldn't help,' she said tentatively.

He was tempted to let her worry about it for a while, but remembered that he had almost accused her of an even greater deviousness than she had shown with the psychic, and it was not she who had talked to the newspapers.

'I won't,' he said. 'But I'm not sure I'll be repeating the psychic experiment again.'

'Think it over. You might change your mind.' She reached up and gave him a peck on the cheek. 'Thanks, Chris.'

'Oh? For what?' Jessie was leaning against her doorway, studying them with a faint smile.

Hermione was a picture of guilt. 'Jessie! He'll explain,' she said hurriedly, and dived into her room a few doors away.

'I was actually coming to see you,' he said to Jessie. 'Hermione waylaid me.'

'So I see.' She stood back for him to enter her office. 'What was all that about?'

'Nothing much. I was just telling Hermione that I didn't think I'd be repeating the experiment with a psychic again.'

'Ah, so that's why she was so grateful to you?' Jessie perched on the edge of her desk and folded her arms.

'Well, afterwards she was thanking me because she thought I might change my mind.'

She laughed at his expression. 'Hermione doesn't need an excuse to kiss an attractive male, or any other for that matter – that was the correct answer.'

'How about you?' he said, going to her and putting his arms

247

around her. She returned his kiss warmly but briefly.

'You want some coffee?' she asked, going over to the machine. 'I'm sorry it's not a more celebratory drink.'

'You've heard all the news, then?'

She handed him his mug. 'The general gist, I think.' She sat down, clasping her own steaming mug. More seriously she said, 'I was sorry to hear about Phillip.'

'Yes,' he said, wondering if she would make any further comment.

'How did you work out that it was Charlotte behind it all?'

'Apart from belatedly, you mean?'

'Don't be so hard on yourself. She must have been very clever.'

Jessie was being generous, he felt. She knew how readily he had believed in and sympathised with Charlotte. Who wouldn't, though, given what seemed to have happened to Emily, and her history too? The problem was exactly that, even so – that he had allowed his sympathies to be engaged, instead of being more objective about the evidence.

'You were right to warn me not to let chivalry influence me,' he said, feeling that it had to be said.

'But you would probably have been less than human if you hadn't. I had the luxury of detachment.' Jessie moved to sit beside him on one of the chairs in front of her desk. 'So, what was it that made you see through what was going on? It couldn't have been exactly obvious.'

'It wasn't anything in particular, just a number of things that didn't feel right.' He told her something of what had been happening since he had last seen her. 'They didn't seem right, or didn't make sense, depending on who was telling the truth. I suppose it was when I decided to give Dawson the benefit of the doubt that other things as well began to make me feel as if I was being manipulated. At first, though, I didn't imagine it was Charlotte that was pulling the strings.'

'Poor girl!' Jessie said. 'Doing what she did was a way of avoiding her grief, putting it all off. She's really going to have to start facing things now.'

All this sympathy for Charlotte was provoking Simon to look at it differently. Jessie's view as a psychologist was essentially nonjudgemental. She observed Charlotte's actions

248

and offered an interpretation.

'But that wasn't why she did it,' he protested. 'She didn't do it to avoid her grief. She did it for revenge. Does that make her better or worse or the same as Dawson?'

'Don't they say that God can handle sinners?' Jessie said. 'It's the stupid ones that he has trouble with. I'd say Dawson fell into the latter category.'

'We still haven't really moved on from "an eye for an eye", have we? Where does it stop?'

'With the law,' Jessie said calmly. 'That's what it's there for, remember? To see that justice is carried out.'

Simon gave a sound of derision. 'But people aren't satisfied with that any more. They don't seem to believe in it. That's why we've got vigilantes springing up all over the place.'

Jessie watched him over the rim of her coffee mug and didn't answer.

'It makes her just as bad, doesn't it?' Simon said again. 'Worse, even. She deliberately killed Beardsley. But the law won't prove it.'

Jessie said slowly, 'I don't really feel equipped to judge what she did. Mostly, I suppose, because I don't think she did it cold-bloodedly. Oh, I know,' she said, seeing his expression, 'it seems calculated. But I think what happened with Emily was like the end for her. She wasn't really in her right mind.

'And I can understand her feeling that the law could do nothing to make anyone pay for her sister's death. I mean, if she had simply gone to the police and said that Dawson had been supplying drugs to her sister, the ones that she took her own life with, it's unlikely they would have done anything, isn't it?'

It was the same accusation Charlotte had made. And it was possibly true. The police just didn't have the resources to follow up such accusations. Most of the resources they had were directed at the big importers and manufacturers. It was only because Dawson was embroiled in the investigation that the search had happened.

'Did anyone have to pay?' he wondered aloud. 'Aren't users responsible for what they do? Emily didn't have to toddle off with Dawson and take drugs and get herself pregnant. Isn't the victim in this case responsible in some degree?'

'I suppose that depends on whether you believe that society has a duty to protect people against the more predatory members of our society.' Jessie said. 'Oh, come on, Chris!'

'It's not that simple,' he said evasively, because these were issues he didn't really want to examine deeply. Perhaps he was only releasing a pent-up resentment against Charlotte and the way that she had manipulated not just his thoughts but his feelings as well. But he couldn't admit that to Jessie, so he returned to safer ground.

'So you're saying that the law is at fault for failing to prevent people like Dawson from supplying drugs to people like Emily? And who supplies Dawson? And does that make Dawson a victim, too? Anyway,' he added, 'Charlotte wouldn't have been satisfied with what the law had to offer. She wanted Dawson convicted of Emily's murder.'

Jessie shrugged. 'She ought to get him for manslaughter, anyway, now that the whole thing will come out in court. Some judges are treating it that seriously when drugs supplied by a friend or acquaintance kill. Was the inquest verdict on Emily suicide?'

'Yes.'

'Oh, well.' She came and sat down beside him. 'Come on, tell me the rest of it.'

He recognised that she was encouraging him in much the same way, and with the same kind of intent, as he had encouraged Charlotte the day before.

'There were some real vigilantes operating that night.' He told her about the outcome of the investigations into the landlord, Edwards. 'I suppose that influenced my thoughts about Charlotte. But I first began to wonder what really happened when Emily and Charlotte were staying in Wales, after Rose rang me in a state – she's coming home, she says. Another thing was Dawson telling me about the letter that Beardsley had received from Charlotte, about the use she would make of the drugs. Dawson, and Beardsley at first, thought it meant that she was going to make accusations against them as a revenge for Dawson's rejection of her. But she was obviously feeling badly depressed. Charlotte said she was convinced that taking the drugs had harmed the baby. Anyway, it was that and Rose sounding so desperate that made me think of suicide. And the question of where Beardsley had gone before his car was seen near the river. A lot of things combined, I suppose.'

'It didn't make any difference, then, that I wouldn't talk about people in the department?' Jessie pointed out.

An unwelcome thought occurred to him and he had to express it. 'Jess, you didn't know, did you? That Dawson and his mate were handing drugs around like Smarties?'

She held his eyes levelly for a few moments while he shrank a bit inwardly. A stupid question. If she had known, he didn't see how she could have justified saying nothing. And if she hadn't, his question might seem equally unforgivable. He waited uneasily for her answer.

'I can understand that you needed to ask that,' she said slowly. 'Though I could wish that you felt you knew me better. If I had had any idea that drugs were involved, I would have told you and to hell with loyalty to others. I have wondered if Dawson used. But that's not unusual, lots of people do, and it's not for me to say so to the police. I admit, though, that I'm glad I didn't know and didn't become involved.'

'Thank you,' he said.

'There's another reason, Chris, that I didn't want to be involved in any evidence against Peter. Though I suppose it shames me to admit it.' Jessie stood up and went to lean on her desk, facing him.

'Oh?'

'You remember I told you that he was likely to get the professorship when Lamb retired?'

'Which won't be happening now.'

'Right.' Jessie went to pour another mug of coffee. 'And you remember I had lunch with Professor Lamb last week?'

Simon remembered the coolness prevalent at the time. He nodded.

'He told me that I was his own choice and that there was a good chance of my being offered it.'

He shouldn't have been surprised. Jessie had two doctorates to her name and a good reputation academically, even if she did not have Dawson's high profile. His initial reaction was one of delight for her, followed by unhappy awareness of the differences between them, the old envy that she had something that he lacked when it came to her work. 'Is it certain?' he asked.

'That's the point, in a way. With Dawson out, it's even more likely. I just couldn't feel the same way about the promotion if I had had any hand in what's happened to him. I mean, it would make the job impossible if people thought that I'd helped you put him away out of personal ambition.'

She was watching his reaction. He put a smile on his face and said, 'Well, that's wonderful, Jess!' Why did he feel that it placed him even further from the hopes he had had when this whole disturbing case had begun? The more successful Jessie became in her work, the less relevance a man would have in her life, he told himself. What did he have to offer that she needed?

'I need you to be glad about it, Chris,' she said.

'Why?' He couldn't see that she had any need at all.

'Because if you can't wholeheartedly accept me as I am, be glad for what makes me the person that I am, then there is no future for us.'

Despite his thoughts, he was startled that she should express an ultimatum to him. He studied her face in turn. There was a faint flush there and she seemed to be holding her breath, waiting for his answer. As he saw that, his own tension disappeared. She was right and it was that simple, or that complicated, depending on which way you viewed it.

'I do, wholeheartedly,' he said. 'I was just wondering—'

She leaned forward and silenced him with a kiss.